My Name is Lazarus

Lazarus

The First 500 Years
Book I

My Name is Lazarus

Lazarus

The First 500 Years
Book I

It is appointed unto men once to die...
Hebrews 9:27

By Kel Baker

Lynn Horton, Editor

Art Dewar, Consulting Editor

David Anders Publishing House

To Karla

Acknowledgements

In the book of Philippians, Paul wrote, "He who began a good work in you will "carry it on to completion." I know a little more about that scripture now than I did before I undertook this project seven years ago. I want to publicly thank the Lord Jesus, for even when I didn't think I could finish this work, He placed people in my life to encourage me and help me go on. He is ever faithful, ever true.

I would like to acknowledge how grateful I am to the following people:

- Lynn Horton for being my primary editor, mentor, and gracious friend.
- Arthur Dewar for his editing and for acting as my guide through the wonderful subject of history. Without his friendship, this could not have been possible.
- Deb Jahera and Leslie White for their encouragement and criticism.
- Randy Valimont, my pastor, whose blessing and inspiration kept me going.
- Kathy Moore, Karen Davis, Jill Entrekin, Lynn Bruschetti, and Christine Brand for their time, their support, and their eyes.
- Bob Newell and Frank Campo for their friendship and support throughout these years.
- Lincoln Anders, Ginger Mahlbacher, Denise Westerveld, Brent Jackson, and Awilda Cruz for being my test subjects.
- Nora Tocups for her copyright expertise.
- Dawn, Ansley, and Beck Burnette for their valuable input.
- My wife and companion Karla for her encouragement and love.
- My children: Jessica, Eden, Jed, and Mark for their help in writing this book.
- David and Kenya Anders for bringing me on board and guiding me through the publishing process. Thank you for making *My Name is Lazarus* possible.

Great it is to dream the dream when you stand in youth by the starry stream,
but a greater thing is to fight life through and say at the end, the dream is true.

John Osteen
from an Edwin Markham poem

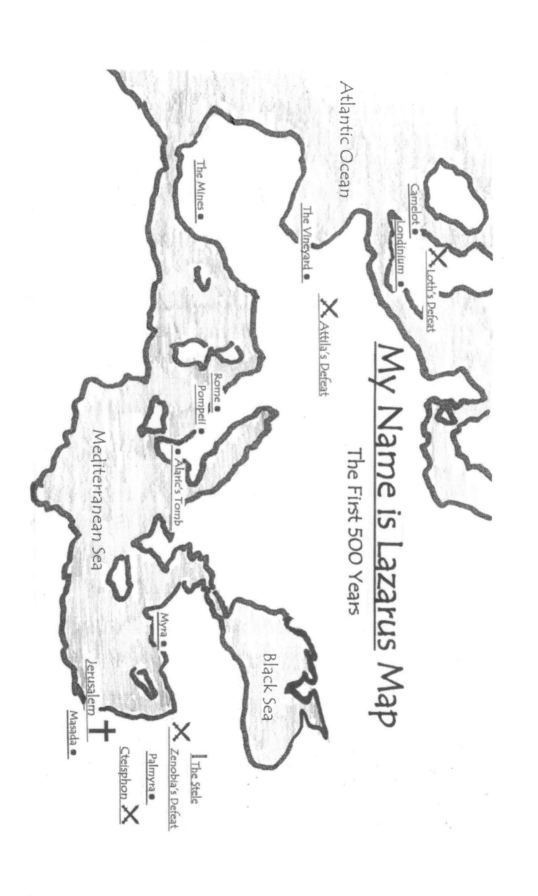

My Name is Lazarus Map

The First 500 Years

Atlantic Ocean

Camelot •
Londinium •
X Loth's Defeat

The Mines •

The Vineyard •

X Attila's Defeat

Rome •
Pompeii •
• Alaric's Tomb

Mediterranean Sea

Myra • •

Black Sea

Jerusalem •

Masada •

X Zenobia's Defeat
I The Stele
Palmyra •
Ctesiphon X

Prologue

197 AD—Persia

Persian kettledrums thundered as dozens of mighty war elephants lumbered forward. The giant beasts moved slowly and predictably at first, but with each step and each hypnotic beat of the drum, they moved faster and faster as their drivers whipped them into a frenzy. More than twice the height of a man, the beasts barreled toward the Roman army's line. Massive brass plates protected the elephant's faces down to their trunks where twin tusks stuck out like enormous ivory lances with brazened spear tips. Two great, grey eyes peered through large holes in the armor. A driver straddled each elephant's neck, and on the animal's back stood archers protected by a wicker battlement strapped to the beast's saddle.

Vologases, the Parthian leader, had brought his army out from Ctesiphon, the Persian capital, to fight the Romans in the field. Nearby, the Tigris River flowed by peacefully, ignoring the elephant advance and the Roman army's quincunx formation that made the plain a mammoth chessboard.

The ground rumbled and quaked under the weight of the war elephants, but the Roman legions stood undaunted. They had been prepared for this kind of assault. The Roman squares, the maniples, consisted of legionnaires armed with short swords, a formation designed for flexibility. Each infantry unit was trained to simply step aside and leave large gaps in the line—creating such lanes would allow the enemy pachyderms to pass harmlessly through the ranks. But this day was different. The musty smell and the trumpeting sound of the charging elephants spooked the Roman mercenary cavalry which bolted en masse into the center of the Roman line.

"Cursed mercenaries," said Severus, the Roman Imperator. "I'll have their heads!"

Suddenly there was no place for the soldiers to go, no room to make passages, and the enormous tusked brutes stampeded through the disrupted legion. Bodies flew through the air as the raging elephants swung their heads from left to right, their tusks goring and swiping soldiers and shields from their paths. Hundreds of men were mangled and trampled in the charge, and still the wave of enemy came onward, now deep into the very heart of the square.

The pace of the attack slackened as Roman soldiers and centurions chopped and stabbed at the great beasts. Even slowed, the wild animals crushed anything and everything. Finally a legionnaire darted in with his short sword and, with a terrific slash of the gladius, severed an elephant's snout that hung from beneath its mask. With another quick hack, the tip of the animal's nose dropped to the ground. A fountain of blood gushed from the wounded brute. The animal shrieked in pain and gored its attacker with its tusk, flinging the soldier into the air. The creature reared up on its hind legs and fell backward, smashing its rider and cage, and flattening half a dozen Romans beneath its bulk.

The injured gargantuan rolled over and back onto its feet and stumbled toward the Persian line, smashing and mashing everything in its way. Large, red pools soaked into the ground where the animal had crushed man, armor, and weapons. The earth was spattered with Roman blood and guts, dead legionnaires as flat and still as if sculpted onto the ground.

Throughout the day the battle raged, moving toward Ctesiphon. Though the elephant attack had wreaked havoc, the Parthian army was repulsed and eventually withdrew; the field and the city surrendered to Severus and his Romans.

At the edge of twilight, the battleground was still and quiet. The victorious Romans had yet to recover their dead from the field where the early fighting had taken place. The war elephant's severed trunk lay in the open like a dead snake, now shriveled from the day's heat. Nearby, the gruesome remains of the soldiers were part of the earth. The stench of blood and death lay heavy in the air. The macabre scene was now hidden by the descending night. No one saw as skin began to move and close over the torso of a smashed and battered corpse. No one heard bones crackle to life or intestines churn and gurgle as rejuvenated muscle and sinew drew them back together. No one tasted the dried blood or breathed the fresh air as the legionnaire's lungs inhaled and his lips began to quiver. No one except Lazarus.

Present Day
July 2, 4:00 p.m.

"Did everybody get out?"

The whole townhouse unit was in flames.

"I think so," said a silver-haired priest who stood with the other onlookers. "I'm Father Braden. I thought I might be of some help, but this is a job for those boys." He pointed to the firefighters who were unrolling hoses from a big hook and ladder truck.

Far off in the distance sirens screamed; more help was on the way. Black, sooty smoke and flames belched defiantly at the yellow-coated men who came to tame them. A local television crew prepped for a live shot while a news chopper hovered overhead, its cameraman already taping.

The three-story apartment building spat fire from almost every portal. Dark smoke funneled from the corner apartment when a tiny head suddenly appeared near the bottom of a window.

"Oh my god!" a woman gasped, pointing to the window. "There's a child up there."

"Father," a man in a navy sports coat shouted. "I don't care what you have to do, but get someone or something and get ready to catch her."

"You can't go up there. It's suicide!" the priest yelled, but the stranger was racing toward the blaze, pausing just long enough to soak his coat in a torrent of water that flooded the curb.

"Just catch her," the man called over his shoulder, looking Braden in the eye.

His gaze took the priest by surprise, a look that echoed weariness. Thirty? Forty years old? Braden wondered. Clean shaven and handsome, the stranger appeared to be a man of substance, a man of means, running to his death. The moment lingered until Braden heard his own heartbeat, louder than the roar of the flames, the sirens and the chaotic din. He crossed himself and began to pray for the stranger who, covered with the wet coat, ran into the burning building. An explosion quaked the complex, and another siren signaled that more help had arrived. Braden ran to a fireman.

"There's a child up there," the priest pointed to the window. "A man went up for her. Can you catch her?" he begged.

"Get the cushion," the lieutenant barked to his crew.

The air cushion inhaled its compressed air beneath the window and they waited, staring at the portal through the sooty haze. The scene assumed a slow motion quality as the black smoke, the smell of cauterized wire, the broiling heat, and the struggle between hope and fear gripped the hearts of the onlookers. As the priest continued to pray, a chair shattered the glass window where the child had been.

Through the smoke Braden saw the stranger toss a dark bundle out the window and onto the cushion below. The EMTs pulled the little girl from the inflatable pad.

"Jump!" The firemen shouted. "Jump!"

But the figure was suddenly engulfed in flames; he staggered and fell to the window sill. As if exhaled from the mouth of a dragon, another whoosh of flames sent the burning body through the broken window and over the edge, scraping along the brick wall as it fell, landing in the smoldering shrubs below. Help reached him in seconds, but the man was charred beyond recognition.

Already two EMTs were examining the blackened corpse.

"Get this man to the hospital," the priest yelled.

The big EMT, a young man in his 20s with a badge that declared his name was Johnson, said, "Too late. This guy's toast."

"You idiot!" his female partner, Smith, said. "How can you say that?"

"I'm sorry. I wasn't thinking," he said. "We should just take him to the morgue."

"Well, say it then. This man saved a little girl's life," she said.

His cameraman now recording, the reporter asked, "Who was he? Did anyone know that guy? How about you Father?"

"I don't know him, but I'll never forget him," said Braden, and for a moment the image of the stranger reverberated in his mind. "He told me to get something to catch the little girl, and then he just ran into that inferno!"

"That's the bravest thing I ever saw," said the reporter.

Johnson and Smith covered the body.

"How's the girl?" Braden asked.

"She'll be okay," said Smith. "She's inhaled some smoke and has a few burns, but she should be fine."

Braden stared at the angry flames that drank gallon after gallon of water.

Wednesday, July 3, 8:09 a.m.

"Hey Keller, Coroner Jacobs said he wants to do an autopsy on that body they brought in from that fire yesterday," said Williams.

"Why? He pronounced the man dead as soon as he came in. Wasn't it obvious? That was one of the worst I've ever seen; that guy was BBR. It was ugly."

"I dunno. He'll be over in a few minutes."

"Thanks for the warning," said Keller. "It's right over here in the D cooler." He grabbed the handle of the stainless steel cabinet and pulled. The cooler drawer was empty.

"Alright Tom, what gives? Is this some kind of a joke?"

"What?"

"Right. I walk in the door this morning and you show up saying Jacobs is on his way over. And by the way, the body he wants to see is missing. Kinda early in the day for a prank isn't it?"

"Honest, Sam. It wasn't me. Check the other drawers."

They were all empty. Sam Keller stared at Tom, then turned and stormed out of the room.

"All right. Who took the stiff outta here last night?"

Thursday, July 11, 1:30 p.m.

Father Braden was finished. Late morning service was over, and the priest pulled the heavy wooden door to a close, then turned back into the sanctuary. The afternoon sunlight poured through the stained glass and spilled rubies and emeralds onto the church floor. A man still knelt at the altar. Father Braden gently placed his hand on the man's shoulder.

"What's troubling you," he asked.

A deep voice answered, "More than you'll ever know, more than I can ever remember. Idolatry, murder, adultery, covetousness, greed, lasciviousness, gluttony ... ."

"That's quite an array of sins," the priest said knowingly.

The man turned to look at Braden. The priest's eyes widened incredulously. He was stunned; again that moment from the apartment fire seized the priest. His mind traveled back to the intense heat, the smell of the smoke, and the blaring sirens. He could never forget that moment or that face with its profound countenance. Braden's memory was fresh with a kaleidoscope of images. He could still see the man's determined grimace and his deep, brown eyes, and the priest could hear his own heart pounding again.

Time seemed to take a deep breath as the priest stared at the man. There was no mistaking the eyes and the hair, though shorter than before, but now there was a silver streak running up the man's hairline over the right temple. This was the man—or his twin.

"Forgive me," the priest finally said, "but you look just like someone I ... ."

"Know?" the man interrupted.

"Yes, a man I saw at an apartment fire, but," the priest hesitated, "that man died rescuing that little girl."

The man didn't answer but continued to stare at Braden. The silence gave way to the white noise of the empty church.

"It's not possible," the priest said. "I know what I saw, and I saw him fall from the window. I *saw* him, lying on the stretcher, burned, DEAD! There is no way he could be alive, even in the hospital. You can't be him. He's dead! You must be his brother, his twin."

"I have no brother."

A fearful look came over the priest. "What are you? An angel? A ghost? Worse?" He clutched a Bible he held in his hands.

"Father," his voice was comforting. "*With God, All things are possible.* That was your message this morning wasn't it?"

The priest paused, searching for an explanation, wondering.

"Your eyes aren't lying to you. I am the same man. You know it. You don't want to believe it, but you know it."

5

"But it can't be. There is no way *that* man can have survived," the priest insisted, eyes wide.

"I can explain."

"But it's not possible. The EMTs said you were dead. The newspapers and television reported it. The coroner pronounced you dead on the scene. Even if it were possible to live through it, you'd still be in the hospital bandaged from head to toe."

"With God, all things are possible," the man reaffirmed.

"Are you telling me you had some kind of miracle healing or something?"

"You could call it that, but hear the rest of my story if you will—please."

The priest stared skeptically at the stranger, desperate to know the truth. He turned and motioned for the man to follow him into the church offices. Braden's office was large with a window looking out over a flower garden. The place was inviting, and the priest offered a seat while he poured coffee.

"Cream or sugar?" Braden asked quietly, his hand trembling.

"Both," the man said. Coffee in hand, each man sat tensely in worn leather wingback chairs, facing one another.

"So," said the Father, "I'm anxious to hear an explanation for this 'miracle'."

"I know you're skeptical," said the man, "but I am who I say I am."

"And who is that? Who are you? What are you?"

"A man in every sense of the word," he answered. "My name is Lazlow. Why don't you turn off your cell phone and put away your desk phone? You won't want any interruptions."

Father Braden left the cord dangling like a small black slinky as he stuck the receiver in a desk drawer and shoved it closed.

Thursday, July 11, 1:50 p.m.

"No one knows my story, but I'm supposed to tell it to you."

"Why me?" asked the priest.

"I'm not sure. Call it a gut feeling. I suppose you'll understand after I tell you. You'll be the first."

"The first what?" asked the priest.

"The first person to hear my story in a long, long time. Many knew at one time, but that was a mistake." The man's mind drifted back. "A lot of people were.... It's just that it's been a long time."

"It can't be that long," said the priest. "What are you, thirty?"

"I'm older than I look. Years ago I lived on the other side of the world, a place with an arid, dry climate. My father abandoned us when I was a child. My mother died soon afterwards. The youngest of three children, I was raised by my sisters. My oldest sister Martha cooked and cleaned for people just to keep food on the table for us, but she had little time to take care of us. My other sister began walking the streets at an early age, and I also became rebellious.

"When I was a teen, Martha found me a position selling goods in the market place for one of her clients. I repaid the man's kindness by stealing from him. He caught me and could have had me stoned, but he cared so much for Martha that he only discharged me. Years later I found myself handling canvas, working as an apprentice tentmaker. Through my work, I had fallen in with some criminals who were bent on overthrowing the government."

"What are you? Some kind of terrorist?" Braden asked.

"Hardly. My name is Lazarus, my real name that is."

"Okay, so your real name is Lazarus," Braden said.

"The Lazarus," the man said.

"The only Lazarus I've heard of was in the Bible," the priest said.

"That's right. I was raised from the dead nearly two thousand years ago by our Lord and Savior, Jesus Christ."

Braden stared at the man incredulously, shook his head, and began to chuckle.

"You're Lazarus? Come on," the priest said with a look of disbelief on his face. "First you tell me you're the man who survived that apartment fire. Now you expect me to believe that you're Lazarus? *The Lazarus?*" Braden growled.

"Believe me, I know how this sounds," the man said.

"So you're more than 2000 years old? Well, you've really kept your age well. You don't look a day over 35," the priest said sarcastically. "This happens all the time, you know. Why just last week Methuselah dropped in."

The younger man smiled. "It's preposterous," he said. "I can prove it."

"How can this be proved? Or even disproved?" Braden asked. "You might not even be the man from that fire! This could be some kind of a trick."

"It's not and you know it. You don't want to believe it, and I don't blame you. Just call the morgue and ask about the body of the man who was burned to death. See what they say. Just promise me you won't tell them that you've seen me alive. That kind of information has caused me great pain in the past, but then that's part of my story."

The priest nervously took out his cell phone and punched in the number.

"Sam Keller works at the morgue. He's a friend of mine. Let's put this on speakerphone," said Braden, dialing the number.

"County Morgue," said a voice on the phone.

"Sam Keller please," the priest said.

"One moment."

There was a long pause.

"This is Sam Keller," a voice sounding canned and tinny came over the speakerphone.

"Sam, this is Father Braden at Holy Trinity."

"Yes, Tom. What can I do for you?"

"You remember that apartment fire last week?"

"The four alarmer at Windsor Oaks? What about it?"

"The man who died in the fire—did you ever get an ID on him?"

"No. We, uh, never did."

"So, there was no funeral? No one claimed to know the man?"

7

There was a long silence.

"Something wrong, Sam?" Braden asked.

"Uh, Father, I'm not supposed to tell anyone this, but um—we've misplaced the body."

"You *misplaced* the body?"

"Please don't tell anyone, but it's like it just got up and walked off or something. I hope it's some kind of a joke. If it doesn't turn up, there'll be trouble. Why do you ask, Tom?"

The priest glanced sharply at Lazlow before speaking into the phone. "So you never identified him."

"Nope, never found out his name."

"Thanks, Sam. See you at church."

Braden hung up the phone and looked intently at the man in the leather chair. "Mr. Lazlow, I mean Lazarus, you have my attention."

Thursday, July 11, 2:05 p.m.

One summer I became ill. The season was so warm that year that even the dust was hot. One day Martha sat me down to warn me about my zealot friends when Mary, my other sister, came through the door. You know her as Mary Magdalene. She was smiling, her face angelic."

"Mary? You look different. What has happened to you?" Martha asked.

"Sister! Brother!" Mary exclaimed tearfully. The most wonderful thing has happened. I met a man who changed my life. He took my sin and my shame. I will never sell myself again."

Martha and Mary cried and we all hugged. "Who is this man?" I asked.

"You'll meet Him soon enough. He will be here for the evening meal."

"What!" Martha exclaimed. "People will be in our home tonight? I had only planned for a fish soup."

"That will be fine. I'll bake some bread," Mary said.

Later that day, Jesus and his disciples arrived. He was the most extraordinary man I'd ever met. He looked at me fondly, and the way he spoke made me understand why men followed him. He was kind and humorous.

"Lord," Simon Peter said, "Lazarus is in league with some of the men who want to overthrow the Romans. Is this how Your kingdom will be established?

"How many times must I tell you," Jesus shook his head. "My kingdom is not of this world. I go to prepare a place for you, and I will return for you. Lazarus will not overthrow this kingdom, but he will see many kingdoms."

We all laughed, but no one had any idea what the Lord meant. The rest of the evening passed calmly as Jesus was the ideal guest, warm and complimentary. The next day I awoke early and arranged a meeting of the zealots at our home.

"Not those men, brother. They are dangerous," Martha said. Her disapproval of my friends erupted into a huge quarrel. "If the soldiers found out about this meeting you're planning, we could all be imprisoned! Our home confiscated!" she cried.

Anger consumed me, and in my rage I began coughing violently, eventually coughing up blood. I had felt sick for some time, but I had hidden it from Martha. Now I suddenly felt weak. I had contracted tuberculosis. We became desperate for some kind of treatment, but there was none.

The Quick and the Dead

Have the gates of death been shown to you? Job 38:17

I

There was no cure. My death was only a matter of time. As the fluid in my lungs increased, I began to run a high fever. I became weak from coughing. With each cough came more congestion, more fluid, until even my breath stank of blood. I told Martha not to cry as she stood over me. I closed my eyes. Mary wailed as she ran her hands through my hair trying to comfort me.

"Lazarus, I know you have bitterness in your heart. You must let it go," Mary pleaded with me. "You must forgive our father!"

For years I'd harbored anger about my father. Even at death's door, I felt my animosity swell up. I tried to let it go, but before I could answer I heard the whispering air escape from my own lungs for the last time. There was a great dark silence.

I was dead. With my last breath I slipped out of my body just as easily as taking off a cloak. I was weightless, floating in space as if in water. I could see my body supine on my pallet as I was being pulled away, but I could hear nothing. My sisters cried silent tears. I spoke to them, but I had no audible voice. I faded into another dimension, and before me I saw the gateways to two worlds. I could see beyond and into each one. To my right was a world illuminated by a beautiful luster, a sea of clear light, deep in the cosmos. From it I heard a synthesis of pure harmony and music—the stars were singing. Emanating from the light was a sense of wondrous love such as I'd never known. Beyond the gate to my left was a dark vortex that sucked in light. From it there screeched discordance unlike anything I'd ever heard, a swelling cacophony of hideous cries with pain at their core.

I wanted so badly to move toward the love, the beautiful music and light, but I had no power. I hung there, motionless. Then I found myself lost in the inside of a sphere, and I saw millions of convex mirrors pointed at me; each held an image of some facet of my life. I saw my best moments and my worst sins; my entire life was there, spinning around me, creating an audible whirring noise, like the sound of thousands of cicadas strumming. Then the mirrored images began to vibrate. Their light and color faded as if being siphoned from them. The images grew gray, then darker like molten lead, and I began to feel heavier and heavier, as if I were a piece of iron being drawn to a distant, powerful magnet. The liquid images swirled violently around me until they became a whirlpool of ashes that suddenly blew away like spices in the wind.

I found myself standing, staring up at a charcoal sky and listening to an unearthly drumming. A great angst came over me as I sensed an ominous, foreboding presence. I saw a huge, towering fortress with coal black walls that stretched forever into the darkness, a massive gate at its center. Chiseled into the gate were words I could not decipher, but I knew what they meant. This was hell. The air was foul and reeked of sulfur and the nauseating pungency of rotting, maggot-infested flesh. As I turned, seeking escape, I realized with horror that I

10

was held firm by a formless creature with prickly, malignant tentacles. Its slimy touch overwhelmed me with sheer terror.

The pulsing beat grew louder as the gates came alive—a ghastly, hungry grumbling accompanied a deep, sardonic laugh. A sickening stench ushered in a din of agonizing cries. It was filled with malice, dread, and pure madness. Black and crimson flames dimly lit the smoldering tableau. The screams became louder, deafening, swirling around me as I was held captive before those toothy gates and their gigantic black mandibles. The jaws of that dreaded place spewed forth a demonic hiss and an incessant drumming sound that became the source of an infinite, throbbing pain, like the soreness one feels from a pus-swollen boil about to burst. Waves of fiery heat and frigid misery pulsated through me like an odious fever, causing me to shudder. I'd never known such dismay, such horror.

I struggled to free myself, but slowly and malevolently, my captor dragged me to the entrance of the gates. I wept and begged for mercy, but there was no one there to hear my cries. Even though I had no physical body, I felt unimaginable pain from those thorny tentacles, the molten heat, and the steady cadence. I was dragged over the threshold; everything that I had ever known as love, hope, or faith was instantly seared away, for they could not enter into that pit. They simply ceased to exist.

Hate, murder, lust, envy, suffering, despair, and torment greeted me, all embodied in gargantuan, gargoyle-like beings. The creatures were ghastly and as black as night. Scaly and winged, they had the deformed heads of mutated men. Fangs protruded from below their wormy, serpent-like tongues. Their entrails spilled from their abdomens, and slimy doglike creatures slithered in and out of them, eating the gargoyle's bowels while baying their unbearable howls. This was pandemonium, a macabre asylum of pain and horror that was never meant for man. Terrified, I heard the gates begin to close behind me, knowing that once they were shut, I would forever be one of the damned. "Forgive me!" I screamed. "I forgive. I forgive all," I cried, weeping.

In the midst of the fiendish bedlam a powerful bolt of lightning flashed across the hellscape, illuminating the place and bringing everything to a sudden halt. At first I was afraid, but the rush of a strong breeze ushered in a thundering Word; a Word that I didn't understand.

The Word stunned all to silence. Hell itself seemed to stagger as if it had received a terrific blow to the head. In that moment there was relief. The heat, the hate, the oppression, the putrid odor, even the drumming temporarily abated. Again, yet at a faster pace, the dark workings of the abyss resumed. But no sooner had they restarted when another bolt of lightning, louder and larger than before, lit up the darkness. All of hell was silenced again as a more powerful wind and the Word, louder and clearer exploded and penetrated the depths in a flash. It was as refreshing as the scent of rain, and for a moment even the cries of suffering ceased.

Defiantly, the heaviness and heat of the inferno intensified, and the machinations of that dreaded place quickened. The yowling hounds, the unending drumming, and the revolting horror worked at a frenzied pace. Fear

11

pulsated through me while the gluttonous jaws of that maelstrom frantically tried to consume me.

A final thunderbolt bathed the sky in light and hell's terrible gates burst open as if two gigantic unseen hands had simply ripped them apart. There was a mammoth, rumbling explosion as bright as a thousand suns that quaked the very heart of the black pit. This time it was the thunderous Word that roared like a thousand waters and reverberated throughout the blinding light. Nothing could hide from the illumination which rocked the blackness to the core, and the underworld cowered at its power. The hounds yelped and squirmed back into their masters' entrails while the gargoyles hid in hell's smoky crevices; the drumming ceased, the pandemonium silenced. Then, from its darkest recesses, the abyss responded with a monstrous banshee shriek that echoed the demon's own anguish! My tormentor released me and vanished, and a forceful surge vomited me back through the gates into another darkness. I fainted.

II

I desperately tried to wake up, afraid, hoping what I had seen was a nightmare. There was a voice calling to me from some cloudy unknown. Confused, I felt myself slip back through the images. I awoke taut with fear, but the voice I heard was irresistibly comforting. I tried to move as the voice of Jesus kept calling me. I got to my knees and struggled toward the words. I managed to stand and staggered through the darkness, tearing at the cloth that hindered me from walking. I heard the words again, but this time I understood them. **COME FORTH!** Blurry eyed, I followed the light through the emptiness and then through a small opening.

Jesus' words drew me out like water from a well into the blinding light. My eyes streamed at the sun's intensity. The air was hot and dry, but it smelled wonderful to me. Even so, my mind still reeled from the nightmare of hell. Was it a dream? Did it happen only a moment before or was it ages ago? His powerful voice called, comforting me.

I tore and ripped at the cloth, and I could hear my sisters laughing and crying joyfully, a silvery mixture of tears, amazement and love. It was like tasting honey for the first time. Their hugs and kisses melded into music as they tugged on the shroud that covered me. They began to sing, "Thank you, thank you, Lord." Martha and Mary helped me pull the shroud from my eyes, and I saw Jesus, tears streaming from His eyes. That was almost 2000 years ago.

The Confession

Jesus wept. John 11:35

I

The priest sat back in the squeaky comfort of his leather chair. "Please continue," he said.

While Martha and Mary sang praises to the Lord, I opened my eyes and saw Jesus. The warm breeze rustled his long dark hair. He smiled through His brown beard as He spoke my name. His dense burnished eyes and tranquil voice were full of light. Sometimes I can still hear Him, and I can still picture the tears that disappeared into His beard. As I came to my senses, I was just glad to be alive. I fell to my knees and worshipped Him. I wept openly and thanked Him for saving me, but then the sight of Jesus crying puzzled me. Why would the Lord cry?

One day, a short time later, Jesus was at our home, taking the evening meal. I waited for the right moment to ask Him about that day. He surprised me.

"Lazarus," He said. "You have something you wish to ask me?"

"Yes." I was caught off-guard, but his eyes assured me. "Lord, why...why did you cry that day?" The words stumbled out of my mouth.

"Come with me," Jesus said, leading me outside into the cool twilight. "Lazarus, it is written. It is appointed for all men to die once."

At the time I was too ignorant to know what He meant.

"But why did you cry?" I asked again.

Jesus' warm eyes showed the love of a father. "I saw you and all those others in hell. Man was not created for such a horrible place. That's why I am here." He then put His hand upon my shoulder and said, "Though you will someday sit at my Father's table, you have much to do before that time, much to do before I return."

"Mary said that You also called me Your friend before you brought me back. I'm grateful, but I have only known you a short time."

"Lazarus, do not be troubled. For it is also written: our Father quickens the dead, and calls things that are not as though they were."

I didn't understand the ramifications of His words then, either for Him or for me. He knew then what I know now. I would see thousands of years of sin, death, and heartache. Religious fervor, rebellion, excess, frustration, anger, sin, sorrow, and repentance: I lived and relived mankind's often foolish, yet sincere efforts to embrace God. The Savior knew all this before He saved me from hell.

By this time word of my resurrection had swept through the land. Many believed He was the Messiah simply because of my story. God was glorified, but some of the members of the Sanhedrin, the ecclesiastical and judicial leaders of Israel, were worried about their position and power. No wonder Jesus referred to them as vipers. Not all were against our Lord, however.

Late one evening I was making my way home when I felt a tremendous blow to my head. Some of the disciples found me hours later. A tile had fallen from a roof and knocked me out. I was still a little woozy the next morning when one of the priests came to our door. He introduced himself as Joseph of Arimathea.

"You are the one who was raised from the dead. Lazarus," he said.

"I am."

"I heard you received a terrible blow to the head last night."

"Yes, a tile fell from a roof and hit me," I said, gently touching my head.

"That tile was left there to fool everyone," Joseph explained. "Someone hit you with a club. I know for a fact that the chief priests have conspired to have you and our Messiah murdered. I also fear for your sisters. I am a man of some wealth. I make no guarantees, but I believe I can insulate you and your sisters from this evil. I do not believe Caiaphas or his followers will strike at you at my home."

"Thank you, but our Lord didn't raise me from the grave just so that I could be killed by an assassin."

"Perhaps," he said. "But you must think of your family."

After a brief discussion, Martha and Mary and I were persuaded to take Joseph's offer. We took only our clothes and what few valuables we had.

A short time later I saw Jesus crucified. That scene was more horrifying than you can imagine: the cruelty, the pain, the blood. His body was so disfigured that it looked inhuman. No one ever talks about that. The beating, the sin and sickness He bore; all played a part in His death.

And the people cried out, "Crucify the blasphemer!" His people. A few of us begged that He be spared, but the chief priests wanted Him dead. They had power. These were some of the same men who'd seen Him heal the sick and perform miracles. As terrible as His crucifixion was, I know there was no other way. The entire scene had been orchestrated by God. We watched Him carry that cross until He could no longer bear it. We cried out for mercy for Him, but the crowd wanted blood, His blood.

Martha and I stood together on that terrible day. She tried to help Jesus when He stumbled and fell from the weight of the cross. Martha stepped into the street and tenderly wiped the blood and sweat from His face. He looked at her for a moment, but the soldiers shoved her aside and then forced some onlooker to pick up the Lord's cross and carry it on to Golgotha.

Like a coward, I stood and watched as the Romans drove spikes through Jesus' wrists and as they mashed the crown of thorns into His forehead. I saw all and did nothing. I watched as a stormy darkness, unlike any other I've ever seen, cloaked the earth. Jesus had said He would die for the sins of man. Many blamed the Jews and Romans for His death, but it was sin that killed Him—my sin, your sin, the world's sin.

II

Through the gloomy, rain-soaked streets of Jerusalem I accompanied my friend Joseph to beg Pilate for the body of Jesus. The Roman Governor released the corpse to us, and Joseph led us to his home to prepare it for burial. Along the

14

way we were joined by Nicodemus, another member of the Sanhedrin who believed in Jesus.

"If preparing the body of the Messiah makes me unclean, then I choose to be unclean," Joseph said to us.

The horrible mutilation made cleaning the corpse a challenge, but we did so somberly, holding back our tears. Mary, Martha, and Miriam, Joseph's wife, sobbed while we did the gruesome work. Thick droplets of blood seeped from the wounds. Jesus' arm hung from the table and blood began to ooze down His fingertips onto the floor.

Even in His death, my sister found a way to serve Him. Mary took a beautiful golden chalice from among Joseph's precious possessions and lovingly guided it beneath the dangling hand. She wept just as she had months before when she anointed Jesus' feet with perfume.

"The blood is the life," Mary whispered as the blood dripped into the goblet.

Under Joseph's direction we finished dressing the body and took it to his private sepulcher. A Roman guard had been assigned to our small entourage as we walked through the damp streets. Our footsteps muffled the grieving cries of the women.

The air in the tomb was stale when we lay down the body of Jesus. Except for our breathing there was no sound. No one spoke; we were overcome with sorrow and remorse. It took six Roman guards to roll the stone into place, and the cave groaned as the rock came to rest.

The next day an uneasy hush descended upon the city. Jerusalem seemed dazed. My sisters were inconsolable, and fear seized us as we expected to be taken and stoned for being Jesus' followers. We remained inside the entire time, and the day dragged on endlessly as we waited into the night.

The morning of that first Easter Sunday found us still grieving. It was early when Martha came running in to Joseph's home shouting, "The tomb is empty! He's alive! Come with me," she cried as she ran out, waving for us to follow.

The stone lay at the side of the tomb when we arrived. Only the grave clothes remained inside. I took the shroud back to Joseph's home and placed it next to the golden chalice which was still full with Jesus' blood. Just before noon a group of high ranking members of the Sanhedrin appeared outside. With them was a cohort of Roman soldiers who forced the door of Joseph's home and entered without invitation.

"You!" The leader Caiaphas, growled, pointing at Joseph. Caiaphas' dark eyes were steely, his long gray beard almost hidden by his *miznefet*, or headdress. "You went to the governor, TO PILATE and claimed the body of that carpenter. You Fool!" His angry backhand found Joseph's cheek. "You traitor! What have you done with the body?"

Caiaphas' thugs began to ransack the house. They touched neither the chalice nor the shroud which lay in the open. It was as if the holy icons were invisible to the unbelievers.

Red-cheeked with anger, Joseph stood his ground and responded firmly, "You heard the rabbi, Caiaphas. He said He would rebuild the temple in three days. This is the third day."

"LIAR and BLASPHEMER!" Caiaphas slapped Joseph again, knocking him to the floor. The High Priest then turned and pointed to me. "You! Where is the body?"

"I don't know," I said. "But He raised me from the dead."

"BLASPHEMY! You are all blasphemers!" In his rage Caiaphas shoved me against the wall. "We'll be back."

As the soldiers filed out, Reuben, one of Joseph's friends on the council, sneaked back into the room. He spoke loud enough for all of us to hear.

"I do not think Israel will be safe for you or your family, Joseph. Please heed my advice old friend. Shalom," he said and hurried out the door.

"Joseph, you're bleeding," Miriam said, grabbing a cloth. She dipped it into a bowl of water and gently touched the cut on Joseph's cheek.

"It's nothing," he said, pushing away the fabric. "We must leave this country. Caiaphas will have us stoned if we remain."

Thursday, July 11, 2:30 p.m.

"You were at the crucifixion? You were a part of it? You saw His body? The empty tomb?" the priest asked. "Surely the people knew who He was."

"Thousands were at the cross. Those who had seen Him perform miracles, those who knew Him; all abandoned Him out of fear. He was totally alone. Only a few of us saw the empty tomb."

"So what did you do? Where did you go? What happened to Joseph and your sisters?"

16

Boudica

...I will strike the shepherd, and the sheep will be scattered. Mark 14:27

I

The time following the resurrection was dangerous for us, and the repercussions were harsh. The tomb guards were interrogated and put to death for falling asleep on watch. Investigations to find out who stole the body soon followed. A few days later, under the direction of Caiaphas, the soldiers whipped Joseph and Miriam and then rummaged through their home again. Joseph was taken before the Sanhedrin for more questioning. When he told Caiaphas that Jesus had risen from the dead, the chief priest had Joseph beaten again.

For weeks, attacks were commonplace against those who were thought to be disciples or those who had befriended the young rabbi. Fearing for Miriam as well as for Mary, Martha, and me, Joseph suggested we all sail to the western Mediterranean to a place known as Gaul. He told us to sell everything we owned. I kept only some clothing, the shroud, and the grail which still held Jesus' blood. I sealed it with part of a wineskin on which I wrote, *"The Cup of the Lord."* Joseph arranged us passage on a ship to western Europe. Once there, we found that although the land was Roman, it was still undeveloped. With part of his fortune, Joseph purchased a modest farming estate in what is now southern France.

It took years of toil just to learn the crops, the seasons, and finally how to make the place self-sufficient. Our diligence paid off. From Joseph I learned the value of hard work and perseverance. He was driven to succeed, but those rugged years took their toll; Miriam died at the end of our third winter in Aquitania. Despite the death of his wife, Joseph was determined to prosper. He taught Martha to run the household and the finances and trained Mary to oversee the farm and the laborers. I was surprised when he told me that he and I were going into business together.

Joseph's education in Arimathea had made him a gifted teacher and a good businessman, but his greatest calling was as the father I had never had as a child. My own father had abused and abandoned my family. One day Joseph took me on a trip to a small *stannum*, a tin mine, that was in operation nearby. I learned about tin and copper and their role in bronze production as well as pewter. He taught me everything: the mining and panning techniques as well as how the metal is separated from the other minerals and then heated and molded to become gray-colored ingots. Joseph took the time to be sure I knew the entire process of how the metals were combined at the foundries, then turned into bronze for sculptures and weapons and hundreds of other items such as tools, lamps and pins. Joseph treated me like his own son, teaching me the skills necessary to make my way in the world. And that was only the beginning. He also prepared me for the art of buying and selling ore to make bronze, something his father had taught him.

We first began purchasing tin from some small mines in Gaul and then selling the metal to the Romans at a profit. Joseph was always wealthy. He had such an astute mind for business that we became favored merchants, a factor that

17

made us enormously rich when we made inroads across the channel on the island of Britannia. The mines in Cornwall were laden with tin and copper, and Joseph took advantage of it. His organization and distribution skills were unsurpassed. We eventually became the largest tin merchants in the empire.

It had taken a dozen years, but money was easy and abundant. We purchased an even larger estate in Aquitania near a Jewish settlement called Septimania. In Gaul, Martha ran the affairs of the home, and Mary continued as the driving force behind the farm and our winemaking ventures. After a decade of booming trade in Britain, Joseph and I had become very wealthy. We were all in good health; life had never been better. Even our wines were becoming popular. The future looked bright, but elsewhere there was a violent storm brewing, one that would take the life of my mentor and see the annihilation of an entire Roman Legion.

II

Joseph and I were in Britain, spring slowly creeping its way up the island. For years in the region there had been a delicate, though amicable balance of power among the Romans, the Iceni, and the other tribes that inhabited Britain. All were thriving, enjoying the benefits of Roman order and commerce. Joseph and I became uneasy the day we heard that Prasutagus, the Icenian king, had died suddenly. Unsure of how this would affect trade, we hurried overland from the mines in Cornwall. By his will, Prasutagus' death left his kingdom in the hands of his wife and daughters. As a nominal ally of Rome, the Iceni people expected life to resume much as it had before. Roman law changed all that. While Iceni law accepted women as legitimate heirs, Roman law did not. Nero ordered the Roman Governor Seutonious to annex the Iceni lands without considering the consequences.

Seutonious saw the annexation as a legal opportunity to fill his coffers, and he ordered his troops to plunder the Iceni villages. When the Romans were threatened by Iceni Queen Boudica, she was overpowered and beaten, her daughters raped before her eyes. This Roman brutality ignited a firestorm that cost the lives of thousands. Intent on avenging her humiliation, Boudica rallied her own people and inspired the other nearby tribes to rebel against the Romans, something Seutonious didn't expect. Nonplussed, he ordered the Roman IX Legion to put down the revolt.

Joseph was angry at the stupidity of the Roman actions against the Iceni. Not only had the brutality overstepped the bounds of law, the Iceni were a strong and proud people. Joseph and I had actually met Queen Boudica a year earlier. We were interested in mining on Iceni land and were introduced to Prasutagus for some initial dialogue. Boudica, present at the meeting, appeared quite formidable.

That was months before, but now we were on the last leg of our journey from Cornwall, our carts creaking and heavy with tin ingots as we neared Londinium. We had heard no more of the rebellion, yet it was with a sigh of relief that we entered Britain's largest center of commerce.

18

The weather was cold and gray that day, and although the marketplace was busy, the mood of the populace was as gloomy as the weather. Usually a place full of laughter and smiles, there were very few greetings that day. We understood why when we heard about the great slaughter at Camulodunum—present day Colchester. The Iceni and their allies had burned the Roman town to the ground and slaughtered all its inhabitants.

Though there was still no news of the IX Legion, we were sure that 5000 well-trained Roman soldiers could easily handle a group of native combatants and that we were in no danger. But while Joseph knew the tin business well, his weakness was that he would spend days negotiating over mere pittances. His haggling was a ritual that delayed us for almost a week.

The day before we were to sail for Gaul, panic swept through the streets of Londinium. The Roman IX had been massacred. How could this happen? The unit had been wiped out to a man, and the hostiles reportedly were moving on the city. Joseph looked at me with great concern for we had often noted how poorly fortified the city was. Londinium had no stone walls, not even wooden palisades, and now there was only a small garrison force to protect it. If attacked, the city would be overrun and razed to the ground. We hurried to the inn, but before we could get there or even formulate a plan for leaving, the vanguard of Boudica's forces crested the top of the hill.

We froze in our footsteps. The Britons approached from the north. Moments later the main body topped the rise; there were thousands of them. With the exception of the Queen and a few chariots, the entire enemy force was on foot. The warriors moved rapidly. Boudica was beautiful and willowy, standing like an avenging angel as her force moved down the slope. The Londinium garrison fled like frightened children, leaving the city completely undefended. Pandemonium filled the streets.

"We're probably going to die here today," I said to Joseph.

"We can avert this slaughter," he said. "After all, we've met Boudica. Perhaps we can reason with her."

"Right now I'd say she doesn't look very reasonable."

"We have nothing to lose," Joseph said.

The Iceni Queen's heavy war chariot came to a stop on the main road about twenty paces from us. Her warriors halted even as she did.

All grew quiet as Joseph fell to his knees and cried out, "Great Queen! We humbly ask that you show mercy to this city."

Boudica eyed us with cold recognition. "Get up, tin man!" her voice boomed as my friend rose to his feet. "I will show this place mercy, Roman mercy," she went on, raising her arm in the air.

I grabbed Joseph's hand with a jerk and yelled, "Run!"

"Kill them! Kill them all! Burn this place! Avenge my daughters!" we heard Boudica shout as we fled.

The enemy entered the city like a flood, warriors wielding swords and torches, burning everything. There was no organized resistance. Fear swept through Londinium like an epidemic. Panic-stricken swarms of people bolted for the river, trampling others who hoped to get away. Within minutes the city was overrun and on fire. People were cut down or clubbed as they ran, like animals in a slaughterhouse.

Unable to avoid the fleeing mob, Joseph and I were caught up in the panic, but there was no way to escape the carnage. Like stampeding cattle, people ran in confusion. A large group of tribesmen with axes and clubs drove us into the blades of some awaiting Iceni swordsmen, and the butchery began. A tall, black-bearded warrior uttered a war cry and felled Joseph with one swoosh of his bronze sword. My friend crumpled. As I reached down for him I felt something sharp bury itself in my left shoulder. I went down in a heap.

A hazy grey fog shrouded the city when I awoke the next day. My shoulder and head ached, but I was alive. I staggered to my feet, aghast at what I saw. Londinium had been burned to the ground. Bodies were everywhere. Joseph lay dead beside me. The nauseating smell of seared flesh and death hung in the air.

The Iceni were gone, and they took with them anything of value. There were few survivors, those who had managed to hide. There were dogs licking and picking at the carcasses. It was beyond terrible. Joseph was as cold as the morning. My friend, the man I loved like a father, was dead. Tears filled my eyes and my heart. Joseph was gone, and somehow I was still alive. How could I be alive when I should have died in the attack? I didn't understand. I was despondent as I buried my friend.

I stayed in Londinium only long enough to see the Romans and some of the surviving locals begin the task of rebuilding. Without Joseph, the voyage back home to Gaul was long and lonely. He had given me so much, and he had taught me to be kind and generous through his example. I had lost my closest friend and confidant, a father.

Thursday, July 11, 3:10 p.m.

"I lost my father a couple of months ago." Braden turned his head to look at a photo on his desk. "Heart attack," he said. "He taught me how to trust in the Lord and to enjoy life. I don't know what I'd have been like without him."

"He sounds like he was a great dad."

"He was. I try to teach my children what he taught me. I still don't know how I'll get by without his advice. What did you do?"

The Two Sisters

*I still dread all my sufferings...*Job 9:28

The decade following Joseph's death was one of the most difficult times of my life. Returning to Aquitania, I couldn't imagine going on without Joseph, but it was Mary who kept us together. Even though we all had grown so close to Joseph and felt his loss deeply, Mary forced us to keep working and stay busy.

It took me more than a year of grieving to move on, but we concentrated on the estate. I gave up the tin business in order to focus on the vineyard. We were producing so much wine and there was such a market for it that we were making more money than ever before. Although we missed Joseph, we were happy to be together. Martha kept the vineyard operating efficiently by hiring more peasants from nearby villages. Neither she nor Mary had accepted any suitors over the years, not that there weren't men who were interested. My sisters had only two concerns: worshiping the Lord and keeping our family together.

One bitterly cold night, Mary and I returned home from a trip south to Hispania where we had contracted with a merchant who desired to sell our wine. This man had traveled a great deal and talked of the growth of the Church. Mary had insisted on going despite having a persistent cough. It was a pleasant trip. The entire way home we spoke of almost nothing but Jesus and how he gave his life for the sin of the world.

"You were so close to Him," I said "closer than perhaps any other woman except for Mary."

I looked at her and we both laughed.

"How can Mary be closer than Mary?" she asked.

"Maybe even closer than His mother," I added.

"He is as close as we desire Him to be," she smiled. Then her brow suddenly grew wrinkled with concern. "For some reason I feel we need to pray for Martha."

About half a day's journey from the estate, we prayed the rest of the way, interceding for our sister. When we arrived the staff met us at the door. Martha had suffered a seizure and was partially paralyzed. Now well into her sixties, Martha looked every bit the old woman. I'm not sure if she was aware of us, and upon seeing her I knew she wouldn't live through the night. I looked at Mary who was weeping as she prayed. I took Mary's hand and then held Martha's.

"I love you, sister," I said.

I felt a small squeeze from Martha's hand before she closed her eyes and was gone.

Mary uttered a soul-wrenching cry, her head in her hands. I tried to console her; grief overwhelmed us as we embraced. As I held Mary in my arms a cold thought whispered that Mary would be next. Tears burst from my eyes, for I didn't know how I could go on without them.

The day we buried Martha, Mary said, "Some day soon I will be lying in the grave."

"As will we all," I said.

"Lazarus." Mary cupped my face in her hands the way she had done when I was a boy. "Have you noticed anything about yourself?"

"What is there to notice?"

"You haven't a gray hair, and you haven't a wrinkle—not one."

"Some people just don't show their age," I said. Until then I'd never thought about it. I assumed I was like everyone else. But what Mary said scared me because I was so afraid of being alone.

Five months later Mary contracted tuberculosis. The disease started with a drop of blood, the same way it had begun with me. I took care of her personally over the course of the next few months, but each day there was more coughing and more blood. I knew there was nothing I could do except pray. Though she lingered for some time, Mary's body was aged and tired. The sickness finally consumed all of her.

The day she died, Mary called me to her bedside. Her breathing was short and wheezy. "I will leave you today, little brother," she said.

"Don't say that." I clasped her hands in mine.

"It's all right," she said. "It's time. The Lord is calling me home. He spoke to me last night and told me to give you a message. He said tell Lazarus that I will never leave nor forsake him." She shuddered and whispered "I love you" as she closed her eyes and breathed her last earthly sigh.

Everyone I loved was gone, and I was completely alone. For months I grieved for my family: Mary, Martha, and Joseph. During my despondency, the staff took care of everything. I finally pulled out of my depression and devoted my time to my family's legacy. We had all worked hard to make the winery beautiful. My goal was to set up the vineyard so that it could be run for long periods of time in my absence. I longed to go back home to Israel, but I couldn't let all our hard work literally die on the vine.

It took almost two years to find the right staff and train them. Everything seemed in order that summer as I said goodbye and sailed for Judea.

Masada

Trust in the Lord with all your heart, and lean not on your own understanding.
Proverbs 3:5

I

My first return to Israel was largely a matter of poor timing. Of course, bad timing is often a frequent companion of a lack of prayer. I'd heard about the terrible revolt in Judea, but I thought that because I had money, I could do anything. With that in mind, I wrote my own letters of reference, although I failed to research the political climate of the area. I knew the temple had been destroyed and that the Romans had killed thousands of rebels, but more than a year had passed since the heaviest fighting. I believed Judea would be hostile but safe. That was my first mistake. My second mistake was going back.

The trip across the Mediterranean was pleasant enough, and my trip to Jerusalem was uneventful. The year was 72 A.D. Jerusalem had not changed much in four decades. The Romans were there when I left; they were there when I returned. Were they cruel? All conquerors seem cruel, but is there any true freedom? There must always be some kind of government to prevent anarchy. Rome provided stability and the rule of law in the region, something it had lacked.

The situation seemed harmless enough for me and my hired servant Cai; however, all of that changed the first night I was there. I should have turned around when we first entered Jerusalem. I felt a deep hollowness in the pit of my stomach as we rode in and saw the great temple ruins. Large square blocks, almost the size of a man, were strewn about where the building had once been. Their gray and black scorch marks indicated the place had been sacked and burned. Only a part of the temple wall remained upright, and several Jewish men in drab cloaks knelt and wept before what was left of the great structure. Roman soldiers eyed us suspiciously as we plodded past them.

Cai and I had difficulty finding lodgings, but we finally found a modest inn with a room. Later that evening we entered a drinking establishment and wound up in a brawl, a decision I would regret for decades.

Trying to be a good Samaritan, I stepped into the middle of an argument between two drunkards. After a bench-breaking, chin-splitting, bare-knuckles fist fight, I ended up relieved of my purse. More importantly, Cai was killed in the melee. My foolish decision had cost a man his life.

I awoke early the next morning in the dusty street. My head felt as if it had been split open as I was roused rudely by Roman soldiers. No one knew me, and my money and letters of introduction were gone. Even my coat had been stolen. The soldiers, who I'm sure had orders to arrest any dissidents, immediately took me by the arms and threw me bodily into a slave cart. I was now a victim of the Roman stability that I had long enjoyed. I had neglected to procure Roman citizenship over the years because I felt it unnecessary, believing that my wealth made me invulnerable. That senseless decision haunted me for the next 30 years.

I was taken from Jerusalem and pressed into slavery for Gaius Silva, the Roman commander at a place called Masada.

Masada was the former fortress of Herod the Great, who had ruled in Judea a century before. The father of Herod Antipas, the Jewish ruler during the time of Jesus, Herod the Great feared revolt and had fortified the place as a refuge from his enemies. For decades the bastion was used very little, but around 70 A.D. a group of Jewish zealots called the Sicarii overcame the Roman garrison there. Once there, the Sicarii harassed the Romans, attacking small patrols, even destroying some nearby Jewish settlements, killing most of the inhabitants. After these attacks, the extremists would retreat to the fortress which was impossible to assault.

The Jews said that Masada had two temperatures, hot and blistering. I arrived there at the end of the hot season. I was one of thousands forced to work on a giant ramp that led to the eastern side of the rocky fortress of Masada which sat atop a mountain overlooking the desert and the Dead Sea. The only way up was a narrow passage known as the Serpent's Path that snaked its way up the side of the mammoth rock. Inside the fortress were hundreds of Sicarii under the leadership of Ben Eleazar. The rebels believed all of Judea should have revolted against the foreigners. The zealots hated their fellow Jews almost as much as they hated the Romans.

A full-scale attack against Masada was impossible. Not only did it tower over the ground below, Herod had built a strong wall around it as well. Realizing that an attack up the small paths would be piecemeal at best, the Romans were building a giant ramp from which to launch an assault. Fortunately the ramp was well underway by the time I arrived at the massive project. It had been under construction for months, so our work was simple: dig up sand, dirt, and rock, load it on carts and take it to the ramp, then dump it and tamp it down.

The Romans treated us like cattle, yet it was the heat that was most cruel. Sometimes it was a dry heat, sometimes humid, but the blazing sun didn't care if we were Roman or Jew. Slave, centurion, general, all were punished equally as far as the heat was concerned. I don't know whose job was worse, the slave who labored endlessly beneath the sun which hung in the sky like the devil's anvil, or the Roman soldier who baked in his uniform under the same blazing orb, immobile, standing over a line of sweaty slaves.

Day after agonizing day, the routine was the same. The only breaks came when Gaius Silva addressed the rebels perched atop the mountain. On these occasions, he was met with the same treatment time after time. The rebels replied by shooting arrows, throwing rocks, or flinging excrement down upon the Romans. This kind of exchange went on for months, but every day the ramp inched higher—slowly, inexorably, creeping upward toward the fortress.

II

Two weeks before the ramp was done, I was placed with another group of workers where I met an old man named Levi. We became friends, but it was clear to me that Levi's life was not to be a long one. The heat devoured him. He collapsed several times a day, and finally, just days before the ramp was finished, Levi passed out beneath the scorching sun. I reached down to help him up, but he grabbed me by the back of the neck, pulled me close and began to whisper.

"There is something I must tell you, but you must swear to do as I ask," he said.

"I'll do it." I said, brushing the caked dirt from his cheek.

"First you must give me your word."

"Upon my honor, I swear. What is it?"

"There is a great secret that no one knows," Levi said. "My father's father's father was a mason who worked on the Great Herod's fortress many years ago. Herod was a tyrant, but he was no fool. There is a tunnel hewn out of the rock leading to the top of Masada."

"I don't understand. The ramp is almost finished and the rock is surrounded by Roman troops. The zealots could not possibly escape," I said.

"You need only save one," his voice trailed off as he gasped for breath. "You must save my daughter."

"You have a daughter up there with the Sicarii?!" I said incredulously, pointing to the mountain top.

"The passage is the only way to save her from the Romans," he whispered. "Her name is Esther."

"How will I know her? Where is the passage?" I asked.

Forcing out the words, Levi said, "You must look for the door in the rock— beneath the talon."

The old man died in my arms, shrinking like a used wineskin. He was taken to the burial pit, and I was left with his secret.

I spent every night for the next few days looking for something called "the talon." The Romans knew that there was no running away this deep in the desert. The only other way of escape was the Dead Sea which was worse than the barren landscape. Deserting slaves who were caught were crucified, and they were all caught.

Masada was known by all as "the Rock," but no one I asked had ever heard of a landmark called "the talon." Each day, like an earthen glacier, the ramp inched its way up, irrevocably toward the fortress. Security was noticeably lax away from the ramp and the Serpent's Path, since they were the only way up to the top.

The night the ramp was finally finished, I set about searching for Levi's talon once again. I don't know how I noticed it this time; perhaps the way the rays of the setting sun struck the crags, but it was now clear. A deep fissure ran down the side of the mountain and branched into five cracks, giving the semblance of an eagle's claw.

I immediately looked for some kind of opening, but there was none. Whatever was there was not obvious. I searched until the light grew dim, examining the side of the mountain, but I found nothing. I felt along the base of the rock without success. Frustrated, I sat down and leaned against a boulder. It moved, ever so slightly; I felt the rock give. I stood and turned quickly, pushing against the slab again. It was of such intricate design that, with just the right pressure, it swiveled almost effortlessly. The opening revealed a dark cavern.

III

I took a tinderbox inside and lit the torch I had stolen from the camp. The chamber was stale from lack of use and led to some crude stairs carved in the rock. The steps were steep, chiseled out of the stone, and rising so sharply that a grown man could barely stand up. It was as if an army of dwarves had fashioned the clean-cut steps, hewing them out of the mountain itself. I started up the stairway. There were hundreds of steps; they went up, up, and ever upward in a spiral fashion. Each flicker of the torchlight revealed only dust, cobwebs, and more steps as I made my ascent. After what seemed an eternity, I finally emerged at the top of the crude stairwell where there was another small chamber.

A pile of dry, dusty torches lay beside the wall. There was also a door crafted like the one that gave me entry; it too swiveled. Again I entered a dark chamber. I followed a passageway that led to some hidden caves in which were huge cisterns of water. I returned to the top of the stairs and searched for another entry. In the torchlight I noticed another door in the wall. I pushed it open and was suddenly inside a long-deserted room. The air was fresh, but cobwebs and remnants of old, broken furniture littered what must have once been a sitting room in Herod's retreat.

I slipped into the dimly-lit room, took a stone, and placed it by the opening to make sure I could find my way out. As I closed the secret door, it vanished into the pattern of rocky wall. Once inside I tried the door which opened easily with a gentle push. Who else knew this existed?

In the faint light I saw an open door and moved toward it. Again outside and behind a row of columns, I found I was in the lower tier of the northern palace looking down upon the twinkling fires of the Roman camps below. A somber darkness clung to the fortress. I climbed the steps to the highest tier where I smelled smoke coming from somewhere atop Masada. I heard voices close by and singing coming from a distance. I was about to begin my search for Levi's daughter when fate intervened. Two Sicarii lookouts spotted me and I was suddenly surrounded by Eleazar's warriors.

The rebels strong-armed me into a large room in the western palace where I was face to face with Ben Eleazar, the leader of the rebellion. Eleazar taught his band of zealots not only to hate Rome but also to despise any Jews who didn't fight the Romans. Eleazar stood with his back to a large wooden chair on an elevated stage in the center of the room, men surrounding him. He eyed me suspiciously for quite some time.

Eleazar was large for a Jew. He had dark curly hair, olive skin, and deep brown, intelligent eyes that burned with anger. The leader studied me for a few moments.

"Who are you?" he barked angrily.

"My name is Lazarus. I am one of the ramp slaves," I said.

Eyes blazing, Eleazar looked at me suspiciously. "A ramp slave? So you are one of the traitors who is too weak to resist Rome. How did you get up here? There are guards posted all along the Serpent's Path."

"Stealth and darkness helped me slip past the Romans as well as your guards."

"I find it hard to believe you could get past my men." He paused, as if choosing his words carefully. "Why did you come here?"

"There was an old slave below named Levi who succumbed to the heat. Before he died he made me promise to rescue his daughter, Esther."

Muffled steps approached, echoing through the palace as the men of Masada shuffled into the great chamber.

"These are the men of Masada," Eleazar said to me.

"You know you cannot win," I said. "You cannot defeat Rome. No one can."

"Spoken like a servile traitor," the Sicarii leader went on. "We have already defeated them, and we will have victory in this last battle. Bind and gag this man and put him in the antechamber," he said, pointing to his left.

I was led into the compartment off of the great room. Even behind the heavy door I could tell Eleazar was doing all of the talking as I overheard bits and pieces of his speech. The leader's voice was indistinct except for his inflection. After a few minutes the door opened, and I was led back out to Eleazar. Only a dozen or so men still remained with their leader who ordered them to untie me.

"Jebbeth will take you to see Esther and her children," Eleazar said, presenting me to a Sicarii warrior. "Make sure that this man joins us in our final victory over Rome."

IV

As I pondered how Eleazar believed the Sicarii could defeat the Romans, Jebbeth led me back toward the northern palace under the starlit sky to another building, originally the servants' quarters. The dark, stone buildings were used by several Sicarii families. We passed through a large sandy hallway and found a well-lit room that housed two women and several children. They looked fearful as we entered.

"This man has come to see you," Jebbeth said in a gravelly voice.

"Which of you is Esther?" I asked.

An attractive woman came forward. "I am Esther, and this is my friend Tamor and her children." She pointed to the little ones.

Esther's clothes were worn and plain, making her dark eyes and soft features all the more lovely. Her delicate beauty was out of place here, and she carried herself like someone resigned to her fate.

"I do not know you," she said, her voice sadly musical.

"Nor I you, but I knew Levi."

"You know my father?" Her eyes lit up.

"Yes, we were slaves on the ramp. He died only a few nights ago."

"Dead!" She burst into tears and fell to her knees.

"The heat killed him." I knelt beside her and pressed her head against my shoulder. "Before he died he made me promise to take you from this place."

"Take me where?" she asked through her tears.

"Where is your husband?"

"He's dead. I have no one," she said, her large brown eyes full of sorrow. "He died on the Serpent's Path at the hands of the Romans."

The door to the outside creaked shut as Jebbeth stood with his hand on the hilt of his sheathed sword.

"It is time," he said, his blade metallically whispering death as he pulled it from the scabbard. His features were grimly set.

"You're going to kill us?" I asked him. "I thought you wanted to kill Romans."

"Our victory over Rome will stand for all time," Jebbeth said. "By taking our own lives we deprive Rome of its conquest."

I was astounded. "What! That's Eleazar's plan to defeat the Romans? Kill yourselves?" I asked.

"Each man is responsible for taking the lives of his family. These women have no family, so I was assigned to them." He pointed to the women and children. "Then the men will draw lots to see which ten will take the lives of the rest. Finally, one man will take the lives of the ten. The Romans will find nothing."

"The Romans?" I said incredulously. "After this siege and all this time the best Eleazar has is mass suicide? This is your final victory over Rome? That doesn't make sense."

Jebbeth moved toward me, sword drawn menacingly.

"Can we at least pray first?" I pleaded.

The Sicarri soldier took a step back and said, "You may have a moment."

I turned to Esther and Tamor, "Go to the lowest room in the northern palace. Look for the rock against the wall. There's a door there," I whispered.

"That's enough," Jebbeth said as he again stepped forward.

I looked around for something to use as a weapon and backed away, but I found only a blanket. Frantically, I wrapped it about my right arm. The women and children huddled in the corner.

The advancing warrior began slashing with his blade, and I dodged, rolling the blanket tighter with every backward step. Jebbeth now moved slowly and cautiously, forcing me into the corner with the door at my back. I held the blanket at chin level, awaiting his next move. He lunged, and like a madman, I let the cover unfurl to mask my targeted torso. Too close, the blade slipped past my rib cage, cutting the flesh, but sticking in the wooden door behind me.

With my body against the door, I charged and punched Jebbeth's face through the blanket. We went sprawling and sliding across the floor to the other side of the room. Both of us twisting on the floor, I wrapped my arms around him with a bear hug and squeezed. He struggled to break free.

"Run!" I yelled, my hold beginning to weaken.

Esther grabbed the door handle, flung it open, and the women and children ran out into the darkness.

A moment later Jebbeth broke my hold and cuffed me across the chin. We struggled to our feet, and I kicked him in the stomach. He doubled over in pain but rushed me and pinned me against the wall before he caught me with a roundhouse blow to my head. The impact stunned me, and by the time I came to my senses, Jebbeth had pulled his sword from the door and stood behind me, his blade resting against my neck.

"Shalom," he whispered as he slit my throat.

The gash was burning cold, and as Jebbeth pulled away, his long knife was red with my blood. Woozy from the trauma, I grasped the mushy, spurting wound and began to wobble. I stood only long enough to see him bring the hilt of his sword down upon my skull. I was sure I would die at Masada as I felt myself slipping away.

V

Just before dawn I awoke. My head still hurt, and I was groggy as I tried to piece together the events of the night before. I found myself face down in a pool of crusted blood. I pulled myself to my knees and examined the heavy blanket wrapped around my arm. The cloth was soaked with blood. I cautiously put my hand to my throat to touch the gash where my neck had been ripped open. The wound had totally healed. In that fearful moment I realized that I would never die. In sobering silence I began to understand the full meaning of that revelation.

I suddenly realized that I should have died with Joseph in Londinium years before. Afterward even Mary had recognized that I wasn't aging. My mind tried to comprehend what immortality really meant—outliving everyone I knew, watching them all go to their graves as I had Joseph, Mary, and Martha.

I struggled to my feet and looked around the darkened room. It was empty. Outside I saw the first glimmering rays of the sun peeping over the horizon. I began to look around in the apartments and found rooms littered with the dead. No one was left alive. I even went back to the great room where I'd met Ben Eleazar. He was as cold as the slab on which he lay. The smoke from the western palace grew thicker, hanging like a shroud. I didn't have time to search for the two women and children because I heard the clanging of Roman arms. The legionnaires had begun their assault from the ramp. They came over the wall expecting a bloody fight.

There was an uneasy hush among the Romans as they began to grasp the situation. I heard a centurion shouting orders that faded into an eerie silence...the song of the dead. I knew I could do no more for Esther, so I quickly slipped into the early morning shadows and ran back to the northern palace, then down the steps to the lower tier. Once there I found where I'd marked the hidden passage and made my way back down the dark steps inside the throat of Masada.

On the ground below I was obviously never missed. Perhaps it was because of the commotion atop Herod's fortress. The Romans were stunned and angry. The Jews below believed their conquerors were lying to them and that all of the Sicarii had been put to the sword. Later in the day, there came word from some soldiers; two women and some children had hidden and survived in the caves of the cisterns.

I knew the survivors had to be Esther, Tamor, and her children. I thanked God that I had helped save them. I was relieved that the siege and the violent martyrdom of Masada was over. I hoped I would be able to go back to my life in Aquitania. But my destiny was not Gaul; I was taken to Jerusalem in a slave cart and sent to Rome where I was to be sold.

Pompeii

When the people saw...the mountain in smoke, they trembled with fear.
Exodus 20:18

I

Pompeii was one of the most beautiful places I'd ever been. Close to the sea, most of the buildings had flat roof patio terraces so residents could view either the serene Mediterranean to the west or the towering Mt. Vesuvius to the east. In many ways Pompeii was the world's first resort city. I was sold into the service of Senator Marcus Antonus, a good Roman of wealthy means. Pompeii was his family's summer home; the family's primary residence was in Mediolanum, present day Milan. The Senator purchased me because of my knowledge of languages. I was to become the tutor for Marcus Antonus' five children, instructing them in Latin, Greek, and Gallic. Within two years time I was second only to the steward of the house, Labiathus, a stubborn but likeable man who personally saw to the interests of the family and had done so for decades.

I find it ironic that those seven years as a slave in Pompeii were among the happiest years of my life. It was my first experience as part of a family with children. Antonus was often home as we traveled between the family's primary residence and summer retreat. The *domina* of the household, Apollonia, a beautiful, moody brunette, was a loving wife and mother. There were four boys: Augustus was ten, Marcus eight, Romulus and Remus were six. Liddy, a little girl, was born after I was purchased. They were all dark haired like their father. The children were not always eager to learn. After a short time under my tutelage, they realized that I had high expectations of them as well as the full backing of their father, so discipline was rarely an issue.

Marcus Antonus was one of the most forward thinking Romans I ever knew. Because I was not a Roman, the Senator was all the more anxious to learn as much as possible from me, especially on the topics of history, politics, and religion. He was surprised to find out that I was a Christian and asked me for a full account of my beliefs. He told me that publicly he was expected to believe in the Roman gods, but privately he had reservations. The Senator even desired that I explain my beliefs to his entire family, which was risky to do at that time.

The children were very inquisitive about Jesus, the nature of sin, and why God would have to die to save man. Augustus, the oldest as well as the leader, believed Christianity was a weak religion.

"If your god is the only god, then why does Rome rule the world? It just doesn't make sense. Besides, how can a god or a son of a god die?" he asked.

"Man's flesh is corruptible and dies," I explained. "God wants man's heart because He loves man. The power of love is greater than any other and is eternal. Only by becoming a man and sacrificing His own flesh could God prove His love for man and save man from sin."

Augustus shook his head in disbelief. He was serious about the family and its good name. He was impeccable in matters of manners and dress, believing that it was up to him to set the example for the other children. He would often scold the young ones, accusing them of laziness in their studies, drilling them and constantly warning, badgering, and harassing them about doing their best. His younger brother Marcus was the comedian of the family and frustrated the dour Augustus.

While Augustus was serious, Marcus' goal was to make the others laugh. Sometimes, during a lesson, Marcus would contort his face weasel-fashion and gyrate wildly while making bird noises. The other children chimed in with a chorus of giggles. At first I reprimanded the boy, and Augustus threatened to tell the Senator. But by the second year even I could not keep a straight face at Marcus' antics.

The twins were young boys whose heads were full of the ideals of courage and valor. They loved to play Rome versus Carthage, arguing and quibbling over who was going to be Roman general Scipio Africanus and who was to play Hannibal, the enemy general whose army terrorized the Italian peninsula for almost two decades. With centuries of victory as a foundation for Roman culture, finding stories the boys wanted to hear about war was never a problem. The twins were good-hearted lads. They would often pool their money to buy gifts for the Senator and their adoring mother. Romulus and Remus were also interested in the Ten Commandments, especially the commandment about honoring parents. Marcus and Apollonia had taught their boys well.

The most loveable of the children was Liddy. She was born three years after I was added to the household, and she was the darling of the family. Apollonia joked that Liddy began walking and talking in the womb. She had such wild black hair that the other children called her "Barbar," short for barbarian. Liddy would wake each morning, climb into her parents' bed, and shower her mother and father with big, sloppy, wet kisses. The entire family was enamored of her, myself included. She charmed us all with her smiles and her songs. She was always singing. One day when she was four, I overheard her singing of God's love for little children.

"Where did you learn that song?" I asked.

"Jesus taught me," she whispered. "I see Him in my prayers."

Then Liddy jumped into my arms and with the tenderness of a moonbeam said, "Jesus says He knows you."

I held her in my arms for a moment as tears welled up in my eyes. I asked, "Do you talk with Him?"

"Oh, yes. He is..." Liddy tilted her head as she searched for words. Then she opened her arms wide and said, "He is big love!" She gave me a quick peck on the cheek before wriggling down to the floor and scampering out of the room.

II

Each day during that spring and summer the children and I spent two hours on language studies. They were all smart and quick to learn. After lessons, we often went up the side of the mountain to pick berries and wildflowers. The little ones loved our hikes as did I. It took the remainder of the morning to go up into the woods, find flowers, and enjoy our noon meal.

I will never forget the horror of that August day. Liddy was four and the boys were in their teens. We decided to go up on the mountain and left midmorning. The day was golden as we began our climb to our favorite spot. Berry season was over, but wildflowers were abundant. The children begged to pick as many blossoms as possible as their offering for the celebration of Vulcanalia. The pagan festival celebrated Vulcan's power to stop fires at this vulnerable time of the year, just prior to the harvest. There would be food, dancing, and bonfires in the city.

Our ascent that morning was nothing unusual, a series of climbs interrupted only by the twins' antics, almost always a screaming ambush followed by laughter and wrestling until everyone was gasping for breath. What was unusual was the atmosphere on the mountain, thick and oppressive, unlike anything I'd ever known. The wood was overly quiet; we had not seen any wildlife, not even so much as a bird. I thought it odd but dismissed it. When we reached our picnicking spot, the twins ran off again. As I began to prepare the meal, I heard Romulus calling for me; I followed his voice in the direction of a nearby stream. It was gone; a trail of muddy silt told where spring water once flowed.

"Look," Romulus said, pointing at Remus. His brother was walking ahead of us toward a dead buck lying in the mud that was once a vibrant stream. A hazy cloud bubbled up from the mire and hung in the air near the carcass. The boy's curiosity drew him.

"Remus," I cried out, sensing danger. "Don't go near it."

Mesmerized and ignoring my warning, the boy moved ever closer to the hart. It was as if a spell had been cast over him. I ran to intercept, but the child stopped a few paces from the dead stag and stood as still as though he were made of wood. Then the boy swooned and dropped to the ground like a felled tree. I ran, quickly scooped him up, and backed away from the area. Moments later I lay Remus on the ground; his breathing was irregular, his skin ashen.

The rest of the children pressed in to see their brother.

"Is he alive?" Romulus asked as they clamored even closer.

Remus groggily awoke, but he was as pale as a vapor. By the narrowest of margins he had avoided death.

"We're leaving," I said.

Without protest from the children, we turned back and hurried down the mountain and back to the safety of Pompeii. But when we reached the city I felt a sense of imminent danger, a heavy angst as if a boulder were on my chest. I knew that we needed to get away from the mountain, away from Pompeii.

Upon arriving home, the children were starving and poured into the kitchen.

"You're back early," Labiathus greeted me as I entered the pink, stuccoed villa.

"We've got to leave. We need to head back to Mediolanum," I said.

With a look of questioning surprise on his face the steward said, "The Senator and his wife are away. We cannot just leave without consulting them. What's wrong?"

"Labiathus," I said. "On the mountain—no life, no water, no birds. Something's terribly strange. Remus almost died up there! We saw a dead stag; the whole place is dead. We're lucky the boy is still alive. I don't know why, but I feel we must leave here as soon as possible."

"We can't just pack up and leave without Marcus Antonus' permission! I can't allow it. Besides, maybe the boy just fainted? If the area was bad around the animal, why didn't it affect you or the rest of the children? The Senator and his wife will return in three days; surely this can wait."

"You don't understand; something terrible is about to happen. It's dangerous to remain here."

"You're just spooked; I've never seen you so jumpy."

"Labiathus, I'm not jumpy. Something is very wrong!"

"No matter. We're not going anywhere until the Senator returns," he retorted with a glare of finality.

Before the echo of Labiathus' words faded, we felt the earth tremble, and we heard a terrific boom as the mountain whose very shadow we had lived under exploded. Running outside we looked toward Vesuvius which was disgorging a large black cloud into the once cerulean sky. At first we thought it was just smoke, but soon a light flaky ash began to fall like dirty snow.

"Does this convince you that we need to go?" I growled at Labiathus.

"There is no need to fear; the gods will protect us," he said. "We will wait until the Senator returns." He hurried back into the villa.

III

The rest of the afternoon crawled by. The mountain continued to grumble, and the ash became heavier, causing darkness to fall like twilight in mid-afternoon. Night came, and the evening was thick with heat. Shards of pumice clattered against the roof and sides of the villa, then noisily down the walls outside the home. I couldn't sleep and got up to pray, but another great rumbling shook the house to its foundation. I spent the rest of the night pacing like a caged animal before a storm. Early the next morning the mountain continued groaning as if it were a blacksmith's forge. Vulcan, the Roman god of fire and metalworking, hammered away, deep within the mountain's innards. Other families had begun to flee the city. Even so, Labiathus refused to let us go.

Late in the fourth hour the falling ash began to wane somewhat. We became hopeful when light began to sift its way through the cloud, and we went from near darkness to a heavily overcast sky. We thought the worst might be over, but suddenly the mountain top blew apart; a massive explosion rocked the earth to its very core. Vesuvius raged and spat, and a terrified Pompeii lay in hiding, like a child under a blanket. Our household hurried onto the terrace, now ankle deep in ash, to gaze at the mountain. Through the gray sky we saw a monstrous black cloud growing out of the mouth of the volcano, heavy and thick, as if the mountain were a boil oozing with black pus. The dark cloud climbed high into the air like the fist of Zeus. "We cannot stay a moment longer," I said.

"I fear we're already too late, and I'm to blame," Labiathus whispered, hanging his head, his eyes red and swollen.

The black cloud roiled like a swarm of locusts winging on the wind and flying directly toward us.

We hurried back inside. I felt compelled to travel east, but Labiathus argued that the ocean was the most logical way of escape. Labiathus, young Marcus, and I each grabbed a shield from the Senator's armory. Before we could leave, it seemed as if someone had pulled a shade before our eyes; there was no light to guide us as we opened the door. Pompeii was already a wasteland. Burning coals sang through the air like flaming arrows. We left the villa and moved single file through the hot ash. I piggy-backed Liddy while the boys struggled to fend for themselves. We pushed through as quickly as we could, using the shields to plow through the ash and cover our heads.

The entire scene was surreal. The blanket of ash muffled every sound except that of the hot coals which fell like whistling brimstone from heaven. I thought it might be the end of the world. Meanwhile, the mountain continued its rumbling, vomiting coals which exploded against our shields. After what seemed an eternity, we finally made the sea gate, but as we passed through, a wave of people was coming back, running away from the docks.

"It's no use; the boats can't move," a voice shouted. We stopped in our tracks, shields held over our heads. I moved toward the voice I'd heard amidst the roar of the mountain and the ever-whizzing hot pumice.

"What do you mean? Why can't the boats move?"

"The gods have it in for us. Even the rocks are floating on the water, and the ships are burning."

Knowing we should have gone east, I clenched my teeth and turned back to the family.

"Now what?" Labiathus asked grimly.

IV

In the leaden light, the children looked to me for an answer. I stood Liddy on the ground and tilted the shield back a little to look at the falling ash that pelted us. It was blowing toward the southeast. Since west took us to the sea, south in the direction of the ashfall, and north to Vesuvius, east seemed our only choice.

"We'll head for Nuceria," I said. "We'll have to hurry."

Liddy climbed on my back, and the boys again fell into our serpentine column with Labiathus bringing up the rear. Though covered with ash, the road was easy to follow because of the buildings. The Nuceria gate was open and abandoned. We wrapped our faces with our clothing to keep from breathing in the ashy air, and we shuffled southeast along the road, hoping to get out from under the ash cloud.

With each step the heat grew more unbearable as Vesuvius hurled thick burning rock and ash at us. Red glowing fragments whistled through the dark sky and clattered off of our shields before burying themselves in the ash. All around us the landscape glowed like dying embers; tree trunks burned like gigantic torches. As we trudged onward, the children whimpered, their bodies stung from the hot ash. The eerie setting was a vivid reminder of hell. Moving became increasingly difficult as the ash was now almost shin high, and hot pumice blistered our feet as we walked. The children cried aloud from the oppressive heat; even Augustus winced from the pain. Visibility was only a few feet, and still the ash continued to fall. It was as though we were wading through a scalding river. The ash became thicker and hotter as we continued to plow it out of our way, like shoveling through the hot coals of a bonfire. Even the shields became so hot I thought they'd catch fire. We had to wrap wads of cloth around our arms and hands just to hold them.

Liddy clung to my back. Because of the sweltering heat, we were soaked through from perspiration, but we had to keep moving. I held the shield in front, and the boys and Labiathus huddled tightly behind me, continuing to use the shields for protection.

"This is like the testudo formation the legions use," said Romulus bravely.

We walked like convicts manacled together for quite some time before stopping to rest. Though we couldn't sit, we did try to catch our breath in the sulfurous air. The children complained that they were thirsty. We'd brought no water. I looked around, trying to get my bearings amidst the blackness and the fires that glowed dully in the dark.

I was afraid. The children were now my responsibility; we had no safe place to rest. While the tree line offered us some idea of where the road was, some burning pines had fallen and forced us to go around them, impeding our progress.

Still we trudged onward. Staying on the route was painstaking as we plowed the ash out of the way to make sure we hadn't wandered from the road. We were not moving quickly enough. The children and Labiathus were exhausted and dehydrated. I too felt the pangs of thirst and fatigue.

I was so stupid. Even though Labiathus was the undisputed head of the household when the senator and his wife were gone, I should have ignored him. Why had I not left with the children? I should have brought water. I should have insisted that we get out when I first sensed danger. These thoughts peppered my mind as we shuffled along in the fiery darkness like shackled prisoners.

The volcano mocked my fear with another tremendous rumble, and ash began to fall harder and heavier. Long red streaks of molten heat dropped from the sky. I could barely breathe, and I knew the others were having a more difficult time than I. I began to take large steps, trying to get the children to move quickly, but it was as impossible as running through a sea of scalding sand. I could see nothing but the mountain's red streaks sizzling through the air.

Romulus and Remus were the first to drop. I handed Liddy to Augustus while Labiathus and I each carried one of the twins. Our progress was even slower, but after a few more paces, we stepped out from under the heavy ash fall. Here the ash was only about shin deep and fell much more lightly.

"We have to rest," said Labiathus. "I can't go on."

"Please, Lazarus," said Marcus. "Let us sit for a moment."

Although I knew we were still in danger, I acquiesced. We found some respite beneath the archway of an aqueduct. We scraped the ash away and sat down. I don't know how long we rested. We were all so weary that we may have dozed off, but I was awakened by a terrific explosion. I looked up and saw a huge orange blast blow out the side of the mountain.

When I struggled to my feet, I heard a loud whirring noise and remembered only the obnoxious odor of sulfur as a large chunk of burning rock knocked me unconscious.

V

I don't know how long I lay there, but I was buried beneath a light blanket of ash when I finally came to my senses. A piece of red-hot slag from the volcano was burning through my tunic. I felt smothered by the layer of volcanic dust. I coughed violently as I stood and shook the ash from my head. Chunks of red, burning rock speckled the landscape with a dull, bloody glow. The foul odor of sulfur again assaulted my nostrils, and the stench of hell and death shocked me into the realization that the children and Labiathus were gone. I frantically looked around in the dim light and found a shield only a few feet away. But where had they gone, and why had they left me? Did they think I had died? Which direction had they gone?

In the crimson glow I searched in vain for the children and Labiathus. The ash and darkness made finding tracks virtually impossible. Calling out for them in the desolation, I sought them until some semblance of dawn, a lighter shade of gray, crept onto the wretched scene. I finally fell to my knees, weeping, before I passed out.

I dreamed I was once again in hell, and that the horrible tentacled creature was shaking me. I awoke to the earth trembling beneath me. I was buried again but this time under my shield. As I surfaced again, the ash was falling heavily, the sky a pewter gray. I stopped for a moment to pray for the children. I headed east with a heavy heart, hoping to find Labiathus and my beloved little ones in Nuceria.

I quickly found my way out of the ash. The depth of the dust and cinders decreased as I moved eastward. Then, as if walking into another room, I stepped out of the volcanic dust all together, and the sky suddenly became brighter. There was a distinct line on the ground where the dust had fallen heavily. On the other side, the ash covered the ground lightly. Only a few flecks of it still trickled to the earth. I moved quickly.

Gray and filthy, I strode into Nuceria, praying that Labiathus and the little ones were there. I managed to get some locals to help me search and made every effort to retrace my path, but the volcano and the depth of the ash prohibited any real effort. The children were not among the other refugees who had come from

Pompeii, and no one had seen them. The boys, Liddy, and Labiathus had vanished. Would I ever know what happened to them? I thought I would go mad.

Those children had become my family, and the scar from losing them was a deep one. I knew we should have gotten out of Pompeii when we had the chance. I should have acted, even against Labiathus' wishes. At first I blamed God. I became so angry that I cursed, and I accused Him of murdering the children. I knew it wasn't true, but I harbored my anger for weeks before I fell to my knees and repented. I was sure it was the Lord who had told me to get the children out. I know it was He who told me to go east instead of to the sea gate. I had not listened to His voice; I had not acted. If I had only been obedient, perhaps they would have made it. How much was I to blame?

I didn't do what I knew I should do. I suppose that's a sin of omission. I don't know. I only know that I loved those children. I failed them—I had let them all down. I can still hear Liddy crying as she held on to me, tears streaming down her cheeks. I can still feel the gentle touch of her tiny hand, and I can still hear the magic of her angelic songs. To this day, they sing to me. There are some things on this earth that I will never understand; the death of children is one of them. I couldn't sleep. Each thought of them washed over me in a wave of sorrow.

As Marcus Antonus' slave, I was sent to Rome where I thought I would be brought before my master, but instead Apollonia was there.

"Where is the Senator?" I asked her.

"He was visiting our friends in Herculaneum. He was on the beach with many who were trying to escape from the terror of the volcano. They were all killed by the heat." Apollonia's eyes were hard, her face cold and expressionless. "Where are my children?"

I sobbed throughout my account, explaining how we were lost and how I was knocked unconscious. "When I awoke I searched for them, but they had vanished."

"How is it that you lie so easily? Do you think I am blind?" Her voice was now accusatory. "I've seen the survivors. They're burned and wounded. You have no burns. You said something knocked you unconscious, yet you have no cuts, no bruises. You expect me to believe you tried to save my children? You ran away and left them to die, didn't you? Didn't you!"

"No. I tried to save them. I loved those children."

"Because of you, I've lost everything. It would have been better for you if you had died. You will be sold to Livinicus, a bondsman who procures slaves for the silver mines in Spain. Slaves rarely return from the mines."

Thursday July 11, 4:00 p.m.

Braden turned in his chair and reached for two mugs from his bookshelf. He then stood up and walked over to a table, reached into a drawer and produced a box of tea bags. The priest filled the cups with hot water from a kettle and plopped the tea bags in the mugs. "We've all been guilty of failing to heed the voice of God," he said.

"Perhaps, but how many people died as a direct result of your disobedience?"

"None? Some? I don't know," said the priest. "But how many will spend eternity in Hell because they didn't hear about the love of Jesus? Those children may have died, but you told them about our Lord and Savior," the clergyman said. "Besides, all we can do is trust that God is faithful and just."

Lazlow nodded and accepted the tea. After a few sips he continued his story.

The Mines

Do not hate a fellow Israelite in your heart. Leviticus 19:17

I

I could not blame Apollonia for having me sold. She had suffered so, and at her order I was taken to one of the main slave traders in Rome. Livinicus took one look at me and uttered the Latin word *servitium*. Even though I felt I deserved whatever punishment awaited me, I just wanted to go home.

"I'm not a slave," I argued with the trader. "I have money."

"Where is your money? Show it to me," Livinicus spouted back.

"I don't have it with me."

"Of course you don't because you're a slave. The domina said you were a slave when they purchased you seven years ago."

"Yes that's true, but I can prove I am not a slave," I said.

"Are you a Roman Citizen?" he asked.

I shook my head.

"Then you are a slave."

"How long must I endure this bondage?" I murmured to myself.

"You'd best hold your tongue before I have it cut out," Livinicus said, "but it doesn't matter; no one comes back from the silver mines."

I was shackled, sold to the state, and placed aboard a galley bound for Spain. The voyage across the Mediterranean was agonizing; the air in the belly of the galley was dank from mold. I was one of a large group of prisoners held in the ship's bowels. The cargo hold of the vessel was dark; the heat was oppressive as was the heavy odor of rank salt water, sweat, and human feces. A few miserable days later the ship docked at the port of Tarragona in Hispania.

We slaves were finally released from the galley's hold, grateful for the fresh air but blinded by the white-hot sun. Once we were off the ship, our keepers tied us behind a rough-hewn wagon filled with tools. The ox slowly pulled the cart along a rocky road and to the banks of the river Rio Tinto. For days we wound our way through the dusty heat before we arrived at the silver mines. The sun was ascending, and the hard music of the morning had already begun what would become a familiar rhythm to me—the clinking thud of sledges, gads and wedges.

II

After a brief rest, we were fed bread and water and were outfitted with leather tunics and aprons before we climbed down into the mine. Immediately we were put to work using iron picks to make initial digs; later we were issued pry bars and chisels to break away exposed ridges. The most difficult job was relying on our brute strength to bust up the large pieces of rock and quartz. Such work resulted in bones throbbing from the chiseling and eyes stinging from fragmented shards of shattered minerals.

The initial pit was a large hole that led to the main shaft below. The shaft went straight down and led to a large horizontal gallery at its base which was lined with stone and timber for support. Workers climbed up and down from the gallery by using footholds in the stone and ladders. Some mines were deeper and had several levels. Buckets and trays attached to ropes lifted precious silver ore from the mine.

The first time I climbed down, I noticed the footholds were pronounced and easy to follow, but with each downward step, the foul air of the mine grew heavier and warmer. Heat, humidity, and the odor of humanity awaited us as we descended into hell; the darkness grew as I approached the floor of the torch-lit gallery, the cavern where the ore was mined.

The gallery was a hive of activity, and life there was difficult and dangerous. The work was tedious as day after day we made war against the earth. Hammers and chisels were our weapons, and the earth fought back with impenetrable rocks, mysterious rumblings, and darkness. Even when we found silver, it was often intermingled with lead and copper. But in the gritty earth there was no mistaking the bright sheen of what the Romans had at one time called *luna*.

I was partnered with Tok, the son of a Numidian. He had been a slave all of his life. Tok didn't know why he had been sent to the Rio Tinto, but he did know that the life expectancy there was short. Cave-ins were frequent; the air was bad, and the food was terrible. Water drainage was another problem. Digging below the waterline usually meant the end of the shaft unless it was heavy with ore.

In tunnels that looked promising, water was combated with a water-wheel. Water-wheels were large, crudely-fashioned, wooden wheels, similar to the wheel of a gristmill but larger and vertical. Two of these wheels were held together by rough, wooden troughs that lifted water out of a ditch and then poured it onto a raised aqueduct built solely for drainage. The water-wheel was powered by a man, sometimes two, whose job was to "walk the wheel." At least, that's what we called it. The unlucky slave whose duty this was would stand on the troughs at the top of the wheel and begin walking on the notched side pieces. The slave climbed the wheel using the weight of his body to help turn it as he walked. It was considered punishment to have to walk the wheel because of the wear and tear on the bare feet and legs. Dealing out this punishment was the shaft's taskmaster.

Our taskmaster was one of the most evil men I've ever met. His name was Malo, an Iberian and a former slave who had eventually become foreman. He was large, with black hair, a bulbous nose, and dark, hateful eyes. His voice was deep and severe, and when he barked out orders, he expected instant obedience. His muscular frame was built for hard labor, his legs rock solid from years of lifting. He used a whip on us as if we were beasts.

Malo was a bully; he loved to terrorize new slaves, particularly those who were timid, and would literally work them almost to the point of death. He would either put them on the wheel for hours, or he would lash them while they worked. Malo was the type of man who seemed happy only when he was intimidating someone. I suppose he hoped to break me quickly when I was assigned to his work detail, because on my second day I was forced to walk the wheel.

I don't know what I did to merit such attention, but I remember working with a wedge and feeling the tip of Malo's whip biting into the flesh on my back. Wincing from the pain, I turned to see the taskmaster standing behind me with a sinister grin on his face.

"Slave," he said in his rugged voice. "You will walk the wheel today."

Turning, I dropped my tool belt, and he cracked me again with his whip.

"Did I tell you to drop your tool belt, slave?" he jeered.

I stooped to pick the belt up, and he lashed me yet again.

"Did I tell you to pick the tool belt up, slave? You had better learn to do only what I tell you to do. I am your master."

I nodded grudgingly and moved toward the wheel. Another slave climbed down, and I climbed the ladder to step onto the wheel. As I moved to the footing, I noticed the wheel looked worn and broken in places. All of the pegs on the left crosspieces were loose, some broken.

Looking down at Malo, I said, "Taskmaster, these pegs...." But before I could finish I felt the crackling pain of leather across my chest.

"Did I tell you to talk, slave? You speak only when I tell you to speak." He climbed halfway up the ladder and this time caught my shin with the tip of the whip. "Now get on the wheel."

When I stepped on the water wheel's left side it groaned and snapped beneath my weight. Suddenly, the entire left side of the wheel split from the right and fell away. I lunged and grabbed onto the right side which had lodged in the ditch and remained upright. In the commotion I looked down to see that the other slaves had gathered around Malo. His body lay face down beneath the weight of the wheel. He wasn't dead, but it would have been better for us all if he had died. The end of his right arm was a bleeding stub where his hand had once been. A large, splintered section of wood had severed the man's limb. One of the guards made a tourniquet to stop the blood flow, and they finally carried Malo out on a litter.

III

The next day another slave, a kind man named Brutus, was promoted to taskmaster to take Malo's place. Brutus set up a daily schedule for walking the wheel in order to even the workload among the slaves. He cared for the well-being of the men under his watch. Without Malo there was little tension, and we were all happier—at least as happy as slaves working a silver mine could be. But several months later our misery returned. Malo was back, and Brutus was sent to the less brutal world above.

The former taskmaster's malefic grin had not changed, and where his hand had once been was a long, brown leather tentacle that extended from his right forearm. In lieu of his hand, Malo now had a whip fitted to the end of his wrist. The lash was harnessed to his left shoulder by thick leather thongs that stretched around his neck and back. The whip itself extended from a woven leather sleeve that climbed up to his elbow.

I'll never forget his grimacing grin or the rancor in his eyes the day he came back. He wasted no time letting me know his temper.

"You made me a cripple for life," Malo said. "That is going to cost you."

Over the next few months, Malo put me on the wheel, sabotaged my work, and beat me. In that deep, dark gallery he learned to use his new toy with even greater effect. But by the end of the third month, the bully finally realized I wasn't afraid of him and that I could take any kind of punishment he tried to inflict. Using a new strategy, he turned to hurting me indirectly by attacking anyone I had befriended, and he started with Tok.

Tok was assigned to walk the wheel, something even Malo usually limited to half a day's work for a slave. On this day he made Tok stay on the wheel from early morning until late afternoon. By the end of the day, exhausted, Tok fell down on top of the wheel which plunged him into the watery channel below. It was an easy and insignificant way to die. Tok broke his neck in the ditch, and when we pulled him out of the water, Malo looked at me with a smirk.

The rest of the slaves growled at the news, but as I stood looking at Malo's evil grin, I felt something flare up inside of me—a hatred that matched his own.

I lowered my head like a bull and charged Malo, knocking him to the ground. I punched at his face with my fists until the guards pulled me from him. While they were holding me, Malo retaliated, beating me until I was unconscious. I fell to the ground where I lay for the rest of the day.

For months, every time I saw Malo I remembered what he had done to my friend. My mind was set on avenging Tok's death—his murder. Meanwhile, Malo made sure the other slaves knew I was a dangerous friend to have. I was shunned as if I were a leper. My days of isolation grew into weeks; the weeks turned to months and the months to years. Still, we worked, moving from mine to mine, along the mineral-rich land of the Rio Tinto. For ten years I lived in seclusion, pounding away at the earth.

Since slaves rarely lived more than a few years in the mines, I shunned the new arrivals. I knew that their contact with me would bring them suffering. I felt God had abandoned me, and I was back in hell. I let the seed of hate Malo planted inside of me grow. My hate for him was a grinding, grueling, grating type of malice whose roots ran deep, and the taskmaster watered it daily.

IV

Malo was evil and bitter, the type of person who made himself feel good by demeaning others. I knew he felt his lash, his new hand, gave him great power. It did. Malo became so proficient with the whip that he could put out a man's eye if he had a mind to. I saw him do so on more than one occasion. He was easy to loathe, and hating him was the only pleasure many of us had.

I became so obsessed with hatred that I let it consume me. With every swing of my pick and every blow of my hammer, I vowed to rid the earth of Malo. For years I entertained ways of murdering him. I wanted to take his whip and wrap it around his neck or beat him with it the same way he beat and abused others. I made myself believe that I was God's avenging angel. I justified myself by repeating the Torah law: *an eye for an eye*. Seething with hate, I found it easy to ignore Jesus' words: *love your enemy.*

I looked for opportunities to do away with my tormentor, but I refrained because if a slave worker rebelled or made a mistake, the other workers shared in the punishment.

One hot summer day the air in the shaft was particularly clammy, and the heat was stifling. We were deep below the waterline of a mine we believed to be almost depleted, but we had recently found another rich vein of silver. It was a large deposit and appeared almost white in the flickering torchlight. As usual, Malo bellowed at us to work harder and faster, cracking his snake-like appendage while he barked.

The earth's first tremor was subtle, barely noticeable, but when the second quake came, the ground shook as if it were having a seizure. Seconds later the mine timbers shuddered and released dust into the cavern. The earth squeezed against itself as if it were having a spasm. Some slaves ran for the ladders, but Malo, having climbed to the upper level, whipped anyone who tried to climb up.

"Did I tell you slaves to quit working," he bellowed over the grumbling of the earth. He lashed three men from the rungs of the ladders before I finally attempted the climb, though I never intended to make it up. Like leathered lightning, Malo began whipping me in a fury of anger, but I was ready for him. I snatched the end of the lash and quickly wrapped it around my arm. What followed was a rabid tug of war. By the time Malo realized my intentions, it was too late for him. I jumped from the ladder and pulled the fiendish taskmaster down to the rocky floor below. The other slaves cheered and scampered up the ladder to escape the falling earth.

Dazed from the fall, Malo struggled to his knees while the earth turned and shook. Even with the walls of the mine crumbling in on us, I managed to get to my feet and made the most of my opportunity. Driven by hate, I took Malo's whip in my hands and wrapped it around his neck and began to strangle the life out of him.

A moment later the ground broke violently, and I was swallowed up by an earthen gash. Darkness and the world fell in on me.

V

Time passed as I was dreaming—I was high up and could see from afar that there was a large hole in the earth, and ants carried rocks, broken timbers, and dirt away from the crater. The ants became men who were removing parts of a water wheel, boulders, and human bones. They dug up large rocks and shoveled away the earth.

"There is a rich vein of silver here," one of the men said in a faint voice.

Then in my dream I recognized Brutus and another slave sifting through the sand searching for something. The slave found a long, black root and began pulling it. More and more of the strand came up through the dirt, but the root was deep in the earth. Brutus too dug and pushed away the sand with his fingers, pulling on the dark cord. He plunged his hand beneath the gritty sand.

In my dream I felt something touch me, and I grabbed it with my fingers and held on with all of my might. It jerked and tugged and tried to pull away, but I would not let go. Suddenly, I awoke and realized that I was buried in the earth which still held me in its grip. I clutched the human hand that continued to pull and yank furiously, but I was determined not to let go, like Jacob when he wrestled the angel.

I twisted with my torso and legs to free myself from my grave, and I felt the sandy soil give slightly. A moment later the earth released me just as the hand onto which I clasped tugged powerfully. Like a tree in a storm, I was uprooted from the ground where I was buried. I quickly fell to my knees. Sand and caked dirt fell from me as I finally let go of the hand. I coughed fiercely, vomiting out black slime. My lungs stung as if I'd breathed in an army of angry ants. I scraped the crust from my eyes and face as I wretched and stood up. I bent double and out came more sand and grit, and still I choked and heaved and purged my lungs and stomach. Finally, I took a dusty breath and shook the soil from my head and hair. Through crusted eyes I realized that there were two blurry figures standing in front of me.

Picking the dirt from my ears, I became aware of someone screaming. I squinted to see Brutus backing away like a man who had seen a ghost. He shrieked wildly and ran away like a madman. The other slave stood frozen in shock.

I leaned over again, put my hands on my knees and inhaled deeply before I coughed up yet more dirt, finally expunging the last of the sandy grit from my lungs and throat. The air tasted good. Disoriented, I slowly looked around and tried to clear my head. The sun was beginning to slip behind the lip of the crater, and the mountain cast a long shadow over the pit where I stood. Then I remembered the whip, the mine, Malo.

Soon afterwards, Brutus returned with the foreman and some other workers. I spat out yet another mouthful of muddy grit, wheezing like a man with pneumonia.

"That's Lazarus!" Brutus cried out. "I was here the day of the cave-in. He's been buried for years." The words leapt out of his mouth.

"He's still a slave," another voice said. "We should make this devil do our work."

"You fools!" The deep voice of the foreman growled. "Pluto has favored this man, and we would be wise to honor him. Let him go. Any debt he owes has been paid."

No one moved. For a moment I thought I might be attacked, but the men backed away. Some of them even fell to their knees. I said nothing, but I noticed Malo's long whip that had been pulled from the earth. It was the root from my dream. I picked it up, climbed the ladders, and stepped onto the dusty earth that surrounded the mine. No one interfered. I looked at the sun hanging low in the western sky, and I began walking north, back to the home from which I'd been estranged for these long years.

VI

On foot, I slowly made my way toward Gaul. From the outset, I was somewhat disoriented. Although I could walk easily enough, my brain tended to shut down at times. I often fell asleep, even while standing. I also had a difficult time remembering specific details of my past. Almost like amnesia, the effects of being buried for several years were something I hadn't counted on.

After a period of what must have been weeks, I was picked up by a farmer who drove an ox cart. Conversation with the man was difficult for me. My mouth had also forgotten how to speak. We followed the main road along the Ebro River to the city of Caesaraugusta, present day Zaragoza. Though I hadn't spoken for the entire trip, my slow tongue finally forced the words, "Thank you," to the farmer as I climbed down from his cart.

Once in the city, I again felt a heavy fatigue coming upon me, and I fell into a dead sleep while standing in the market place. When I awoke it was dark and raining. A stranger was leading me by the hand.

"I will take you to the Lady of Mercy," the man said. "She will know what to do."

Confused, I groaned and nodded my head. We plodded through the mud as the rain became heavy. In a dark alleyway, we stopped as a wooden door opened. Light from the room flooded into the dark passage where we entered.

"My lady," my guide said, "This man has neither food nor money. I believe he is simpleminded for he cannot speak, and he falls asleep where he stands."

"Thank you, brother," a beautiful voice responded. "We will take care of him."

Before the man left, I again managed to blurt out the words, "Thank you."

"Come with me," the woman said, taking me by the hand. "You need food and rest."

She took me to a kitchen, sat me down, and fed me some warm chicken stock. I still remember the hot soup with its garlic and leeks. I don't remember what happened after I ate, but when I awoke, I was sleeping on a warm, feather pallet. This marked the first time I had slept on a bed in more than 20 years. I felt refreshed, and my speech had come back. I no longer felt mentally fuzzy, and I could remember the mines, the earthquake, everything. The woman who fed me, a raven-haired beauty, tapped on the door and entered the room.

"I see you're awake," she said. She wore the traditional beige garb of a Roman woman.

"Thank you," I said. "And thank you for feeding me last night."

"You can speak now." Her voice was reassuring. "You must have really needed to rest. You've been asleep for three days. You also need a haircut. I can do that for you."

"Three days?" I said. "How can I thank you? What is your name?"

"They call me the Lady of Mercy, but that's not my name." Her eyes softened as she told me her story. "My father was a notable Roman politician. Most of my family was killed at Pompeii. As a young woman the Lord found me. I have been serving Him since, even though it is a crime against the state. But there is little persecution here; I've even tended the magistrate's children."

At that moment I recognized her—Liddy. It wasn't possible. "Was your father Senator Antonus?"

"Yes. How do you know that?"

"I knew your brothers. You were all given up for dead."

"It's true," she said. "I alone survived. I was a young child, so I don't remember much, only what my mother told me. I was found months after the eruption at a farmhouse near Nuceria. How did you know my brothers?"

"We played together as boys. I'm sorry they didn't get out, but I'm glad you did. You are Liddy aren't you?"

"Yes. God had His hand on me there. He had much work for me to do, the work I do now. Do you know the Lord?"

"Yes," I said, tears running down my cheeks. "I know Him well. I also have work to do, so I must be going."

"But you only just arrived. You're not fully healed."

"Jesus ordered my steps and brought me here. I am well enough. Thank you for your kindness. It is no wonder they call you the Lady of Mercy."

I thanked God as I left Caesaraugusta with a warm feeling in my heart. Liddy had not only survived, but she had grown up to be a wonderful, Christian woman. I made my way to Gaul, grateful that Liddy was alive and warm with the knowledge that I was going home, something I desperately needed.

A month later I finally arrived in Aquitania; nothing had changed. It was early spring, and the fertile land welcomed me with its greenery and wildflowers. I stood on a rise overlooking the place. For a long while I breathed in the air and enjoyed being home. Kido and Rael, slaves I had freed years before to run the estate, still did so. They were both gray and bent with age.

"Master?" Kido said as I stood at the doorway. "Is that you?"

The man squinted at my face incredulously. I had no wrinkles, and my hair was full and long, falling upon my broad shoulders. I wanted to say yes, but instead I said, "You must be Kido and Rael. I am not your master. I am the son of Lazarus, though I feel I know you already. My father told me much about you."

The vineyard was in extraordinary condition. The green grapes were far from ripe, but the vines promised a large yield. Money here was no problem, so my first goal was to purchase Roman Citizenship. Kido and Rael chose to remain with me.

"We never felt like slaves around your father," Rael said as she smiled her agreement. "You are so much like him."

The couple continued to oversee the workers in the vineyard while I took on the tasks of production. Our wines became more popular than ever. Success was wonderful, and my years as a slave made my freedom all the more pleasurable. Years later, death finally took Kido and Rael, and though I was successful, I was lonely. However, exciting events in Judea were to lead me in another direction in search of the returning Messiah.

Son of the Star

*Evildoers foster rebellion...*Proverbs 17:11

I

The year was 131 A.D. I had spent the last three decades managing my estate in Gaul, having settled into the routine of property ownership and wine making. By this time I was well aware of my immortality, and I had decided to be as productive as possible. The estate thrived, and I felt like I was one of the wealthiest men in the province. The vineyards were beautiful. Our varieties of deep purple, red, and green grapes produced some of the best wine in the world.

One evening I sat with some friends at an inn eating, drinking, and playing *tali,* a popular dice game of the time. During the course of the evening, I chanced to overhear a silk merchant relate news from the Middle East.

"They say the Jews have kicked the Romans out of Judea," he said. "They've taken Jerusalem and destroyed an entire Roman legion."

"Is that just another rumor of rebellion in Israel?" I asked.

"No rumor. I heard this from the governor."

Shocked at the news, I leaned over the table and said, "They destroyed an entire Roman legion? Are you sure?"

"I believe so. The rebellion is widespread. Those Jews are cutthroats," he said.

"I know the Jews well. They are so divided in their beliefs that I find it difficult to believe they could destroy a legion without some kind of a miracle," I added.

"They say their new leader can perform miracles. His name is Simon Bar Kokhba; the Jews call him the Son of the Star. Some say he is the Messiah."

"The Messiah?" I asked, my interest peaked. "The Messiah has returned?"

"I do not know, my friend. I just know he is called Messiah by some. He will need to be, for the Romans are gathering a large army, almost a dozen legions, to deal with the rebellion."

"A dozen legions? That's almost half of the empire's strength," I said.

I sat back in my chair, and a million thoughts raced through my mind. I felt gleeful. Perhaps Jesus had returned to create His kingdom. Jesus had said that he would come back. I had to go back to Jerusalem to see for myself.

It took a little more than a month to set my affairs in order and once again put the winery in a position to function independently. For this, my third trip to Jerusalem, I was prepared for almost anything. I was determined to avoid any imperial entanglements that would prevent me from seeing Jesus.

II

Rebellis—it was a word commonly associated with Judea. Yet even more unbelievable was that the Jews were winning. Perhaps this time Jesus had returned as the lion instead of the lamb. Perhaps He had come back as a military conqueror. I did not go back because I wanted to get caught up in a civil war; I went back to find out if the Messiah had returned.

48

I took plenty of money this time, and since I was a citizen of Rome I had no fear of becoming a slave again. But the rebellion drew me to Israel, drew me to the Messiah, drew me to the Son of the Star—Simon Bar Kokhba. Jesus had said he would come back, and if He had returned, I wanted to be with Him.

The insurrection was well into its second year, and the Romans had yet to move on Judea. The Jews were even minting coins with Bar Kokhba's likeness stamped on them. Rome seldom saw such leaders rise up against them. I believed Bar Kokhba must be Jesus because of the rebellion's success.

Again I boarded a ship and sailed across the blue Mediterranean to the ancient port of Sidon. Once there I purchased a small caravan of camels so all would believe my merchants were headed east for the desert. When Roman patrols stopped us, this story with a small bribe assured our passage through rebel territory. Two weeks later the caravan entered Jerusalem.

The Romans had been booted from the country, so my citizenship did nothing to help me get into Israel, and entering Jerusalem was difficult for the mood of the capital was extremely fearful. The new ruler had a reputation for ruthlessness, which I found odd, but he also had a reputation for the fantastic. Many spoke of Bar Kokhba's exploits, but none had seen them.

The fact that there were no eyewitnesses to Bar Kokhba's miracles gave me cause for concern. The most common notion of the time was that the Son of the Star needed neither sword nor spear in warfare. According to one man, Bar Kokhba spewed forth flaming breath like a dragon. When I asked the man if he had seen this with his own eyes, he said his nephew had heard it from a trusted friend.

Another man said Bar Kokhba had single-handedly defeated a host of Romans by burning them up with a great firestorm. He said he had witnessed the event in a vision. Naturally I became somewhat more skeptical. The Jewish Christian church had suffered severely under the rebel leader, something I found most distressing. If Bar Kokhba were the Messiah, why would he punish those who were believers?

III

After only a few days in Jerusalem, I was able to accomplish what I had set out to do, meet Simon Bar Kokhba. This was no easy task since he was well guarded, but I was able to meet the leader face to face after some well-placed bribes.

We met in the governor's palace in that city. Bar Kokhba was a large, olive-skinned man with wild black hair and a long, heavy beard. His dark, triangular eyebrows gave him a sinister countenance. While his military prowess stood on its own merit, I was disappointed in his manner. I went to the appointment looking for Jesus, but I found someone who was almost His opposite. Where Jesus had been humble, warm, and loving, Simon Bar Kokhba was arrogant beyond belief and paranoid as well.

My introduction was short as I walked across the room to greet the rebel leader. "This rich man desires to meet you," Bar Kokhba's lackey said, pointing to me.

"What do I need with another rich man?" he asked blankly.

"Perhaps he can help us. He is very wealthy, a Jewish wine merchant from Gaul."

"Very well, bring him in."

The puzzled look on my face bewildered Bar Kokhba at first.

"You look surprised," he said, his brown eyes riveted to mine.

I hesitated for a moment. "I thought I might know you—that is, you might know me."

"But we have never met," he said, turning away nonchalantly. It was obvious that he had no idea who I was. "Why should I know you?"

"I know who the Messiah is," I said, "and the Messiah knows who I am."

"Are you sure about that? You bribed your way in to talk to me. What do you want?"

"I'm here to see if you are the real Messiah, but I already know you aren't the Christ who raised me from the dead."

"Hmm, I smell a Christian." He raised an eyebrow and smugly said, "Let me see if I can test your faith, for you will either renounce it, or you will go to be with your master."

"Your days are numbered," I told him. "Even now almost a dozen legions are descending on Judea to squelch this rebellion. What will you do? Breathe fire on the entire Roman army?"

"How do you come by this information? Are you a spy?"

"If I were a spy, why would I tell you? I am a wine merchant, and I heard it from some other merchants in Aquitania. Surely you must know this is common knowledge."

"The Romans have closed ports and roads leading into Judea. How is it that you were able to get past them?" he asked gruffly.

"Money—the same thing I used to get in to see you."

"Hmm. The trouble with the wealthy is that they are blind. They cannot understand that riches mean nothing," Bar Kokhba said as he clapped his hands.

Two guards entered the room.

"This man is a Christian," Bar Kokhba said. "I believe he is also a Roman spy. Bind him and send in that other spy. Send in the Rabbi."

I was bound with leather straps while a rabbi was brought in for questioning.

The Rabbi Elazar HaModai was an old man dressed in traditional Hebrew robes. He looked weak and weary as the guards shoved him to the floor. "This is a terrible day for my family," Bar Kokhba said. "My own uncle a spy for the Romans—a rabbi, a member of the Sanhedrin, a Jew—what would make you stoop to become a Roman spy?"

"I am no spy," the rabbi said.

"My sources say you are, Uncle!" Bar Kokhba retorted.

"What sources? Where are my accusers?"

50

"Who are you to question my sources? I am your accuser. Don't you think I, the Messiah, would know who is for me and who is against me? Don't you think the Son of the Star should know these things? You were seen collaborating with the Romans. What do you have to say for yourself, Uncle?" Bar Kokhba rose and walked through the sunlit room to face the teacher, bullying his frail uncle with his large stature.

"I am a rabbi," the haggard old man answered. "I am your flesh and blood. You yourself have spoken with Roman spies. Does that make you one? I am innocent of such charges."

"Liar!" Bar Kokhba said, and he slapped the rabbi across the face with the back of his hand, drawing blood from the man's lip. He then called for a guard and ordered, "Beat him until he confesses."

Another guard joined in and the two, using short wooden rods, proceeded to double the old man over with jabs to his ribs, then knocked him to the ground with blows to the head. The rabbi, mute with innocence, never confessed; he was beaten to death before my sickened gaze. He was no spy, and Bar Kokhba was no messiah. While it is true that the rebel was a great military leader, he was also a ruthless, self-serving, megalomaniac. The deluded leader suffered from the disease of too much power. He was accountable to no one but himself, so he became judge and his henchmen, executioners.

"Now, citizen of Rome," he said turning his attentions to me. "Let us test your faith; you will be thrown from the battlements of the governor's palace unless you renounce your claim that Jesus of Nazareth was the Messiah. There is only one Messiah, and I am he. I have no qualms about sending Christians to see their so-called savior. Let's see if the Nazarene decides to save you," he said smugly, his eyes glaring in condescension.

"I only hope He can save Israel from you," I retorted. "You have led this nation to ruin. No wonder some of your own people call you the Son of the Lie."

Bar Kokhba angrily buried his fist in my gut, and with red-faced rage shouted, "Who says that I am the Son of the Lie?" Then regaining his composure, he snarled to the guards, "Take him away with the other Christians."

IV

Two ruffians led me up some steps and to the parapets of the governor's palace, a tall building that looked to have been recently fortified. I didn't see much, though, as they punched and prodded me along the way. I was led onto a walkway off the backside of the palace, several stories above the ground. The battlements at the rear of the building overlooked the city walls. I could make out a grisly sight below, the bloody bones of those who had met their fates pushed off of the walls, left to die, and to be eaten by wild dogs. I was left outside of a small room filled with Jewish Christian captives.

Bar Kokhba followed us into the room, speaking to me before he entered.

"You will observe," he said smiling. Turning to the group, he barked, "You will renounce Jesus of Nazareth as your savior and acknowledge me, the Son of the Star, as the true Messiah. If you refuse, you will be thrown from the ramparts

51

to the rocks below where the dogs will tear the flesh from your bones." Three women immediately fell to their knees, renounced Jesus and began to proclaim Bar Kokhba the Messiah.

"The Son of the Star is the true Messiah," they whimpered through tears.

Guards then took two of the other prisoners, their arms tied behind their backs, and forcibly shoved them out the door and over the side of the wall. Their brief cries ended in dull thuds as the prisoners' bodies hit the ground and split open.

Another woman went to her knees begging for mercy but would not renounce Christ. She screamed and flailed as a burly guard literally picked her up and tossed her over the side. There was a sudden silence when she hit the ground, her neck obviously broken. Then a terrified, plump, dark-haired man began to shake. His knees wobbled, and a puddle of urine slowly spread on the floor beneath his feet. Losing heart, the little man quickly renounced the Lord and was placed to the side with some others.

Quickly and mercilessly, the rest of those who remained faithful were shoved over the battlements like refuse onto the ground below. I was disgusted at how casually Bar Kokhba and his men went about the ghastly business of murder.

Bar Kokhba finally looked at me and said, "We saved you for last."
He turned to the guards. "And these are now believers?" His eyes like a serpent, he smiled balefully and pointed to the four prisoners who had saved themselves.

The guards nodded.

"Good," he said. "Over the side with them! They're liars and traitors."

Despite the prisoners' protests, the guards ruthlessly seized those who had only moments before renounced Christ and threw them over the side onto the bloody ground below.

I looked at him. "You are no messiah. You're just a murderer."

"They're not all dead. Not yet anyway. Take a look," Bar Kokhba said.

The guards held my arms and led me to edge of the fortification, forcing me to gaze upon the grisly scene below. Some people had died in their falls, heads crushed or bodies smashed. Others had survived the fall and were squirming like worms on hot stone. The ground had absorbed most of the blood, but the moaning, twitching bodies were sickening.

Without warning or fanfare I was shoved over the side by Bar Kokhba's thugs. For a moment in midair, I was unafraid; I was reminded of jumping off of steps as a child, the feeling as if I were almost flying, but just before hitting the ground I could feel the fear and the earth both rushing up to meet me. Now, as I fell, I could see the bones and bodies beneath me drawing closer. I smashed into the rock-hard dirt, crushing my legs which broke trying to cushion my fall. I passed out, unconscious until that night when I awoke to some growling dogs fighting over a carcass.

Somehow I struggled to my feet, my broken legs now straightened though still feeling fragile. The dogs were too busy nosing around the dead bodies to notice me. It was then, as I limped away, that I decided I would become a soldier of the Roman Empire. As far as I was concerned, the World was Rome. Other empires, even my own people, had committed crimes as bad, more heinous, more terrible than Rome's.

While some would call me a traitor to my people, I saw something in Rome I believed was worth fighting for. Rome provided a framework of law and justice for its citizens where even Roman slaves could earn their freedom. In spite of all of its shortcomings, Rome provided a way for honest people to work hard and thrive.

Others would call me a traitor to my faith, wondering how I could desire to be a part of the machine which had crucified our Lord. But in my eyes the Jewish leaders, the Sanhedrin, were guiltier than Rome. I would learn to fight with the greatest army the world had ever known! I didn't want to think about life; I just wanted to live, and to be told what to do. The Roman army seemed a likely place to do that.

The Roman

*For I myself am a man under authority, with soldiers under me...*Matthew 8:9

I

Shortly after I left Judea, the Bar Kokhba rebellion was brutally quashed by the Emperor Hadrian in 135 A.D. His anger toward Israel was so great that after crushing Jewish resistance, he passed an edict forbidding Jews from ever entering Jerusalem. I found myself beginning my soldier's career in what would become known as the Golden Age of the Empire, serving a parade of both good and bad emperors while in service to Rome.

I began my new profession in Asia Minor as a part of the *limitanei,* groups of non-Roman recruits stationed in the frontier provinces. These places were usually small, dusty cities where legionnaires would never want to be stationed. Life in the army was not easy, but it was routine. For that I was thankful. After seven years of service, I bribed my way into the regular Roman army, and with my dark hair and brown eyes, I certainly looked like I belonged. As a soldier, I was surrounded by all kinds of humanity; rogues and libertines—rough hewn men with few scruples, but there were also good men who were courageous, honorable, and responsible.

Over the course of many years of service, I put on the scarlet tunic as an old-looking 20 year old only to retire at the end of my term as a young-looking 40 year old. The training was intense, miles of forced marches while carrying heavy equipment, or swimming long distances with and without armor. I became a close friend to many comrades as we shared the soldiers' bond: men who save each others' lives on a regular basis. I went to great lengths to protect my true identity and to remain as unobtrusive as possible. As the decades passed, my fighting skills grew far beyond those of my comrades. Unlike the other soldiers, I could learn from my worst mistakes, often fatal mistakes. Though painful, my education in combat was ongoing. This became obvious during a particularly bloody encounter on the shores of the province of Belgica, present day Belgium.

In a gruesome battle with some sea-borne raiders, I drew my gladius and hacked off the forearm of a burly invader I faced. Any Roman soldier or civilized man would have recoiled in horror at his bloody stump and turned to flee. Not this barbarian. Without pause the brute thrust what remained of his arm in my face, squirting blood from the severed arteries. The salty-tasting gore stung and blinded me momentarily, causing me to gag and stagger. In a flash the raider drew a short, single-bladed weapon called a sea axe and stabbed down the neck opening in my armor, piercing my heart. That was a harsh lesson.

The following day I returned to my unit to the delight and cheers of my comrades. I concocted a tale explaining how the wound had only grazed me and that I had been merely knocked unconscious. Such "training" enabled me to become incredibly adroit.

II

Because I became too good of a warrior, promotions were frequent but problematic. At that time the Roman army was an organization that was based on individual merit and discipline. There was no room on a battlefield for pretense or posturing; only real performance was recognized—skill and success in combat. The recognition of excellence became so much the rule that in the later empire, there were peasants who rose through the army to actually become emperor, such as Maximinus Thrax in 235 and Diocletian in 284 A.D.

Sometimes in camp, I would purposely fail in a simple duty merely to avoid being seen as the perfect soldier. Still, promotions in rank came my way with such certainty that problems began to arise from my notoriety. In spite of my protests to keep from being promoted, I was often overruled and several times awarded the rank of decanus, commander of eight. Sometimes I received field promotions to replace fallen optiones, those second in command to the centurion, although afterward I often managed to foist the position on a comrade who desired the promotion more than I. As time passed I was promoted to centurion, with a hundred men under my command. The position brought with it some recognition. Often, to my dismay, every soldier in my legion of 6000 brave and dedicated men would know my name and face.

Eventually I traded in my scarlet tunic for a black one as I was made a member of the Praetorian Guard. The Roman emperor's personal body guard, we wore black uniforms with gold trim to distinguish us from the regular legionnaires, important since we were the most elite troops in the army, and the only soldiers allowed in the capitol. Our unit's strength was about 700; man for man, cohort for cohort, we could best any warriors known to Rome. In the early years of the empire, a soldier's reputation and heroism would move him toward the praetorians. Commanders proudly nominated their high-caliber warriors for this recognition, much like athletes who competed at Olympia. The praetorians were also the highest paid soldiers in the army, greatly respected and greatly feared. They were above the law. They could, and would, do anything to protect the emperor.

III

I was first made a praetorian in the year 179 under the philosopher Emperor Marcus Aurelius who unfortunately died shortly after I was promoted. Afterward we were forced to serve his son, Commodus, who did little to follow in his father's honorable footsteps. Under Commodus, the expansion of the empire halted as the new Emperor elevated the policy of "bread and circus" to a higher level.

The beauty of the city of Rome at this time was unparalleled. Pennants flew high over the coliseum and the great circus. Crowds thronged the market places and the forum. Rome bustled with humanity and trade as its beautiful polished marble buildings and huge columns glinted in the sun. The populace and the city itself exuded an air of confidence and strength, that of an empire with no rivals.

Commodus' dictum of entertainment kept even the poor busy. Thousands and thousands of people would clog the coliseum to see and place wagers on the violent, gory games. The Emperor himself donned the garb of a gladiator slave from time to time and went into the arena. As praetorians we were wary of the new Emperor who was so unlike his father. I knew the praetorians were valuable and too respected to be sacrificed in the coliseum and that any emperor who mistreated his bodyguards would need—a body guard. But I was wrong about Commodus.

One autumn afternoon my two companions, Varus and Polos, and I were summoned by our centurion. We were then escorted through the streets to the arena and left in one of the waiting chambers beneath the coliseum where our battle armor awaited us. Outside and above us the crowd roared at the day's entertainment. An aide of the Emperor came into the room and told us to dress. Moments later Commodus himself entered. His dark eyes were piercing.

"Lazarus, Varus, Polos," he spoke softly. "Charges have been brought against you by the civil servant Domitus. Don't bother to deny that you have been lingering with Christians. If proven, the charge is a crime against the state, and it would mean your lives and your families' lives would be forfeit. It is not fitting that my praetorians befriend these people."

We stood and said nothing. Each of us knew the charge was true.

"But because I am magnanimous," the Emperor continued smugly, "I make you an offer: You will be the first praetorians to fight in the arena. If one of you dies, the lives of your friends and the lives of your families are forfeit. If you all survive the...uh, entertainment, you will retire with the yearly stipend of a senior centurion."

With that Commodus raised an eyebrow, turned, and smiled broadly, chuckling as he left. Varus and Polos were both Christians, and each had a family. Since we were elite warriors, we reasoned that we were to face something very strong—perhaps an elephant, tigers, or such beasts as we'd never seen before.

The door to the floor of the arena opened and we marched out from our dimly lit chamber into the blinding white sunlight of the coliseum. We three stood alone in the arena, and the crowd gave only mild applause as we approached Emperor Commodus' shaded pavilion. The herald of the games commanded us to make the gladiator's oath to the emperor: *Nos morituri te, salutamus!* In spite of their stern countenances, I could tell by their eyes that Polos and Varus were aghast, for never before had an emperor dared humiliate praetorians like this, demanding the oath of a gladiator slave: "We who are about to die, salute you!" Nevertheless we were all praetorians, sworn to the emperor. We responded with the praetorian's oath: "I die for my Emperor," and bowed deeply. It sufficed. Making examples of his elite warriors in this way meant that Emperor Commodus would not be around much longer. The rest of the Praetorian Guard would see to that!

IV

Then with trumpet and fanfare we turned to see emerging from the far gate a small army, a very small army, an army of soldiers all under four feet tall, some as small as three feet tall. The band of fighters was made up of dwarves from every corner of the empire. These little black, white, and brown men were perfectly outfitted in miniature helmets and armor, and most held tiny swords in their hands and diminutive bronze Roman shields. They stood as a formation of soldiers. This was a lavish show. Someone had gone to a great deal of trouble and expense to outfit these little legionnaires.

The crowd applauded, then roared its approval when two tiny archers standing in miniature chariots charged into the arena. Pulling each chariot was what I can only describe as "war hogs," large pigs with horned helmets on their heads and customized armor on their backs. The little bowmen in the chariots were outfitted as Roman auxiliaries, the light troops of the Empire.

After the musical fanfare, the herald informed the crowd that the members of this little army were slaves confiscated from the subject nations of the Empire. They were trained by the impresarios to fight like Roman soldiers for the amusement of the citizens of Rome. The trumpets sounded again and a chorus somewhere behind us began to chant a rhyme about "three against three hundred." The music stopped and a cadence beat double-time as the enemy closed ranks, forming a 300-man triangle.

One soldier was the tip of the spearhead, followed by two, then three, and so on. Each warrior on the outside of the triangle took his buckler and held it to form a shield wall, while the ones in the center held their shields aloft to form a roof over each man's head, the entire formation protected by a shell of armor. Between the shields in the wall and at the top of each slit in the shield roof, every man held his short sword. My comrades and I looked at each other questioningly. While the formation looked impressive, like a tortoise with steel teeth, Polos, Varus, and I knew such a tactic would be useless in the arena because it was so slow and cumbersome. The little soldiers edged ever closer, now only a few steps away.

"I cannot bring myself to strike the first blow. It's like fighting little children," said Varus, who was the father of six.

"I think Polos is taking care of that," I shouted as our friend took two quick bounds and kicked the front shield of the formation with all of his might.

Polos' mighty boot jolted the human triangle and caused a chain reaction as the dwarves went sprawling to the ground, almost half the small army affected by the blow. The audience howled with laughter as the little men fell into and on top of one another in comedic fashion; however, Polos' kick served only to infuriate our opponents. Like a swarm of angry bees from an overturned hive, the little soldiers charged us with vengeance.

Polos, Varus, and I formed a circle as best we could and soon learned that these little fighting men were indeed dangerous. They came at us from all sides while the two archers began firing their tiny darts at us from their chariots.

57

Fortunately for us, their aim was not very good. In fact, several times they shot their own men.

The child-sized warriors hacked and stabbed away at us, but the three of us were experts in war and moved together in unison. Within seconds we had slain a dozen of our opponents and taken their shields as a defense against the archers. Lacking any kind of a commander, the little army came at us in a series of uncoordinated attacks. My comrades and I, though, fought as a unit moving together and covering one another. After a short time the little army was unable to cope with our skill; the slaughter began in earnest.

Each of us was sickened by what we had to do, but if even one of us failed, the others and their families would pay with their lives. I felt bile rising in my throat every time I hacked and stabbed with my sword. All three of us were great warriors, but this was different from war; this was butchery for the amusement of the callous thousands sitting in the coliseum. The bowmen kept circling us and one of their arrows found Varus' arm. In a flash my praetorian friend picked up a sword from one of our victims and flung it at the archer, slicing deep into the bowman's throat, his chariot crashing wildly against the wall. The war hog broke from its harness and created mayhem as it ran into and through the ranks of the midget warriors, trampling some, goring others.

The audience soon lost interest in this festival of gore; some began to boo. The rest of the little army backed away; the small warriors knew they couldn't win. More than half of them lay dead on the floor of the coliseum. Suddenly the trumpets blared and the arena gates opened again. What was left of the dwarf troops scattered like rodents into the recesses of the coliseum.

Panting and ashamed, I waited for what was next. Such a fanfare usually signaled something stronger and fiercer to come out for the fight. A detachment of praetorians marched out, men we knew; they headed straight for us. Only a few paces away, they stopped and opened ranks. Emperor Commodus, dressed in a white praetorian uniform, stepped out from among them. The crowd was instantly silent.

"I was assured that this army of little men was well trained and could hold its own with our very best soldiers." He looked down with disdain upon the little bodies strewn on the ground. "Obviously the impresarios were mistaken. I will deal with them later, but I promised each of you a centurion's stipend if you were victorious. Awaiting you inside is a small chest of treasures that will keep you all well into your old age. Now, take your winnings and leave Rome before I change my mind."

Stunned that Commodus would honor his word, we all responded with the Roman salute and placed our fists over our hearts. Varus and Polos were suddenly men of means who retired to Sicily. I returned to Gaul even wealthier than before. Months later I received word that Commodus had been murdered in his sleep. Thus ended my first term of service in the Praetorian Guard.

V

Late in the second century, more than one hundred years after the crucifixion, I had again become a soldier of the empire. Emperor Severus seized power from the praetorians in the year 197 and turned Rome into a military dictatorship. Handsome, tall, and regal, he was as ruthless in the political arena as he was on the battlefield. Severus' great skill as a general pushed the boundaries of the Empire all the way into Persia and to the banks of the Tigris River. Serving as a legionnaire at the battle of Ctesiphon, I was awed by the beauty of the two armies facing each other on the sandy plain. Banners stood at attention as the steady breeze carried the sound, the cadence of the enemy's massive kettle drums.

We stood in checkerboard formation, trained and ready for what we knew would come—war elephants. The huge elephants almost blinded us as sunlight glinted off their brass masks. The beasts' tusks were deadly points, iron spear tips. Riders sat atop the animals in wooden cages, and when the trumpet sounded, the armored giants lurched forward, urged by their drivers. The mammoths stepped slowly at first, but moved faster with each step until they were running toward us at full tilt.

"Discipline! Steady!" our commanders yelled, for we had been drilled to side step and create giant passages for the elephants to pass through without harming the legion. The ground shook beneath our feet as the attack approached, the men tense with anticipation, awaiting the order. Suddenly we were blindsided by a unit of our own heavy cavalry. Spooked by the pachyderms, the mercenaries' horses had bolted causing a great commotion, and our unit never heard the order to open ranks.

The elephants plowed into us head on, tossing legionnaires into the air, trampling and goring others. From atop the beasts, riders threw spears or shot arrows from their perches. The elephants came to a halt just in front of my cohort, shoving other Roman soldiers back into our disrupted ranks. Suddenly emitting a shrill cry, the mammoth nearest us reared up and keeled over on top of us. The pain was hideous, and I choked on my screams as helmet, armor, and shield were smashed into my crushed body. Days later I found myself in a torn and bloody tunic, walking in a line of wounded Roman stragglers. Other than the elephant attack, I could remember nothing except a vague recollection of trying to breathe in the darkness.

After that incident I retired to my farm, but a few years later the tedium and restlessness I felt created in me a need for adventure. Desperate for the comradeship and excitement I had once known, I reentered the Roman army. After several years I was once more selected for the Praetorian Guard, this time under the Emperor Elagabalus. From my first day as one of the defenders of the purple, there was tension between the Emperor and his personal bodyguard.

There was much grumbling among the praetorians about Elagabalus. This Roman Emperor was devoted to the Syrian sun god El-Gabal, a deity he hoped the Empire would embrace. His beliefs as well as his depravity cost him dearly though as the Roman populace refused to have a foreign religion forced upon it.

Out of necessity the praetorian officers chose a cohort to eliminate the Emperor. My cohort was chosen. To determine who would perform the actual deed, we drew straws. I drew short, and the grisly chore fell to me. I had never murdered anyone in cold blood before, and I began praying for a way out. The Lord spared me, for the night before I was to assassinate Elagabalus, he was found strangled to death by one of the slave boys he had viciously abused. I was grateful, because I believed I could never murder a man in cold blood, no matter how much he deserved it.

VI

Almost two decades later I was considering retiring from the legions once again. I was serving as a decurion, a squadron leader, under the command of one of the more brutal and ambitious officers I'd ever encountered in the Roman Army. His name was Quintus Tardus, and he seemed to gain favor with the generals through a macabre deception he practiced on the battlefield.

During lulls in melees, Tardus ordered us to drag the corpses of fallen foes from nearby areas to add to the heap of bodies directly in front of our own formation. That deception made it look as if we had killed more of the enemy than we actually had. This abominable work was so transparently dishonest we never imagined that anyone would be deceived by the trick, but we were wrong. After the battle, our commander, Maximinus Thrax, and his staff would ride through on horseback, nod approvingly, and salute our deceitful officer. Tardus made a good impression and rose to gain the confidence of the commander.

Tardus' cheap trick worked for him, for Maximinus would soon find himself named emperor, and Tardus would be promoted. Maximinus, a Thracian, was well over six feet tall, almost a giant. The man was a ruthless warrior and good general. He became one of several men who would wear the purple in the year 238 A.D., a time that eventually became known as "The Year of Six Emperors." The Romans counted their years from *Ab Urbe Condita*, Latin for "founding of the City." Rome was founded in 753 B.C. in Christian reckoning, so the year was 992 A.U.C. to Romans.

Maximinus was popular with his troops because he doubled our pay. He detested aristocrats but knew he needed some of them for his political ambitions—he wanted to be emperor. Tardus used Maximinus' trust, as well as gold pilfered from a pagan temple, to establish our unit as the would-be emperor's Praetorian Guard. Once done, Maximinus took the gold Tardus had stolen and added more to it in an effort to bribe the Roman Senate. Taking the gold, the Senate named Maximinus Emperor. Once in power, the Thracian hoped to consolidate his political influence, raise money through taxes, and oppress all opposition.

VII

Under Maximinus we had subdued Germania and, after a long march, were returning to Rome. Thanks to the new Emperor's bribe, Maximinus believed there would be little opposition. Although the politicians had supported the

Thracian from afar, the Roman Senate balked when it discovered that Maximinus was marching on the capital. We were told our Emperor would assume power with relative ease, but we were misinformed. Our army was stalemated at Aquileia in northern Italy, where the city had locked its gates. Sieges were arduous work in the best of times, but our army had been marching for months and was almost out of supplies. We were also told that Aquileia's residents were going to pour out to hail the new Emperor. This setback did not bode well for us.

Maximinus had assumed Rome and her allies would welcome him, but he was grossly mistaken. He had justifiably gained a reputation as a ruthless power monger who lived off the fortunes of families he ruined. The Senate and wealthy families of Rome had heard enough and had raised an army led by a man named Pupienas, one of two co-emperors the politicians had hastily voted into power—one to handle the civil government, the other the military.

As a soldier I had little to do with the political workings of Rome. On occasion, duty would place me holding a spear standing in rigid stillness and silence while white-robed senators, nobles, and generals came and went from the Emperor's tent outside the walls of Aquileia. Inside the tent with Emperor Maximinus, the politicians argued policy and future actions. Most of the soldiers believed it was only a matter of time until the city capitulated, so they took little notice of the words our rulers spoke—more because they didn't know or care of these matters than because they were commanded not to listen. Of course, I did not obey this command.

I was always fascinated by the workings of the Empire from my past life as a merchant and traveler, and from my long-lived view of seeing history unfold within my centuries on this earth. I hung on every word spoken by these high-ranking patricians, pretending indifference. At one meeting I was disturbed to learn of Maximinus' plan to use imperial authority to murder supporters of rival claimants to the purple, even in areas he did not control with his legions.

This was the power the Emperor held over his rivals. He could send commands through the vast administrative apparatus of the Empire to be obeyed by the city governments. For even if a rival's legions controlled a province, the Emperor still commanded the imperial servants who kept the roads, the post houses, the aqueducts, and the machinations of a great empire, including local policies.

During the months-long siege of Aquileia, we learned how tenuous Maximinus' hold on power was. Spies and agents of his rivals filled the camp. I caught wind of some of these dealings: the whispered conversations, the furtive glances, the concealed purses. I knew for certain that my commander, the ambitious Tardus, was scheming with at least two agents offering bribes. I believe he accepted both. Tardus was cheating the Emperor as well as the bribers!

These were the times the praetorians' power was most feared. Suspicion of a plot against the Emperor could be suppressed with unmeasured ruthlessness. There were no trials, no hearings, no protests heard. On nothing more than a rumor, Tardus could command the torture and execution of almost anyone. He rarely had anyone killed before confiscating the property of alleged suspects. The entire guard knew that Tardus received commission on funds seized for Emperor Maximinus.

Matters were strained both inside and outside of the city of Aquileia. Such an atmosphere of tension and instability wore on everyone's nerves; this was doubly so for our army as each day brought news of rival claimants' advancing troops and no word of surrender from the town. Arrests and torture were commonplace; the effect of fear on the populace was paralyzing.

Many nobles feared that if they guessed wrong on where to place their loyalties, their lives would end in a horrible death in the arena or in a secret dungeon somewhere. Rival armies were also approaching Rome, and the situation in the capital grew as frantic there as it was in Aquileia. Several men wanted the title of emperor, and each tried to position himself to take it. Maximinus' claim to the throne started to slip when his influence began to wane with his legions. The men were tired and hungry as supplies and rations were meager. The soldiers hadn't been paid in months, and there was sickness in the camp.

VIII

One chilly morning I stood as a silent guard in the Emperor's command tent. Maximinus strode into my presence flanked by aides and a group of nobles from Rome. They were conversing about some dispute but were in a good mood, for they had just received some heartening news. I could overhear only some of their excited words: "...killed them all...", "...a great triumph...", "...show those who defy the Emperor...."

My interests heightened as they spoke of southern Gaul, Aquitania specifically, the land I called my home, the province of my beloved farm. One of Maximinus' enemies had marched through the province. Many of the cities in the region had supported the rival with their cheers, their purses, and their arms. The Emperor had vowed revenge and sent his minions to Gaul with orders for retaliation. My mind focused on what they were saying while my body remained a statue, standing silently, like my companion guard who stood on the other side of the entry.

Then I heard the words that drew me in completely. Maximinus explained how he used Imperial power by ordering his henchmen to murder supporters of the Emperor's rivals in Gaul. He was jubilant with the results—entire villages and cities had been razed.

When the Emperor spoke of Aquitania my heart began to ache, for I loved the area and its people. Then, to my horror, Maximinus spoke of my own estate as though he knew it. He described the unique tree by the Roman road that marks the way to my vineyard. I realized that he and many others knew of my estate as a mysterious possession of a "wealthy Roman." Later I could appreciate that my mysterious life had attracted the wrong kind of attention to my farm.

I listened intently and heard that Maximinus had ordered the murder of all the workers on my estate, overseers and servants alike. His messengers laughed and belittled the lives of those slain, saying the dead were "probably

Christians." They went into detail about the torture of the villagers who lived nearby, women raped and butchered, children with their brains dashed out on the road. The Emperor laughed at these descriptions. I was sickened by the thought of the brutal extermination of families I had known and loved for generations. The bile rose in my throat, and my pain and anger turned to white-hot fury. Enraged, I drew my short sword, strode two steps, and plunged my blade though the heart of Maximinus. Never did I imagine that I was capable of murdering on such blind, unthinking impulse! Gurgling, he slid to the floor in a pool of royal blood. I looked at those remaining in the room, waiting, expecting retaliation. They did nothing. Not even a ripple of surprise, only silence.

Then one of the white robed civilians, the one with a purple border on his toga, calmly tossed me a purse filled with gold coins. He and his conspirators turned and walked from the room. The other soldier standing guard, my comrade Publius, spat his words in anger, "You filthy jackal, that's supposed to be my gold!" I had unwittingly become an assassin. I threw Publius the purse and left for Aquitania, asking God's forgiveness and vowing never again to murder in cold blood.

I worked for years to help rebuild villages and repair my farm after the ravages of the Emperor's men. Years later I grew uneasy, and I hired people to run the estate. I had a taste for battle; I again felt the need to fight and reenlisted in the Roman army, this time as a cavalry officer.

IX

My first few years as a squadron commander were relatively peaceful, but eventually my horsemen were deployed to the north of Rome. My unit distinguished itself at the battle of Mediolanum, present day Milan; this battle turned out to be a significant step in my career.

In 259 A.D. the Emperor Valerian's army was campaigning in the east when northern Italy was invaded by a tribe from Germania, barbarians called the Alamanni, a tribal word translating as "all men." These fair-skinned peoples were from the highlands in Germania; the Alamanni were strong and rugged, afraid of nothing. They poured through the Alps and moved on Mediolanum. In Rome there was a public outcry that the capital itself might even be threatened. The danger was so great that the Senate hastily drafted a citizen army. Valerian's son Gallienus was given the task of driving the Alamanni from the Italian peninsula. Fortunately the Roman general was a good strategist and tactician.

Gallienus' use of mounted auxilia, light cavalry, during the ensuing battle earned him the title of Germanicus Maximus and convinced Gallienus that mounted troops were vital for Rome's safety. Our mobility and ability to react defensively helped the Emperor's son wage a successful campaign against overwhelming numbers.

In one such attack, our army's right flank was in disarray. The barbarians sent thousands into the assault, and a large gash in our line was created when a legion of our mercenary infantry routed. My squadron of cavalry had received orders to wait in reserve behind the lines, but the fleeing units left such a large hole in our battle line that defeat seemed imminent. Acting against orders, I led my squadron in a charge against the lead enemy units that were pouring into the gap.

Our daring assault had no hope of winning as we were vastly outnumbered, but the attack stunned the Alamanni vanguard, which broke and ran. The fleeing enemy troops disrupted other enemy units moving in for the attack. One huge tribal warrior, a blonde-haired giant, turned and stood his ground, holding his sword aloft trying to rally his fellow marauders. I flung my lance at the brave brute; the spear's iron tip struck him between the eyes and red gore hung out the back of his skull. Seeing him fall, his followers lost their will to fight and fled. The chaos that followed our quick jab at the enemy saved the day and bought time for Gallenius to plug the gap with Roman reserves.

Because of that success I was promoted. I was to become the military attaché to Palmyra. Located between Syria and Persia, Palmyra was a wealthy client state, a Roman ally on the eastern border of the Empire that protected Rome's interests from Persia.

Thursday, July 11, 5:00 p.m.

"A hundred and fifty years in the Roman army—didn't you ever want a family?" Braden asked.

"I've been wed many times, but I've never fathered any children. There's much more to say about my time in the Roman army, but my story is long so I must go on. Becoming a military advisor led me to my first great love."

Zenobia

Charm is deceptive, and beauty is fleeting...Proverbs 31:30

I

The winter sun was setting as I crested the hills and looked down onto the pink stone kingdom known as the City of Palms. The locals called it Tadmor, but to the Romans it remained Palmyra, and the world *was* Rome. Palmyra's love affair with the empire was in its honeymoon. Though considered a colony of Rome, the city was allowed great freedom in governing itself. This made the Palmyrenes feel autonomous, and since Palmyra was on the far edge of the Empire, it gave Rome a buffer state between itself and the Persians. Besides, Palmyra was a center of commerce, and both Rome and Palmyra benefited from trade from the east.

The Silk Road was the artery for trade between east and west; it was the economic heart that pumped money into Palmyra and the eastern half of the Roman Empire. Nestled between the two great dominions of Persia and Rome, Palmyra stood majestically on an expansive plain looking as if the pagan god Zeus himself had chiseled the columned city from pink marble and dropped it into an oasis of palms. I don't know that I've ever seen a more beautiful place.

A large thoroughfare ran from east to west like a great river. Everywhere there were people, camels, and horses. The heart of Palmyra was a gigantic bazaar situated in the center of the city. It was the place where merchants and caravans melded. The citizens and merchants gathered there to buy and sell goods such as silks, dates, and spices. Palmyra had been part of the Roman Empire for 50 years but had been a part of the Silk Road for centuries.

According to the Roman army, I was a military attaché, a title that took me several years to achieve. I was there technically to advise Palmyra's army, but my primary assignment was to note the increasing influence of the Persians. At first, the years I lived in Palmyra were so delightful that they were almost like retirement. With the exception of the Persian advances to the north, there was little else to report. The people were pleasant, and the climate was tolerable. While Palmyra grew strong and flourished, the Roman Empire tottered with a series of dreadful emperors and civil wars. During this time Rome and Persia would come to blows, and Palmyra would be called upon for support. Though the King, Septimius Odainat, was an able monarch, it was his Queen, Zenobia, who became a bold and formidable head of state.

If ever there were a daughter of Eve, it was Zenobia. She stood like an empress, erect and commanding. Her sharp, obsidian eyes were alert. Her delicate high cheekbones and short nose accentuated her voluptuous lips. She was a bronze goddess, her skin as smooth as gardenia petals. Willowy, tall and thin, she was shapely and graceful, her voice sensuous as honey. Zenobia's every movement was a temptation; her every word was a song. As if beauty were not enough, Zenobia, confident and ambitious, was a warrior in the truest sense of the word. She was accomplished with the sword and could fire a bow accurately while riding her horse at a full gallop.

I first met the great warrior Queen the night of my arrival in Palmyra. I was introduced at a political dinner at court. At King Odainat's side was Queen Zenobia, who scarcely did more than glance in my direction. She said nothing, though her eyes spoke of ambition, power over men, and lust.

After our meal Odainat asked his Queen to perform for her guests, something that she was apparently accustomed to doing. The musicians struck up a Bedouin tune, and the ouds, lyres, and dafs followed in time. Like a sensuous leopard Zenobia rose and made her way to the center of the room, striding to the pulse and tempo of the music. She moved elegantly and lasciviously to the beat, like a living aphrodisiac. Her supple figure swayed to the rhythm of the music, enticing, ensnaring, enchanting. The Queen's black, gold-tipped tresses swung seductively to the melody as she dipped and swayed like a primal Salome.

Zenobia swirled and spun in a performance that held every man in the room captive, including me. I couldn't turn away from her, and I would have sworn she was eyeing me like prey during her dance. The court was spellbound, not wanting to miss a moment of this suggestive exhibition of womanly beauty, passion, and grace. Zenobia's body undulated, obeying the cadence, and when it was over, every man desired her. The King was bloated with conceit at his wife's immodest talent as he enjoyed possessing what other men coveted.

Even before I met the Queen I had decided I didn't like her. There were rumors of her infidelity as well as her disdain for slaves and common people. I was told that Zenobia had once had a woman whipped for accidentally brushing against her in the market place, and also that the Queen had tripped a young girl who was carrying flowers to the King. I believed that Zenobia was conniving and spoiled; however, my trifling concerns were put away as political upheaval shook the Roman world.

II

The crisis of the third century was at hand, and the two great empires of Rome and Persia were finally at war. The Roman Emperor Valerian led his army to relieve the forces besieged in the city of Edessa, a large center of commerce in Mesopotamia, northwest of Palmyra. His relief force defeated the Persians, but it was a Pyrrhic victory as immediately afterward the Roman legions were stricken with the plague from the East, a disease that killed one-third of the army. The Roman Emperor shared the fate of many leaders whose stars are out of alignment—matters proceeded to get worse. Sapur I, the King of Persia, was approaching with a large army. Emperor Valerian had hoped to give battle, but his army was suffering the ravages of the ague, chills, fever, and diarrhea so debilitating that few could even stand. Though there were no good solutions, the Emperor opted for a commendable, but foolish, action.

Valerian decided to seek terms with his foe. Certainly this approach was nothing new, but he fell into the trap of believing his enemy would live up to Roman ideals of honor. Valerian, with only a small escort, agreed to meet the Persians on their own ground, an idiotic move. Consequently, Valerian holds the distinction of being the only Roman emperor ever to be captured. If that weren't ignominious enough, he was killed, stuffed by Persian taxidermists, and hung on a wall of Sapur's palace! Valerian's shameful death set in motion the events that triggered the Great Rebellions, one in Gaul and the other in Palmyra.

Upon learning of the Roman emperor's death, Odainat, who by this time had become Septimius Odainat, bearing a Roman consul's title, readied his army for war. Odainat and Zenobia were meticulous in their preparations. I was surprised to see how heavily involved the Queen was in this enterprise, and I was impressed by her knowledge of heavily armored, cataphracted cavalry, and battle tactics.

Since I was an advisor and in command of a detachment of Roman cavalry, Zenobia and I often spoke about the use of light and heavy mounted troops. During these discussions she was always knowledgeable and inventive. The Queen appeared all business and straightforward, but I felt there was something submerged, some hidden attraction between us. In spite of my initial disdain for her, I found myself admiring this woman.

III

Although it took months to prepare for war, Palmyra was finally ready to move against the Persians. Early one morning the trumpets blared, and the archers and cavalry moved out of the city to meet the forces of King Sapur I.

I suggested to Odainat that he send jewels and riches to the Persian king in an effort to ease tension, a move that might also help in the element of surprise. The King took my advice; however, we intercepted the gifts a week later as the Persian ruler had insolently sent them back. Angry at the insult, the Palmyrene King prepared a clever ambush for the Persian forces returning east after successfully sacking the city of Antioch.

The Persian army, fat with booty, staggered home like a sot, sated with its victory over Rome. The enemy troops were crossing the Tigris back into Persia when the Palmyrene army fell upon them like a giant scythe. The Persians, little more than a mob of sleepwalkers, had neither scouts nor sentries when we took them completely by surprise. I was in command of a Roman cavalry unit that was still anxious to avenge Valerian's murder and disgrace even years after his death.

We met little resistance as the Persian army had become intermingled within its baggage train. It was like warring against a traveling brothel of prostitutes and drunkards. The bloodbath began with the enemy split in two, part on each side of the Tigris. Those soldiers on the western side of the river were cut down or driven into the water where they drowned or became easy targets for our archers. Many were trapped by the ambush, and these were killed to a man. There were no prisoners.

I estimated Persian losses at about 5000. It was a stinging defeat for Sapur I. The main body of his army did turn and make a stand on the other side of the river, but there was no pursuit by the Palmyreans. The slaughter was over, and by nightfall those who hadn't made it across the waterway had died by the sword or by the river. Ironically, we seized most of the booty the Persians had taken from Edessa and Antioch.

Our return to Palmyra was glorious, and mimicking the great Roman conquerors, Odainat arranged a triumph, a Roman-style grand procession, for himself and his army. My detachment rode directly behind the King's silver-plated chariot. The entire city turned out waving palm fronds. We followed the King, pausing before the people and the nobles. When we stopped to acknowledge the Queen, she nodded seductively. The evening turned into one of great revelry, a feasting bacchanal that continued for almost three days.

The battle had been well planned and grand in scope, but it changed Odainat and Zenobia who both became drunk with power. As a show of thanks and trust from Rome, the Senate named Odainat *Restitutor totius Orientis*, Corrector of the East, a title carried only by the Empire's emperors. In this, the Roman Senate made a mistake—Odainat's success went to his head, and he became bolder politically. Rome was still embroiled in a civil war in Gaul. With the Empire's attentions focused elsewhere, the Palmyrean King gave himself the ancient Persian title of "King of Kings." Rome paid no attention. Zenobia ascended with Odainat, her glory second only to her husband's.

In the months that followed, I began to feel like an unwelcome houseguest. I was rarely consulted, summoned, or invited to any state function. I was completely left out of the line of communication until one evening when the King requested my presence.

"Old friend," he greeted me as I entered before him. "I should have summoned you sooner because I have missed your honest advice. But that is in the past; I called you to hear a proposition. The Roman Empire is weak and cannot sustain itself. Rome is drowning in many wars. Now is the time for Palmyra to stand alone, to create her own place in the sun. Campaign again with me; become one of my generals and you shall rise with Palmyra."

I was stunned. I stood for a few moments, befuddled by the awkwardness of the situation that followed as the King and his entire court awaited my answer. The Queen stared at me intently, her eyes hungry and suggestive.

Graciously, Odainat sensed my hesitation, saying, "Take some time to consider it—a day—perhaps two. Then return and let me know your decision."

He nodded his dismissal, and I was ushered out of the room. It was the last time I would see him alive. The next morning Odainat and his firstborn son, Hairan, were both found murdered in their beds. The Palmyrene healers were summoned to the fallen leader's chambers, but they could not revive him. The dead men's yellow skin suggested they had both been poisoned. Suspicion fell upon Odainat's advisors as well as the heir who was next in line, the Queen's only son Vaballathus. Wary eyes were also cast upon Zenobia, who was named the new regent, a title that gave her control of the throne.

Warrior Queen

It is better not to make a vow than to make one and not fulfill it. Ecclesiastes 5:5

I

Upon Odainat's death, I sent word to Rome that the King and his son had been assassinated and that the Queen's son Vaballathus was to be king with Zenobia to reign until he came of age. The Roman Emperor Claudius approved the situation through negligence, and because of Rome's silence, months later I was summoned into the Queen's presence.

Exotic eastern music accompanied lively sword dancing and filled Zenobia's court as I entered. The mid-eastern instruments slowed to a halt, and I was taken before Zenobia. She sat at the top of an elevated platform, upon a royal chaise on an immense crimson tapestry. As if posing for a sculpture, Zenobia sat on a gold, gem-encrusted throne which embraced her. The seat of the chair rested between two golden lions, their regal heads forming arm rests. The back of the settee was adorned with a golden lion's head around which its mane emanated like the rays of the sun. The royal chair was a work of art crafted for an emperor, but Zenobia found that it fit her well.

As beautiful as the throne was, even more dazzling was the bejeweled Queen who graced it. Zenobia wore a golden crown with a lion's head at the front and rubies for its eyes. Her gown was golden silk; she wore gem-covered golden bracelets and rings on every finger. Around her neck hung a large gold necklace with a lion's head covered with diamonds, but it was Zenobia's eyes that sparkled and lit up the room with a seductive sovereignty.

At her side were her two most trusted counselors, General Timagenes and General Zabdas. Timagenes was an Egyptian mercenary general who had sold himself to the highest bidder. He was known for his skill with a blade and his ability to motivate his soldiers. His graying hairline suggested wisdom and his leaden eyes, purpose. Zabdas was a native Palmyrene who was always the subject of court intrigue. He was both a diplomat and a general whose spies were everywhere. Zabdas was bald and had a jagged smile. His eyes were deceitful, like those of a crow. Although he was wealthy, Zabdas was unable to mimic the stance of an aristocrat. His mannerisms were stilted and awkward, and his clothing, though expensive, looked out of place on him. Zabdas and Timagenes acknowledged my presence with a bow and backed away.

I stood before the stunning Queen, enthralled by her imperial elegance, her unparalleled beauty. "Commander Lazarus," she addressed me, her eyes piercing the moment. "As you can see, General Zabdas and General Timagenes have joined me in my efforts to strengthen my kingdom." With a wave of her hand, the two bowed again and retreated from court. "Please be seated," she said, pointing to the stool that awaited me.

Zenobia's eyes locked onto mine. There were no words for this moment, only attraction. She was breathtaking. I thought her sensuous and exotic before, but there was something about power that agreed with her, like a lioness after a fresh kill. Perhaps it was her confidence; perhaps it was her control, but her eyes devoured me. I was falling under her spell; a woman I had feared, a woman who I thought might be a murderess, had won my heart with a glance. How fine the line is between love and hate. My disdain for Zenobia had turned into polarized admiration and infatuation in a single moment.

She stood regally. "Months have passed and yet Rome has not responded to my regency," she said, awaiting an explanation.

"I can only imagine that the Emperor has been distracted. His attentions are elsewhere."

She sat gracefully. "You mean Gaul," she said. "My sources tell me that the civil war there still rages. They say Rome may not win and that there are other areas of unrest as well. The Empire is on its knees."

"Rumors, your highness; Rome will survive as it always has."

"It was my late husband's wish that you become one of his generals." Her voice was beguiling. "You are a skilled warrior and have shown great courage and leadership. It is my desire that you would join Palmyra as she ascends to her place at the center of a great empire."

She rose and stretched out her hands as if she were offering me her dominion.

My silence enveloped the room.

II

I stood, unable to speak, mesmerized by Zenobia's beauty, torn between my desire for her and my loyalty to Rome.

I lowered my eyes, muttered hoarsely, "Queen Zenobia, I must have time."

"You insult me. You insult Palmyra," she hissed, eyes flaring, her voice cold. "It has been months since the King asked you to join him. You have had plenty of time to consider."

"No, my Queen," I insisted. "A man can be true to only one oath at a time. I swore an oath to Rome."

Zenobia's eyes unexpectedly softened. She clapped her hands twice, and immediately the room emptied. The Queen motioned to her attendants who took the torches, followed her, and exited the room. I was alone. I stood for a moment, letting my eyes adjust to the darkness, not knowing what to expect. I shuffled slowly toward the door to make my way out of the chamber, careful to slide my feet along the floor to avoid tripping over the luxurious carpets. The great door was barred from the outside.

I slid my hands along the wall, seeking another exit when a dim light filtered into the room followed by a distant rhythmic beat, a stirring murky melody, accompanied by the sultry fragrance of jasmine. Then someone found my hand. A woman's velvety touch led me through the darkness into a softly lit chamber. The twilight glow revealed a golden room and a beautiful woman in a flowing gown; she moved across the floor in one liquid motion, like a tigress. Stunned, I realized it was Zenobia. The Queen took my hands and kissed them, sliding her arms around my neck and pulling my lips to hers.

Zenobia whispered, "I must have you."

Her inviting lips pressed against mine, and my heart was ablaze. I kissed her long and firmly, pausing only to breathe in the air of passion. Like two polar opposites suddenly brought together, our embrace was volatile.

"All this can be yours, Lazarus. Think of the power and the glory," she said, gently running her hands through my hair. "And every night you shall have me."

Like a mythical siren she enticed me. I was in love. I kissed her again and again on those moist, voluptuous lips. I wanted to shout "Yes!"

The room felt like it was on fire as she turned and led me to a silken feather pallet, and then she slowly moved around behind me and began to untie my sash. I turned, took her hands, and held them against my chest. Then I pulled her to me, lovingly kissing each finger, then her neck, then her lips again and again. I desired her more at that moment than any woman I had ever loved, but I knew our love would be short lived. Making war against Rome was futile. Besides, even after the years I had spent as a slave, even after all the injustices I had seen done by the state, even after all the cruelty I had seen done in the name of the state, I believed that Rome was a necessary evil, one that provided a foundation for civilization. Kingdoms rose and kingdoms fell, but Rome was more than a kingdom. It was a vision; it was a dream; it was the world—my world.

"I want you. I want to say yes," I said. "But I cannot have you by betraying Rome, for if I betray Rome, I betray you also. Palmyra cannot sustain a lengthy war against Rome."

"Rome is weak," she said confidently, circling behind me and rubbing the back of my neck with her possessive touch. "Palmyra will rule the East."

I pulled her hand away and again brought her face to face with me in the dim light. "Palmyra's rule will be short. I have both served and studied Rome for years. There was, is, and will always be Rome. Rome is like the wind. Sometimes the wind is strong; sometimes it seems as if it does not exist, but the wind always returns."

"I would never have thought that you would be a coward," she growled and backed away.

"I fear neither man nor death," I said. "Claudius is weak; in that you are correct, but there is a new emperor. Aurelian is strong and within months will quell the uprising in Gaul. Then he will turn his attentions to the East. No matter how much success you have, no matter how large your empire, Rome is more powerful. Is not what you have enough? You are a queen who wields great power. You have riches most monarchs in the world can only dream of. You lack for nothing. You can have me without making war. What can you possibly hope to gain?"

"Wealth is not enough!" the Queen said. "We must have power. There will be glory in the fight. Rome is falling and Palmyra rising. We will write the history of the world together! So you must either join me now," her voice rose as she issued her ultimatum, "or you must leave Palmyra." She finished with a sweeping, majestic movement of her bare arm.

"I cannot love you and make war against Rome!"

She inhaled then turned away sharply. "Get out," she ordered coldly.

I bowed deeply and retreated toward the door to which she still pointed. How could I leave Zenobia and Palmyra? I loved her more desperately than ever.

III

As I was leaving the Queen's chambers I saw a figure skulking in the passageway. Zabdas confronted me as I drew near.

"What did the Queen offer you, Roman?" he snarled.

"You'll have to ask her about that, Zabdas," I said.

"The fact that she dismissed you is enough. I need you to listen closely to the offer that I have for you," he said with a sinister grin.

I don't remember what happened next, only that there was a tremendous pain in my head. My guess is that one of Zabdas's ruffians knocked me unconscious. When I groggily awoke, I was lying on my back tied to a horse; my arms were pulled over my head and then around and under the neck of the beast. My legs were spread over the back of the animal and tied together by a rope underneath the equine's abdomen. I could barely see out of my right eye because of the crusted blood, but in the torchlight Zabdas came around to gloat.

"I'm surprised that you awoke from such a terrible blow, Roman," he said in the flickering glow. "It is my custom to send traitors into the desert to die. Do you have anything to say before we send you to meet your death?"

"Does the Queen know about this?" I struggled to ask.

"The Queen?" he said. "What does Zenobia know about anything? She rules only because I chose her instead of Odainat and his halfwit son."

"So you killed them?"

"Oh no. I pride myself in having some honor. He was my King. I would never stoop to murder a sovereign with these hands." He held them before me as he smiled.

"Hell will be waiting for you with open arms," I said.

"There is no hell. There is no heaven. There is only here and now."

"I know better, Zabdas. I've seen it."

"Listen to the Roman prattle about the afterlife," he said sarcastically. "You bore me. By the way, this is a terrible way to die. If the sun does not bake you to death, the horse may crush you when it dies. If neither of those kills you, the stinging flies or thirst will. If you are unfortunate enough, you may even live long enough to see the vultures peck out your eyes."

With that he laughed derisively and slapped the horse on its hindquarters, sending me into the dark desert night. I eventually passed out but dreamt of Zenobia. The blistering desert sun on my face woke me. I was confused until I finally recalled Zabdas' words. By twisting my neck I could see that my horse was slowly walking toward some boulders that offered some shade. The pitiful creature stood for hours panting, but God was with me, and as the pathetic mount finally keeled over, the rope that bound my legs snapped.

Although in pain, I managed to flip my legs and trunk backward so that I was stomach down on the horse's neck and head. My shoulders ached unbearably as they had separated from their sockets, but somehow I was able to slip the rope from underneath the dead animal and pull myself free. Again and again I relentlessly rammed my shoulders into a boulder, slamming each back into its socket. The process was agonizing, but eventually I felt relief. Although I had no idea where I was, the rock formation offered some shade from the relentless sun. I untied the rope and I slept.

I don't know how long I lay there, but when I awoke the sun was setting. I decided my best option was to travel northeast. I hoped that Zabdas had taken me north of the city where the land was the most barren. There were no settlements in that area, but there was a seldom-used trade route four days or so from Palmyra. I hoped the old road was only a day's walk.

I found a trail late the following morning and stumbled upon a small caravan guarded by a Roman mercenary named Favius. He gave me food and water and took me as far as Antioch. From there I made my way to Byzantium and reported to the garrison commander there.

IV

For the next two years, Zenobia's lust for power went unchecked. Her armies conquered lands and people, to the north as far as Asia Minor and to the south deep into Egypt. To the east she carved out part of what belonged to Persia, and to the west as far as the Mediterranean.

In Byzantium I met the consul Baltus who said that the new Emperor Aurelian's strategy was to avoid any major conflicts against Palmyra until Rome could consolidate its position in the west. Aurelian was wise politically and militarily, and he believed in rewarding loyalty. The first move he made was to quash the rebellion in Gaul. In less than six months, the situation was rectified. Once done he began gathering his forces to defeat Palmyra.

I first met Aurelian in the spring in Byzantium. Unlike most of the emperors before him, Aurelian was unpretentious and practical. He was an appointed man for an appointed time—probably the only human being on the earth who could have accomplished what he did in such a short time span. He entered Byzantium, one of the oldest cities in the Empire, without fanfare and went to work immediately. I met with him within two hours of his arrival. He was warm and friendly. His long face was regal, sporting an aquiline nose and a well-groomed beard and mustache. His kind eyes indicated that he genuinely cared about his people.

In our meeting Aurelian began questioning me about the Palmyrean army and its tactics. He then asked me to go into detail about the Queen Zenobia. Although I felt guilty for betraying the woman I loved, I had chosen Rome over her. I told the Emperor all, even that she had asked me to turn against Rome.

"I understand she sent you into the desert to die," he said.

"Not the Queen; it was her cutthroat general Zabdas. I look forward to killing him," I said coldly, relishing the thought and forgetting the vow I'd made when I'd killed Maximinus Thrax so many years before.

The Emperor immediately made me an advisor. As such, I counseled him on engaging Zenobia's forces and was privy to his plans for restoring Rome's Eastern Empire. He was a great strategist.

"We will force Zenobia to make war on two fronts," Aurelian said, pouring over maps of the eastern Mediterranean. "The southern army will land in Egypt and fight its way east and then north through Palestine. The northern army will move from the east out of Byzantium and meet the enemy at Antioch." He pointed to the city on the map that lay before us. "Capturing Antioch will open the way to Palmyra. She will have to fight us there or we will threaten her capital."

Within a year, the southern army was driving up the eastern Mediterranean against General Timagenes. The main army, under direct command of the Emperor, had captured much of the East without a fight and then driven directly toward Palmyra. As Aurelian forecast, Zenobia could not maintain war on two fronts. Withdrawing most of her troops from what was the western half of her empire, Zenobia made her stand just outside of Antioch.

On the eve of the battle, the weather was beautiful. The Queen had chosen a good defensive position, and her army was larger than that of Rome. But the Romans had fought larger armies for centuries with great success. Soldiers fighting the Romans were usually vastly overmatched when confronted by the empire's well-trained, well-disciplined troops.

Like any good general, Aurelian inspected the field the evening before the battle. It was twilight as three of us rode over the long, rising plain Zenobia had chosen to defend. There was only one unusual place on the entire battlefield. The area Aurelian was concerned about was called the funnel, a grouping of large boulders that forced troops into a narrow pass before opening up again. The Emperor, General Cruz, and I had foolishly gotten too far ahead of our escort. We sat on horseback discussing how to use the rocks to our advantage. We believed our scouts had secured the area since we were protected from enemy sight. As we discussed the coming battle, I heard the clang of sword and rock above us. I glanced up just in time to see the flash of a javelin hurled at the Emperor.

My reflexes alone saved Aurelian's life as the edge of my small shield deflected the heavy spear tip from his head, sending the weapon crashing harmlessly into the dust. The Emperor's horse reared, throwing him to the ground, and another spear sailed past my shoulder lodging in General Cruz' throat; he toppled to the earth with a bloody gurgle. The clamor of hooves announced that horsemen were charging in through the gap in the rocks. My mount and I stood our ground in front of the Emperor, and I took on the riders as they came one at a time. Sword held high in my left hand and shield drawn back, I moved my horse forward quickly a pace and slammed the first of the light cavalrymen to the earth, punching him with my buckler, knocking him senseless. I turned sharply and shield-punched the second with the same result. The last two riders charged abreast. I engaged one, while the Emperor, now on his feet, fended off his opponent with a spear until moments later when our escort arrived to drive away our attackers.

Heading back to camp, Aurelian said, "I owe you my life."

"I am a soldier," I said. "We fight for a dream called Rome."

The Emperor looked at me with grateful eyes. "Let us continue to dream," he said with a warm smile.

V

Back at camp, battle maps lay before us in the light of flickering oil lamps. I suggested that we wait and let Zenobia attack first. Her best troops were her cavalry. They were heavily armed, and the heat could work against them. It was her combative nature to go on the offensive. While her own army was as yet undefeated, I knew that her men had never faced an army like the grizzled veterans who made up Aurelian's legions.

"The Palmyrean army will find it difficult when it sees that the Romans will not rout at the first charge," I said. "They're used to fighting inferior troops."

"They certainly have the numbers on us," the Emperor said. "Constantius' scouts say that the Queen Zenobia has upward of 10,000 more than we."

"It is only her cavalry we have to fear. The rest of her men are undisciplined brawlers. We'll see how tough they are marching into the teeth of our legions."

"We shall have our cavalry out front near the funnel. The two battle lines will be almost a mile apart. The legions will line up just ahead of this hill," the Emperor said, pointing his finger along the map. "When the Palmyrean cavalry attacks, we will retreat in disorder. The legions will turn and run as if they've wet themselves, then move into tight formation behind the rise. We will prepare the position with a semicircle of caltrops, sharp stakes, and spurs. We will allow the enemy cavalry to move deep into our lines before we retreat behind the thicket. The spikes will halt their advance; then we will close in on them from the flanks in tight formation. We will defeat the enemy cavalry there." He pointed to the position with his finger. "Away from their supporting infantry."

I was to command the cavalry on the left wing. Aurelian and his legions would stand dead center in the battlefield, and General Constantius, who replaced the deceased General Cruz, would command the right wing.

"Victoria pro Roma," the Emperor said taking his fist and putting it over his heart.
"Victoria pro Roma," the staff snapped to attention and responded, our fists over our hearts.

VI

The heat the next morning was scalding. By dawn the Emperor had his army lines formed and waiting, acting as if we might launch an attack at any moment. Zenobia's forces, believing an assault was eminent, hastily assembled and mustered without breakfast, awaiting the onslaught. Whenever the Queen's force began to relax, Roman trumpets blared or our drummers tapped out a cadence as if we were going to attack. This distraction kept the enemy army at attention for the entire morning. Aurelian's plan worked to perfection. Not only did the Palmyrean cataphracted cavalrymen stand in their metal scales and wait in the blistering heat, they were unfed. It was almost noon before the Queen began to lose patience and ready for her own attack.

As was the plan, the Roman drums sounded, and I went forward with the cavalry and waited for the enemy to charge. The Warrior Queen rode in a stately war chariot, up and down the lines of battle shouting encouragement to her army of 40,000 warriors.

Even in battle dress Zenobia was beautiful. She wore a golden lion's head helmet with a golden cuirass or breastplate, over a white tunic. My heart stirred just watching her. She stopped in front of her cataphracts. Her 10,000 heavy cavalrymen were almost entirely covered in shiny scales of iron, so skillfully wrought that it looked as if thousands of silver coins had been gilded to their bodies. Even the horses were heavily protected with similar armor scales, and they had been standing in the sun, roasting for almost six hours. The Queen raised her sword in the air and brought it down, pointing at the Roman line.

In one monstrous gleaming wave of man, beast, metal, and dust the charge swept toward us. It was magnificent. The shimmering heat of the sand made the Queen's figure flicker like a flame in her chariot as the cataphracted cavalry passed her. Not wanting to confront her elite cavalry with my light units, I signaled retreat before the enemy's heavy cavalry was half way across the field. Slowed by the weight of the armor and the heat, our opponents could not hope to catch us, and the dust from our retreat choked them as they relentlessly pursued us.

Aurelian's legions then made a good show of feigning a rout, and like hounds smelling blood, the Palmyreans whipped their mounts into a froth, charging over the open plain. On the other side of the crest, the Roman army had quickly regrouped with only light troops dispersed in front of the large crescent-shaped thicket of ground spikes which still remained concealed. The Palmyrean cavalry, disrupted and already fatigued from the long charge, blindly moved into the snare. Believing they were finally closing in for the kill, the enemy horsemen charged down the slope to overrun the slingers and archers. Once again though, before the heavy cavalry could close, the light foot troops quickly made their way through the thorny pricket of spikes, drawing the cataphracts deeper into the gigantic, crescent-shaped trap. Meanwhile our heavy Roman legions moved up on the flanks into tight square formations, enveloping the cataphracts and closing the position from the flanks and behind.

What culminated was the destruction of some of the finest cavalry the world has ever seen. Unable to move, fatigued, and disordered, the enemy riders realized their situation was hopeless as the heavy infantry pressed them against the thicket. Some riders tried to brave the spikes, but moving through the caltrops was almost impossible as the steeds in their armor were easily snared by the man-made thorns, causing horse and rider to fall into the thicket. The rest tried to fight, but their heavy armor and exhausted mounts became a hindrance as movement was so restricted.

The shielded legions drove deeper and deeper into the ranks of the great cavalry, cutting down horse and man. While the enemy's armor protected them from slashes and cuts, thrusts with lance or sword could penetrate and find the mark. Even if the stab did not pierce the armor, the horses were less protected, and a dismounted cavalryman made easy prey.

Aurelian's Palestinian infantry were wreaking havoc as well. These warriors wielded heavy clubs that battered the large, easy targets of horse and man. I saw one rider swiped from his mount by a single, mighty blow. Another one of our infantrymen bashed a horse to the ground where the rider was bludgeoned to death on the spot. As the battle raged, the cataphracts became more and more compacted and cramped. Completely exhausted, the troops were unable to move or even engage in combat effectively.

Zenobia arrived in her chariot at the crest of the hill, fully expecting to see her horse soldiers mopping up the fleeing Romans. Instead she watched her cavalry being decimated. She frantically motioned for her foot soldiers to move up, but they were slow and undisciplined. With the Palmyrean cataphracts in disarray and engaged, I signaled for the entire Roman cavalry to follow me in a charge against the advancing enemy infantry which was totally unprepared for our onslaught. Initially the enemy units held their ground, but when one unit turned and ran, the rest fled en masse.

The rout was on. Weapons, stragglers, the baggage train, even the Queen's personal items were left behind. I searched for Zenobia, but she was gone, escorted by Zabdas and her personal bodyguard. Zenobia's only hope had been to defeat the Emperor's forces in one large battle. Her heavy cavalry, the great weapon she had wielded so successfully until now, was utterly annihilated. Her army in tatters, the Warrior Queen withdrew to Palmyra knowing that Rome would not be far behind.

VII

The Emperor did his best to follow up his victory by harassing the residue of Zenobia's army. Commanding the Roman cavalry, I pressed the pursuit, but the Queen and some of her troops quickly and successfully made their way back to Palmyra. In an effort to protect himself and Zenobia, Zabdas had dressed up a slave as the Roman Emperor and paraded him through the city as their prisoner, claiming a great victory over Aurelian.

The Emperor sent orders to capture Zenobia to make sure she would not escape. Aurelian and General Constantius were already driving hard on the city. I decided to move north with my cavalry, wheel around Palmyra, and south to block off any eastern escape routes. I divided my cavalry into three groups, each one covering a way east out of the city. I personally led my detachment to cover what I believed was the most direct route to Persia.

After dealing with the usual Silk Road travelers bound for the East, we were approached by two people, each on camel. The captain of the guard was questioning them when I recognized Zabdas's thorny smile.

"Seize them," I said.

In an instant Zabdas pulled a blade from beneath his cloak and waved it menacingly at the captain who promptly cut the saddle harness, accidentally gouging the camel as well. The animal reared up from the wound while rider and saddle slid to the ground. The camel came down on top of the Palmyrene general, crushing Zabdas beneath its weight. The general's black eyes bulged as he lay gasping. I knelt beside him and pulled the dark cloth from around his head.

"Remember me?" I said.

A look of astonishment crossed his face, followed by one of agony. "It cannot be possible." The words crawled painfully out of his mouth as he winced.

"With God all things are possible," I said.

"But you...should...be dead."

Zabdas left this world with those words, and I paused triumphantly before I realized that I had momentarily forgotten about the Queen.

I looked up to find that Zenobia was still atop her camel. She sat quietly, offering no resistance.

"They told me you were dead," she said with a momentary look of wonder on her face.

"That was Zabdas' plan," I said, pointing to the dead general.

We escorted the captured Warrior Queen back to Aurelian. Palmyra surrendered without resistance. Trying to reduce Zenobia's humiliation, I allowed her to ride unfettered back into the city. She was still beautiful and proud, but the dark circles beneath her eyes and the smatterings of gray hair indicated that the stress of the campaign had been great. The once bold and powerful Zenobia was a defeated woman.

It took less than two days for the Roman army to loot the city while the Emperor tended to administrative business. By the fifth day Aurelian, I, and most of the Roman legions were on our way back to Rome. The Emperor brought along Zenobia as a prisoner. The voyage back to the world's capital was uneventful, and as we entered the city I could tell that even Zenobia was awed by Rome's grandeur.

The first order of business was the Emperor's Triumph, a gargantuan, grandiose procession. Leading the parade were hundreds of trumpeters and drummers in scarlet tunics trimmed in gold. Their job was to announce the glorious Emperor Aurelian to the public. Aurelian followed in a golden chariot pulled by white stallions. He wore a laurel crown of gold, and before him beautiful young maidens tossed crimson and white rose petals that gently fluttered to the ground. The crowd cheered the Emperor as he drove by, followed by the beautiful Warrior Queen in shackles.

Arrayed in a white gown, Zenobia walked behind the Emperor's chariot. She wore the golden lion crown, and her braided hair was tipped in gold. The Queen's fetters were gold as well. It was ironic that the more chains Zenobia wore, the less she looked like a prisoner. At the end of the massive procession, the captive sat rigidly at the feet of the Emperor, who then rewarded his soldiers.

Aurelian sat at the top of a dais, a raised platform in the middle of the square. This stage was elevated above the throngs so that all could see. As I passed by, I paused, and by a wave of Aurelian's hand, I was signaled to come to the Emperor. I was in a Roman Praefectus' dress armor that blazed like fire in the sunlight. In an attentive stance I stepped toward the top of the dais where I could see the Emperor. Zenobia sat at his feet. The crowd cheered wildly.

Lifting his hands to quiet the people, the Emperor spoke. "Commander Lazarus, you saved my life. You demonstrated great courage and skill during the eastern campaign. You have my gratitude. Now, what is it that you desire? How can the Empire repay you?"

It was then that I realized there was only one thing in the world that I desired—Zenobia. For a twinkling instant, my mind recreated the moment when I held Zenobia in my arms, hearing her say she would be mine every night.

"Great Emperor," I said, not quite knowing how to frame my request. "The one thing I desire from Rome is to take Zenobia for my wife."

Like a magical echo, the repeated words whispered their way through the plaza. Mystified, the Emperor raised his eyebrows and then smiled.

"That is quite a request. It is customary for such rebels to be executed in public by strangulation. Come to the palace tomorrow and we will speak further of this." He motioned for me to leave.

I didn't even look at Zenobia, although I wondered about her reaction. All I knew was that I wanted her to be mine. I wanted to save her. The next day I arrived at the palace in the early morning. I waited nervously. Finally, Aurelian was seated and rose to greet me as I entered the room.

"Welcome, Praefectus," he said, motioning for me to be seated. "Yesterday I asked you how Rome could repay the debt it owes you. You asked for the Warrior Queen, Zenobia, a woman who led a rebellion against Rome. You must be aware that it is not Rome's custom to allow prisoners of war to go free."

"I know my request is unusual," I said.

"Allow Rome to be magnanimous," he continued. "Your loyalty to me and your faithfulness to the state dictates that special consideration is necessary." He turned his head to an attendant. "Bring in Zenobia," he said.

When Zenobia entered, it was as if Venus herself had come into the room. Dressed in a slave's attire she looked more regal than any of the women at court. A hush settled over the crowd; everyone, even Aurelian, appeared dazzled by the elegance and grace with which she carried herself. She regarded me with her smoldering, ebony eyes, and I felt my heart bounding with hope.

"She is your slave to do with as you please," the Emperor said. "There are but two stipulations. First, I will hold you personally responsible for Zenobia's captivity. She must never be allowed to escape and stir up unrest in the Empire. Secondly, you must assume a post of my choosing somewhere within the confines of the Empire."

"I accept," I said, unable to contain my broad smile. "Where does Rome require my services?"

"You are granted a provincial governorship in Hispania. I understand it is very pleasant there. Rome hopes you will prosper and continue to serve her well."

I was overjoyed at the prospect of life in Spain. The Emperor had graciously given me a soft position in an affluent region that required little governing.

As we left the palace, Zenobia, no longer the Warrior Queen, stared coldly and said, "I am your slave, nothing more."

"I had hoped you would be pleased," I said.

"Pleased?" she said in a contorted grimace. "You helped destroy me. You chose Rome over me. Pleased?"

"I chose to fight for Rome before I ever met you. The plan for the attack was Aurelian's. Had I been with you, Palmyra still would have been defeated. You offered me love for my treachery against Rome. Being a queen was not enough for you."

VIII

For more than a year I courted Zenobia at my home. I did my best to show her Christian love and spoke with her often about Jesus and His teachings. Though my fear of losing her made me want to hold onto Zenobia, I felt that it was the Lord's will for me to offer her freedom. In either case, Emperor Aurelian would hold me responsible for Zenobia's actions. I was afraid I might lose her if I freed her, but I also felt I might lose her by keeping her captive. I was distraught at the thought of life without Zenobia. After weeks of prayer and meditation, I released her and told her that she no longer had to remain with me.

"You are a strange man, Lazarus," she said, her dark eyes now softer. "You could have forced me to be yours, but you willingly give me my freedom, like the trainer who releases his falcon."

"And yet it is the falcon who releases the trainer and then returns," I said.

Several days later I tapped on the door to Zenobia's room. She sat staring at the golden lion's head medallion that had once bejeweled her as sovereign. Tears flowed from her eyes as she held the magnificent piece in her hand.

"Do you wish you were Queen again?" I asked.

"Hardly," she said quietly. "I would not go back to that life. I was so vain, so arrogant. My foolishness resulted in the deaths of so many. I am grateful that I am forgiven, but I cannot understand how God can give me so much after what I've done."

"What has He given you?"

"Peace, freedom, and the greatest love I have ever had for a man," Zenobia said as she rose and pressed her lips to mine.

I stood there dumbfounded as she continued.

"You're the only man I've known who has ever desired me for more than just my body, the only man who wasn't interested in the power I could give him, the only man who has ever been patient in courting me. And more importantly, you are the only man who has ever cared enough to be concerned about my future after this life is over. That's why I am giving you this." She held up the imperial medallion she had worn on the throne. "This is a symbol of what I once was as well as a symbol of what I will be. I once was Queen of Palmyra. Now I will be your queen and you will be my king, and we will serve the Lord together."

I took her in my arms and kissed her passionately. We were married a week later, and I was reminded of the scripture: *The Lord will give you the desires of your heart*....The next three decades were wonderful. Zenobia and I were deeply in love. During the first ten years she often joked with me about how

I maintained my youthful look. She also taught me a great deal about giving joyfully. In fact, she gave me my first birthday present.

"On what day were you born?" she asked one day.

The entire Roman Empire was celebrating the emperor's birthday at the time. I had rarely thought about my own, but now I recalled the date of my birth.

"It is the very middle day of the Roman calendar year in the month of Julius," I said.

Then she dropped the subject. But later that year, on the day that we now know as July 2, Zenobia gave me my very first birthday present. How happy she was that morning, more vibrant than ever. After we awoke from our slumber, she took me by the hand after breakfast and led me outside. She was giddy as she guided me to our livery where the gentle rays of the sun promised another beautiful warm day.

"Why did you choose me to be your wife?" she asked.

"Because I love you," I said.

She smiled, and as we rounded the side of the stables, our horse trainer stood proudly alongside a magnificent white stallion.

"What a fine animal," I said.

"He's so high and mighty, proud and strong" she said. "But he loves to eat the skin off of trees, so I have named him Bark." She smiled and added, "He's yours, my love, for your birthday."

I was overwhelmed with joy, not so much with the gift of the impressive steed as by the fact that I was truly loved by the most beautiful woman in the world. Tears streamed from my eyes as I thanked God and held Zenobia in my arms. I could smell the wonderful scent of jasmine in her hair.

Every year afterward she always gave me gifts to celebrate my birthday and always asked me why I had chosen her for a wife. After two decades Zenobia realized that I was not aging.

"You look as young as you did the first day you entered my court in Palmyra. Why is that? Why do you not age?"

I had already decided that I would not lie to Zenobia about my life, my history. By this time, Rome had changed emperors several times, and I had long since retired from my position as governor. I sat Zenobia down, told her my story, and explained why I brought in new servants every ten years. I don't know that she believed me, but she believed her eyes. To my knowledge she never spoke of this to anyone.

Zenobia became ill at the end of our twenty-ninth year together. I had tried to prepare myself for the eventuality of her death, but how could I know the depth of the loss of such a love? It's as impossible as measuring how far the East is from the West. One cold, winter day when she called me to her side, I knelt next to her. Zenobia, now gray and aged, asked me for the last time why I had chosen her to be my wife.

"I loved you," I said. "I still love you. I will always love you."

"You once told me you were more than 200 years old. Surely you have had other wives."

"There has never been one like you." I held her in my arms and kissed her. I closed my eyes through the tears, wishing I could have those years with her again, desiring those wonderful days when we walked together in the rain and then sat by the fire, wanting those moments when she gently pressed her hand into mine.

"Lazarus, I have loved you like I have loved no other. I will be waiting for you in heaven when the Savior decides to call you to Elysium." She closed her eyes and even though I held her tightly, I felt her slip through my fingers and into my past.

The moment I had dreaded for so long had come. My love was gone, and already my years with Zenobia seemed distant. They had vanished like a vapor, and in that abrupt silence I was alone again.

I fell into a deep state of depression. For months I barely ate, and I slept for long periods of time, unable to do anything productive. The servants did their best to comfort me, but I was inconsolable. I could not move past the loss of my wife, my love.

At our home in Hispania—our villa—every room, every path, every tree served as a tearful reminder of what I had lost—Zenobia. Everything we had built together had lost its meaning. I felt abandoned. I knew I couldn't continue this way, and the painful memories of Spain were too deep, too fresh. I decided to go away to the other side of the Roman world. I quietly sold my property and disappeared into the vastness of Asia Minor.

Thursday, July 11 6:00 p.m.

The priest eyed the storyteller who was deep in thought. "I was in love like that once," he said. "My first wife and I were together for more than a decade before I lost her." He paused. "Car accident."

"I'm very sorry," Lazlow said, his expression consoling.

"But the Lord brought me another wonderful wife. She's a godly woman. In fact, I need to call her." Braden took his cell phone from his pocket and punched a button. "Kathy, I've gotten tied up here at the church. I may be a little late tonight," he said.

"Is it the Hammonds again?" she asked.

"No. Nothing like that. There's a man here I met last week. I'll tell you about it tonight." He clicked off the cell phone and looked out of the office window. The shadows of the day were growing long. "People come into our lives and then leave us. All we can do is love them while we have a chance. I've spent a good portion of my life trying to learn that."

"Sometimes it's not that simple," Lazlow said. "I've been alone for so many years that when I do find happiness with someone...." His voice trailed off in thought.

Giving All

...if indeed we share in His sufferings in order that we may also share in His glory. Romans 8:17

I

Angry at the Lord, I turned away from Him. For 20 years I lived a life of debauchery, joining the decline of the Roman Empire like so many other wealthy Romans. I was angry at the Lord for my immortality, for taking Zenobia, for my pain. I consumed money, women, wine, and possessions. For the first time in my life I lived a life of pure indulgence. Like a decadent sponge, I soaked up people, power, position, and riches for my own pleasure.

I had moved to Myra, a city on the southern coast of present day Turkey. Spain and Gaul held too many memories from which I sought to escape, too many responsibilities that I wanted to ignore. My two-decade-long bout with depression had made me a hedonist. Living for anything but the moment seemed void and meaningless. Filling the monotony of every day was another cup of wine, another gold trinket, another beautiful woman. They were all the same in the end—hollow, an empty chamber filled with the whispered echoes of sin. I grieved for what I had done, for what I continued to do. I tried in my own flesh to stop the drinking and womanizing, but I found it impossible—I was an addict.

During that time I didn't live like a Christian. I'm embarrassed to say that while many Christians were being persecuted under Emperor Diocletian's policies, I was wallowing in sin and self pity. I was hardly conscious of the atrocities that were committed against believers at the time. I wasn't even moved when Emperor Constantine was converted. I was convinced that I was so far away from God that I could never find my way back. I believed the lies that continually crept through my mind, that God could never forgive me, and that I was worse than someone who had never accepted Christ.

The embarrassment of my sin was so great that I found it difficult to remain sober for any length of time. One morning I was on my way home from a night of corruption, asking myself how long I would continue to sin only to hear the same answer that I always heard in my brain—*forever*. I found myself walking past a building with a large wooden door. On the dark wood of the entrance was the carving of a fish. I turned abruptly, compelled to go inside. I entered the assembly room of a church. The building must have been a home at one time, but it had been renovated to accommodate a congregation.

A deep peace, like the solitude of still waters, reached through my shame and silenced the condemning voice in my head that told me how unworthy I was. The sanctuary was empty except for a bearded man in a monk's brown robe. I took a deep breath and tried to pray, then turned to go.

"The Lord sent you here," the holy man said. "Seek ye first the Kingdom of God."

"I must leave," I said. The words of the monk, Jesus' words, pursued me as I bolted out of the chapel. The voice of my transgressions once again began to ridicule me. My guilt and shame shut them out as I busied myself even more than usual with worldly feasts and bacchanals, but wherever I turned, *Seek ye first...* resounded in my soul.

Diana, my beautiful chamber maid, poured me yet another flagon of wine one afternoon, and I peered into the amethyst liquid and thought of the Grail and the blood of Jesus. The image of the blood of Jesus and the golden goblet seared my brain like blazing sunlight after a passing storm. My mind's eye replayed that ghastly day: seeing Him on that cross beam, crown of thorns on his head; Joseph of Arimathea and I begging Pilate for His body; Jesus' blood dripping into the goblet. It all seemed so far away, but even after 200 years the blood of Jesus remained fresh. The Grail was still concealed where I'd hidden it years before, near my vineyard in Gaul.

Shaking off those thoughts, I called for a tune, and the musicians began a merry din. I called for dancers, and beautiful women began their scintillating movements to the hypnotic rhythm. I called for more wine, but I knocked the flagon to the floor, its contents splattering upon the white marble—blood on a heathen altar. The wine, the blood, my sins, they all came crashing down upon me. I sent the servants away, and I buried my face in my hands, howling like a wounded animal.

I was a fool. How could I have sunk to such depths of sin? How could I have ignored God? I had given in to the epicureans. In living a life of a hedonist, I had ceased to need Him. I had even scorned Him. I had disregarded people in need. I had become apathetic. How could God forgive me? How could He have anything for me? I could not imagine how disappointed He was in me except to measure the disgust I felt for myself.

My eyes flooded, and an inner voice harangued me: *How can you be forgiven after all you've done; how could God possibly care about you? You don't deserve forgiveness. You can't be forgiven because you knew Him and denied Him.* A morose silence followed. I hung my head in disgrace until I heard His compassionate words resonate deep in my spirit: *Where are your accusers?* And then the Holy Spirit reminded me that even Peter had denied Jesus, yet God had used him. I immediately fell to my knees and repented, awash in remorse, shame, and finally, hope.

The next day I gave my servants their freedom and a year's wages; then I went back to the church. The same bearded monk was there.

"So you've come back," he said quietly. "I knew you would."

"I've come to confess my sins," I whispered hoarsely.

"You already confessed; that's why you're here."

"It's true. How did you know?"

"The Lord told me you would come. I am Nicholas," he smiled.

"I know who you are," I said. "You are the bishop who has given away a fortune helping the needy. You leave your gifts silently and quietly, sometimes at night."

"And I know who you are," he said, his brown eyes gently piercing the depths of my soul. "You are the Jew who saw our Lord and Savior crucified."

I was totally disarmed. "How do you know that?" I asked.

"The Lord spoke to me the first time you came here. He said you would return."

"Oh, Father Nicholas," I said before I shed bitter tears of repentance. Unburdening my soul, I proceeded to tell him all.

The good bishop listened to my story and comforted me with Scripture and his gentle prayers. "James the Apostle said that we should confess our sins to one another," Nicholas reminded. His kindness and warmth helped me to find God again.

II

Now that my heart was unburdened, I wanted to live as ordinary a life as possible. I re-enlisted in the Roman army for a brief time. The Empire was still vast, and I was stationed in Sebaste, a small city in what we now know as Armenia. At that time in the fourth century it was dangerous to be a Christian, but I had made a vow that I would be a witness for Christ wherever I was.

As an enlisted man the routines had changed little over the years. I made friends easily, and one evening I was on duty with a friend named Aulus. The summer breeze was warm, and the campfires were beginning to dim within our stockade.

"You are unlike most of the other men stationed here," Aulus said. He was a robust centurion who had large brown eyes and dark, curly hair. "You don't drink, and you don't chase women. You don't even gamble. Have you no vices?"

"Aulus," I chuckled. "Much to my shame, and to the shame of my Master, I have done plenty of carousing. But I put those things away."

"Some of the men say you follow the Nazarene," Aulus said, his eyes inquisitive.

"Yes, it's true."

"I've often thought that there must be something more to this life, a deep peace. But they say you must be born again. How is that possible?" asked Aulus.

"Salvation is simple. Believe in the Lord and repent of your sin. Invite Him into your heart and be born again of His spirit."

"I followed Mithras. I found it was just a secret fraternity for soldiers, endless rituals that left me feeling empty. I want salvation."

I led Aulus in the sinner's prayer. Reveling in his new life, he soon grew to become a powerful witness for the Lord. We were like brothers and within six months had converted 40 men. Our group met discretely whenever we could. We had to be careful because the Emperor Licinius had reneged on the Edict of Milan, a document he and Emperor Constantine had signed assuring tolerance of

Christians. Political rivals, Licinius encouraged the persecution of Christians, especially those in the military. Such punishment could be severe.

One afternoon in the dead of winter, as our cohort's food was being prepared, we were called to muster. The 500 men in our formation stood together in the biting wind, the sky spitting light flakes of snow. Our group of 40 was called out by our commander, Tertius, a hard, but fair man.

"Men of the XII Legion," Tertius began. "It is known that some of you have fallen under the spell of Christianity, a religion that teaches against the divinity of our Emperor. Today you will renounce your god and pray to the divine Licinius."

Our cohort remained at attention, facing Tertius. Behind him we could see the frozen pond beside our encampment. A small stream flowed into the eastern end of the lake and another flowed out of its western end.

"All men in this cohort who are Christians, step forward!" Tertius shouted.

All 40 of us stepped out of rank and marched to the front. Tertius commanded us to move toward the edge of the icy pond, then to turn about face so that he could speak to us without the rest of the troops hearing him.

"You are all good soldiers," he said. "It would be a pity to lose you from this great legion. If you renounce Christ, I can offer you preferential treatment and advancement in the ranks. You'll have more leave and better assignments. All you have to do is proclaim the divinity of Licinius and disavow this man Jesus."

"What kind of men would we be if we renounced Christ just to get earthly treasure?" Flavius, one of our converts said. "We are 40 Christian soldiers of the Lord."

"Does this man speak for you all?" Tertius asked.

"We are 40 Christian soldiers of the Lord," another man said.

Then all of us in one voice shouted, "We are 40 Christian soldiers of the Lord!" Our voices echoed in the wind, across the frozen lake.

"Very well. You force me to do something I do not want to do," Tertius said.

He stepped away from us and issued orders to the other troops who stood and watched. Some of them began building fires near the lake. A large cauldron was placed upon each fire and then filled with water. I thought we were going to be boiled alive, but I was wrong.

"Christian soldiers," Tertius yelled. "Remove your armor and all of your clothes."

We stripped off our helmets, armor, sandals, and tunics, even our loincloths. Completely naked, we were all marched out onto the ice. It was thick enough to hold us, but the harsh wind and the bitter cold were unbearable. We huddled together."

Tertius then called to us on the ice. "When you find that you are too cold, all you have to do is proclaim that Licinius is your god. Just say it once. The warm water is here to ease your pain."

"We are 40 Christian soldiers of the Lord," Flavius again said.

86

Determined, we all began chanting, "We are 40 Christian soldiers of the Lord."

We stood together and chanted for hours, our teeth chattering, our bodies becoming blue with frostbite. We swapped positions frequently, moving men to the center of our group for warmth, but the icy weather was cruel and unyielding,

"Come. Ease your pain," said Titus, a guard who reached in and touched the warm water. We had often spoken, but he had never accepted salvation.

As tempting as it was to go to the steamy bath, we continued to chant, our voices now hoarse and weak. I wondered how long the men could continue, but one of our 40 finally gave in. A man named Spurious began feebly staggering toward the cauldron. Titus suddenly fell to his knees, lifted his hands, and stared into the cold blue sky. Meanwhile, Spurious slid into the warm water and died instantly.

Flavius immediately began to chant, "We are 39 Christian soldiers of the Lord." We all began to chant with him, but we were interrupted by Titus who came teary eyed, running and sliding to us on the ice.

"No," he shouted. "We are 40 Christian soldiers of the Lord!" He stripped off his armor and clothes and kicked them across the frozen pond. "I had a vision," he said. "I saw the Lord Jesus in heaven, handing out wonderful gifts and crowns to all who stood here, all but Spurious. Christ opened His arms and bade me come to Him." Titus' conversion had a profound effect on us. We stood to a man, long into the night until we were dead or nearly frozen to death.

The cold became so intense that I began to feel warm and sleepy. I simply remember waking up naked by the side of the stream. I was covered by a thin layer of snow. I fought to stand. My skin was blue, and I was colder than I had ever been. I struggled to take one step, then another. With each succeeding step I could feel my heart begin to pump and my blood begin to flow.

Through the icy pain, I felt almost numb. I had no idea where I was, but I stumbled upon an abandoned hut. Inside I found an old rag of a cloak with which I wrapped myself. There was no food, and the roof of the hut was gone, so it offered little protection from the elements. I left the meager shelter and later found a path that led to a road.

III

I walked along the road until I saw two men traveling in an ox cart. I was so tired that I sat down and waited for them to approach. A large bearded man, a hood pulled over his head, spoke to me.

"So we meet again, old friend." It was Nicholas of Myra. "The Lord spoke to me early this morning that someone on this road needed my help."

Unable to speak because of the cold, I simply nodded. The two men helped me into the cart and covered me with blankets. When I awoke, I was in the Bishop Nicholas' church. I sat up as I watched his apprentice, Basilus, packing what few garments he had into a bag made of canvas.

"So you are finally awake," Nicholas said. "You have slept for five days. Basilus has made us some hot broth. He'll be leaving today."

"Where are you going?" I asked the bright-eyed lad. His cheeks were rosy and youthful. His skin was fair, but his hair as black as soot.

"I will be leaving to serve the Bishop of Carthage. I am to be a scribe." His voice was young and energetic. "I have made a nice fish soup for us. We also have bread."

"That sounds wonderful," I said. I rose to my feet and, stumbling, made my way over toward a rectangular table, a wooden bench on either side. Nicholas and I sat down while Basilus served us.

"I will miss the good bishop," Basilus said a bit sadly. "He does a great work here, but over the past few years we have had to do our work privately because of the Emperor Licinius. Father Nicholas has been flogged on several occasions. But what are your plans? Father Nicholas says you're a true Christian brother."

"I suppose you could say that," I said.

"You know how to read and write don't you?" Nicholas asked.

"I'm not terribly gifted at crafting letters, but I know many languages," I said.

"Then you should stay and be the bishop's scribe," said Basilus.

That's what I did. For five years I studied under Bishop Nicholas. The first three years we had to be careful because of the persecution. We were often threatened, but no harm was done to Nicholas or me. Eventually, the persecution was lifted and the church grew. Nicholas often sought my counsel about the meaning of scriptures, partly because he knew I had walked with our Savior, but also because of my knowledge of Hebrew, Latin, and Greek. From him I learned the art of being a scribe as well as how to pastor a growing congregation. There were always people in trouble and needs to be met. No one I've ever known was more giving than Father Nicholas.

If the bishop could not meet people's needs himself, he would find another to help them. The Lord always honored Nicholas' efforts. I remember one instance in which a young couple in the congregation had lost their cow to disease. The animal was their main source of income. No one in our congregation was wealthy, so Nicholas put the matter to prayer. We fasted for several days and thanked God for providing. One day a well-dressed man of some means came into the church and asked for the bishop.

"Father Nicholas," he spoke with an accent. "My name is Soledad of Anatolia. My attendant outside has the cows you requested."

"Hallelujah!" Nicholas shouted. "The Lord is able to do more than we can ask or think. How did you know we were in need of a cow?"

"I don't know. I simply felt inclined to bring two cows to the bishop of Myra."

Nicholas laughed and gave the man a bear hug. Late that evening the bishop and I led the cows to the couple's empty stable and left them. The next day the man and his wife came in excited about what the Lord had done for them. There were many such instances.

"Why didn't we just take the cows to them during the day?" I asked.

"This is the Lord's doing. I want no man to feel he owes me or anyone," he said.

One morning a messenger came to the door of the church and asked to speak to the Bishop of Myra. He handed Nicholas a dispatch.

"It's from Emperor Constantine himself," the wide-eyed bishop said. "We are asked to quickly come to Nicaea for an ecumenical council. The Emperor wants us to meet in order to settle quarrels and establish a standard doctrine. We also must address the teachings of Arius of Alexandria."

Constantine, now sole ruler of the Roman Empire since the defeat of Licinius, offered bishops the use of public conveyance so that they might meet expeditiously. By June we found ourselves sitting amongst the most notable Christians of our times, the bishops of Rome, Antioch, Alexandria, Jerusalem, as well as hundreds of others. All of them brought attendants and scribes to the church in Nicaea.

Considering the years of persecution, the church building was in remarkable condition. The first morning of the meeting Nicholas and I sat and watched as bishops from all over the Roman world entered. Some were dressed in fancy robes and cloaks, but most wore the simple, drab garb of a monk. After prayer and a brief salutary address by Sylvester, the bishop of Rome, the council wasted no time in getting to the main item on the agenda, Arius' teachings.

The main debate concerned the nature of Christ. A large majority of the bishops felt that Jesus was divine, an equal part of the Trinity. They used countless scriptures to support their claim. Arius and his followers did not believe Jesus was God. They believed that He was simply the most perfect creature created by God. They found a few scriptures to support their beliefs as well, such as one we now know as Colossians 1:15. In his epistle, Paul writes that Jesus was the firstborn over all creation.

At one point the silver-haired Arius stood in his black cloak. A wooden cross hung from his neck. His sharp, dark eyes looked around the room before he stepped directly over to Nicholas, who had been very vocal about the divine nature of Christ. "I simply can't understand you fools." He waved his finger in the face of my friend.

"Jesus was both God and man," Nicholas said, slapping Arias' hand away. "Let us bring an end to this argument. Let us vote either for or against the teachings of Arius."

In the end, only two bishops sided with Arius. They, along with their leader, were anathematized by the church. What emerged from that meeting was a uniform concept of the Godhead, the Divine Trinity, what we know today as the Nicene Creed.

IV

Shortly after we returned from Nicaea, I left Nicholas and journeyed back to Aquitania where I had secreted away Joseph's wealth. Gold, gemstones, coins; all of it I took to Orlans where I sold it. For myself I kept only the burial shroud of Jesus, the Grail, and Zenobia's lion's head medallion. They remained hidden on the farm which was now in disrepair. I returned to Asia Minor where I gave the money, all my worldly wealth, to the church.

"This is an enormous sum," Nicholas said, touched by my actions.

"I know it will be put to good use, Father Nicholas, and I know that God has something else for me now."

"Each of us has his own path, my friend," he said. "Yours is simply longer than most."

Simon of Stylites

*...my peace I give you...*John 14:27

I

I left the city of Myra with only a brown robe on my back and a pair of sandals on my feet. Like the apostles, I heeded Christ's injunction to carry neither bag nor purse.

I headed east through Asia Minor, then south toward the Palestine. It took weeks of walking, talking, and praying, before I settled in Syria, near Antioch. I found lodging and fellowship in a brotherhood of men. They lived as monks, and their goal was simple: live as Christ lived, do good works, pray for and minister to the sick.

The monks were known around Antioch as "The Brotherhood of the Spear." Life with the Brotherhood was plain and direct. They were as dedicated to the spreading of Christianity as any group of men I've ever seen. This fraternity made the Lord's work its business. The building that housed the sanctuary and the living quarters was inside the city walls, but the Brotherhood went outside the walls, farming and providing for the brethren as well as for the destitute. This group of men emphasized helping the poor, especially distressed widows and orphans.

The Brotherhood was excited about the upcoming visit of Emperor Constantine's mother, Helena, a passionate and influential convert who had been traveling throughout the Empire collecting Christian relics. She had found the True Cross, the nails that were used to pierce Jesus' hands, and there were rumors that she had found the Crown of Thorns. The Brotherhood was elated that Helena was coming to see their relic, the Spear of Longinus.

"Would you like to see the lance?" Brother Julian, one of the longstanding members of the order, asked me. "We have the actual spear that was used to pierce our Lord's side."

I nodded and was taken inside the monastery's chapel, down some steps, and then down again to another level that was the substructure of the church's foundation. The stone steps were dusty from lack of use, and unlit torches saluted us along the corridors as we made our way to the door of a subterranean vault.

Brother Julian pushed open the heavy door. With a hearty laugh and a quick smile he lit four torches and then beamed as he pointed to a long table that sat squarely in the middle of the room. On the table, beneath a precious, sheer gossamer fabric, lay the great Spear of Longinus. It rested upon a white linen cloth. The monk gently pulled the transparent shroud from the lance so that I could touch it.

"This *is* the spear," I affirmed mysteriously, and my memory took me back to that day again. I saw the Roman centurion take the iron tip of the lance and thrust it into the lifeless body of our Lord. Water had literally burst forth from His body, already terribly misshapen and disfigured. The low, dark clouds had gathered and pressed in upon us. We witnessed the sacrifice of the Lamb, God's only Son. And at the very moment when water streamed from the wound, the swollen, charcoal clouds burst with rain and lightning flashed across the black sky.

"Brother Julian," a voice shyly interrupted as a timid monk tapped on the door of the vault. "We have just received a messenger who says that the Emperor's mother has taken ill and has had to return to Constantinople."

Although a disappointed look crossed his face, Brother Julian smiled. "All in God's time," he said and began covering the weapon, gently replacing the translucent fabric over the lance.

I thanked Julian and the other brothers for their hospitality and kindness.

"Would you like to remain here? Join us in our mission?" Brother Julian asked.

"You and the brethren are doing exceptional works, and the food is certainly good. But I believe the Lord has told me to continue on my way."

"You must go then. For above all the Lord desires our obedience," he said.

After I left Antioch, I neither cut my hair nor shaved for months; that and my tattered robe made me look like a wild man. I continued in prayer and fasting, waiting for a revelation. I believed there was only one way to draw near to the Lord, and that was to put down my flesh, to try and overcome the natural cravings and desires that tend to make us worldly, the lust and desire that had nearly destroyed my mind. I wanted to isolate myself from the sin in which I'd often been such a willing participant.

I ventured off of the main road. The arid land was sandy and brittle. After traveling a while, I discovered a rocky precipice in the desert and felt led by God to live there. I sensed a powerful calling to depend solely on the Lord for sustenance and guidance. The place was really nothing more than a large boulder which offered a flat surface about a dozen feet off of the ground. I hoped the stone was far enough away from the heavily-traveled thoroughfare that I wouldn't be easily noticed by pilgrims on their way to or from Jerusalem.

II

My life on the rock consisted of praying and fasting. My body grew weak and I became lean, but my weight and constant hunger pangs stabilized after a few weeks. Since I knew death wouldn't take me, I believed that it was all the more reason for me to overcome my own flesh. Even though I could survive without food and water, I still desired them—not to live, but to avoid the pain of hunger and thirst. For the first time in my life, I felt a deep sense of peace and repentance, as if I'd been buffed and polished from the inside out. I realized that my obedience had little to do with God loving me and forgiving me, but I was doing something to draw close to Him, something that would cost me personally.

On the rock I was apart from the world, and I devoted my life to seeking God's face. In that serene beauty—the orange radiance of the sun, the silent strength of the stone, the parched scent of the desert—God's voice was ever near and might ride upon something as simple as a warm zephyr or even the stillness itself. However, in trying to get away from the world, I had inadvertently called attention to myself, like a lonely star which is noticeable only because it is set apart from others in the heavens.

Forty days after I set up residence on the boulder, I received a pilgrim who strayed from the road one overcast day. He looked confused. The oafish man was lost, looking around like an animal just released from its cage. The pilgrim spotted me and stumbled toward the stone.

"Where am I?" he shouted up at me.

"You are due east of the main road," I told him.

"Holy man," he said. "My name is Baltazar. Why do you live alone on top of this rock like a wild man?"

"I am not a holy man, though I was a wild man once," I said, acknowledging my past. "I live here in order to seek the Lord. I have no need for earthly pleasures. I have been bound by them far too long."

"How do you live up there with no food?" he asked.

"The Lord will provide. Take no thought, saying: What shall we eat? What shall we drink? How shall we be clothed? For your heavenly Father knows that ye have need of these things" I said, quoting Jesus of Nazareth.

"Are you John the Baptist returned? He was a wild man of the desert."

For a moment I remembered watching John the Baptist's hand raised to immerse Martha and Mary and hundreds of others in the river. John's deep voice was unwavering in purpose and command, and scornful of the Sanhedrin. The prophet had been imprisoned and beheaded by Herod.

"No," I said. "I am not John the Baptist. I am only a man who has repented."

"What is your name then, brother?"

"Names mean nothing out here."

"Then since you have no name, I will give you one. You live on the rock, so I shall call you Simon, after Simon Peter, the rock upon which the church is built."

"I am unworthy of such a name. I only live here because of my worldliness, not because I am holy," I said.

The morning sun had climbed almost to noon, and the warm breeze whistled through the desert.

"How do I get to the road from here?" he asked.

"Just keep the crest of the long hill to your right," I said pointing behind him. "As you walk, the road will find you."

He left some bread at the base of the boulder and then thanked me before walking west.

The following day Baltazar was back, but this time there were more than a dozen people with him. They encamped about 30 yards from the boulder. Annoyed, I looked down on them as they sat in a circle where they prayed for several hours. They wore light colored robes covered with the gray dust of the desert road. One of the men pulled a rud from his wagon and began to play it while the rest sang songs of praise.

The wooden stringed instrument had a mesmerizing effect on me as I hadn't heard music for almost a year. I relished the pleasant rhythm as the notes danced and lifted my spirit. The lyrics and melodies mingled with the breezes. I had forgotten that music, even in simplest form, disarms the soul. I felt encouraged and sang along with the pilgrims for a while before I just sat back and listened. I must have dozed off, for I awoke to the sound of people calling out the name of Simon. Stunned from my nap, I was puzzled until I remembered that Baltazar had christened me Simon.

"Simon, Simon. Speak to us," someone said.

I sat up and sat on the edge of the boulder, and again I felt the intimate din of the world come to life around me like a familiar echo. I grew agitated. The world had found me.

"We have come to see the holy man named Simon," a corpulent, wealthy-looking, pilgrim said. The man's skin was sunburned, his pink head perfectly round with a patch of brown on the top that made him look ridiculously like a coconut from my vantage point.

"I am not a holy man!" I said. "I live here in repentance, hoping to put the things of the world far away from me. I came here only to fast and pray."

"Then you truly are a holy man," he insisted. "Your example has caused us all to consider our earthly situations."

"But I am not a holy man," I repeated emphatically.

I was frustrated. First at them for interrupting my solitude, then at myself, for being upset that they were interrupting my solitude. I was angry for being angry. I was certainly not ready to give people advice. Even though I had witnessed to soldiers, I still felt inadequate. I was bombarded by thoughts that reminded me of how I had watched Him beaten and crucified. I had watched Him die, and I was so afraid for my own life that I lifted not a finger to stop it! I had also practiced decades of sin and debauchery, been labeled a traitor by my own people, had killed and even murdered while I was in the Roman army. And these pilgrims thought I was a holy man? I had come to this rock, set myself apart from humanity. Irritated, I fidgeted away the rest of the day and awaited darkness.

III

Early the next morning before the sunrise, before the pilgrims had roused from their slumber, I climbed down and headed east again further away from the road. I felt I had to get away. After three days' travel, I came upon the bones of some long-forgotten city. What had these ruins once been? A palace? A temple? A monument? It was difficult to say as only a few pillars remained. Most of what *was* had long since turned to sand and grit.

I looked at two columns which stood where an entrance or some kind of portico might have been long ago. One of the pillars was broken in half and stood only about 20 feet high. The other half of it lay on the ground and was almost completely covered by the buff-colored sand. Another large stele, made of rounded blocks, lay horizontally across the ground like a gigantic, petrified tree trunk that had flattened almost everything close by. The tallest column was intact and stood upright. I circled it, scrutinizing it, and although it had spots where it was rough and weathered, the pillar was unmarred, towering over its diminutive brothers by about 30 feet.

Centuries of sun had bleached out the column's once dark pink color. The pillar was circular, composed of large blocks that had been specifically carved to create the rounded column. Heavily worn by erosion, the base of the pillar was about six feet square. It increased in girth slightly in its center before tapering off again about ten feet from its apex. On top of the stele sat a large square block of broken, weathered marble, a brace for the remains of what must have been some kind of roof over a porch. These remnants formed a flat deck that I estimated to be enough space on which to live. The portico had at one time extended to another column but was now only accessible from the top of the pillar to which it was attached. What was left of the porch roof was almost square. There was only one problem: how to get to the top of the pillar.

The area near the ruin was desolate. There were a few scraggly trees reaching up to the sky like old withered hands, but primarily the land was rock, sand, and dust. There were even the moist remains of what earlier had been a spring, now barely more than a trickle of muddy water.

I had no tools, but I felt compelled to find a way to get on top of that column. I considered tearing my robe and tying together the pieces to make a cloth rope, but then I would have no clothing. The pillar was too wide to climb up as it was. I finally climbed one of the trees and broke off two green, v-shaped sections of limbs. I spent the better part of the day twisting and winding the branches until they became ropy. I then wrapped them around one another.

I whipped the makeshift tree rope around the base of the column, grabbed both ends of the rope, and pulled it tight, wrapping the sinewy branches around my forearms. I considered using my weight against the line by leaning back and walking up the side of the pillar while sliding the tether upward, but I realized that plan would not work. At some point I would need to use my hands to climb up on the block, and when that time came, I'd fall to the ground and smash against the base of the stele. Although I knew the fall wouldn't kill me, I didn't want to suffer the pain. I studied the pillar very closely and decided that I needed a hammer and chisel.

At that point I walked back toward the road, making sure to mark my path so that I could easily find my way back. It was only a few days before I found the same group of pilgrims. They asked many questions that I could not answer. Even so, they were more than glad to give me the tools and a rope I needed. I crept off one early morning, and a week later I was back at the pillar, ready to begin my ascension.

The task was more difficult than I imagined it would be even though the column was nicked and chipped from time and weathering. Using the rope as a kind of safety harness, I hammered away at places that would serve as leverage points for climbing. Although the grooves between the blocks were easier to chisel, the work was grueling. Sometimes the hot marble exploded to bits. Dust, grit, and salty perspiration covered my body. The glaring light was blinding. Each day the sun bore down, blazing like a blacksmith's fire until evening came. I tried to work in the shade provided by the column, but even then the heat was incredibly intense. As I chiseled, I rounded my way up the pillar as if I were a piece of meat on a spit. Half way up the stele, the column, my fingers began to ache from the constant hammering and chiseling. In cold heavy waves, the rhythmic vibrations pulsed through the iron chisel and into my hands and my brain. My head ached, and my forearms cramped. My tools became heavier, as if I were carrying buckets of water. My legs were like dead stumps, simple props. Yet I continued to batter my way up the column.

For two days I drubbed away, slipping several times. Each time I was able to catch myself either with the rope or on one of the chiseled-out footholds. On the third day I was only ten feet from the summit. I looked up at the broken block on top of the pillar, and for the first time, I became aware of something sculpted into the marble, a gravened disk about the size of a dinner plate. As I studied it, the image began to take shape. In the center of the circular carving was a man who had wings; it was Ashur. This column had at one time been part of an Assyrian temple.

IV

Exhausted from the day's work, I edged my way down the pillar and fell asleep. When I awoke my arms were drawn up, and I throbbed from head to toe. My hands were so stiff I thought they would break as I opened them. The pain caused me to laugh. It was like having had one's muscles massaged too hard. I began to chuckle, a sound I was certain had not been heard in this place for centuries. I laughed harder still, and the tower seemed much smaller.

Every muscle in my body ached and cried out for rest, but I was determined to finish. It was hardly an epic struggle, just me against the tower. Did anyone care how long it took me to finish? God was my only witness. I heard nothing, received no divine revelation, but I knew I would conquer the temple in three days.

Like a punch-drunk brawler, I staggered toward my towering opponent, challenging myself to finish. Wearily, I picked up the tools again and slowly climbed the pillar, grimacing through the pain of every step. I took the chisel and placed it against the marble and then struck it with the mallet. Each swing took me closer to my goal; each clink resonated through my body. I couldn't stop. Finally, though it took every ounce of strength I had, I reached the broken block on the pillar and placed my foot on top of the stone of Ashur. Though only part of the roof still remained, the broken slab was flat and easy to walk upon. The Assyrian temple ruin was now my new home.

I was astonished. Invigorated, I felt freedom for the first time in my life. The view was breathtaking. The sun was setting, and the white-hot orb that had been so relentless had now cooled to a beautiful deep orange. The daylight's majestic citrus rays painted the dust of the day; shadows silhouetted the rugged peaks and rocks like monuments in a temple. The air tasted brand new, and to the east the white moon began its own climb to the heavens. Here I would be able to pray and meditate in solitude. For the first time in many years I felt content. I needed nothing but prayer and devotion. I began life on the pillar.

Atop the column, I towered above the earth each morning. I could see for miles, and I felt that I was literally and figuratively above the sin and the temptation of the world. Over the next two months I lived in total isolation. I made a shade from my robe and some branches for some protection from the sun which rose each day and found me deep in prayer. I endured storms, dry weather, heat, and cold. My skin became as bronze. I meditated and fasted. I was away from the world and its problems. For 40 days I fasted, and I never felt better or more in harmony with the Creator. I was literally on top of the world.

The Summons

*Truly I am your servant, Lord...*Psalms 116:16

I

The evening of the fortieth day I meditated long into the early morning hours, and fell asleep just as the coral rays of the awakening sun began to fan skyward. Fatigue overtook me, until I awoke to the jangling sounds and pungent smells of humanity. A haze of dust hung in the air, a cloud kicked up by donkeys and carts. The parallel tracks that followed the wheels told me they had come from the main road to the west. But even asleep, I was aware of the aromatic odor of life, riding on the breeze like a bouquet of rotting flowers—then the smells of cooked food, animals, and humanity.

The late morning sun painted a golden sky as a large group of people began to encamp. Donkeys brayed, iron kettles clattered, and cloth flapped in the wind as a dozen tents were haphazardly erected into a circular, dark brown hive of activity. From my perch I watched. Like buzzing bees, people floated back and forth, finishing their makeshift tent homes and preparing the noon meal.

For almost an hour, the wafting odor of baking bread beckoned my stomach. The velvet aroma made me hungry and called to mind my sister. Martha loved to bake bread. That was three centuries ago, but for a moment the memory was fresh. Finally, a large man walked toward the column. His taupe colored clothing billowed in the breeze as though he might fly away. He looked up and greeted me with a wave, then cupped his hands around his mouth and bellowed, "Are you the one they call Simon? The holy man? Simon of Stylites?"

"I am not a holy man," I yelled back. I just want to be left alone, I thought to myself.

"It is he," he turned and yelled to his fellow campers. "It is Simon of the pillar, Simon of Stylites, the one the pilgrims spoke of who has crucified his flesh and has shunned the world and its sin."

I was frustrated and tried to ignore them, but they would not be refused. They were like starving children, waiting to be fed. It took me three days to realize that I was the problem. I was angry because they had interrupted me. I had not considered that perhaps the Lord had put me on the stele for them.

"Simon, Simon, pray for us Simon," some would yell. "Absolve us from sin."

Each day more and more pilgrims came. The tent circle had grown to twice its original size, more than a hundred people.

On the third day a woman came to the base of the pillar. She hung her head as she approached. "What must I do to be forgiven?" she called out. "I am a sinner. Forgive me of my sin, Simon."

I looked down and I thought of Jesus' words: "Feed my sheep." I dropped to my knees and repented aloud before God and the congregation. The tent city suddenly became alive. I had been in prayer and meditation for more than a month, and still I had missed the mark. I had been so concerned with myself that

I missed the unction of the Holy Spirit. I was placed atop the pillar to minister to these people. I smiled to myself, contemplating the irony.

"I am no priest, woman. I am only a simple believer," I said.

As I sat down on the edge of my perch, my feet dangled joyfully like a child's on the limb of a tree.

There was an excitement in the camp as pilgrims came out of their tents to listen.

"I'm just a man," I said. "Only the Lord has the power to forgive sin. The Lord Jesus Christ Himself is your priest. Simply go to Him in prayer. There is no need for absolution from me or any man. For the Kingdom of God is within you."

"But what must I do to be forgiven? What must I do for penance?"

As I spoke, many people began to move toward my voice, like sheep to a shepherd.

I looked down at the woman kneeling below. Though her head was partially covered, wisps of her long black hair contrasted against the base of the pillar where she wept. There was something vaguely familiar about her total surrender that moved me. She reminded me of my sister Mary weeping at Jesus' feet.

"Forgiveness cannot be earned," I said to her. "It is as freely given as salvation. That is the simplicity of the gift of Christ."

"But what must I *do* to be forgiven? What must I do for penance?" she asked again.

"If you feel you must do something, obey His commandments. Love God and love your neighbor. *Do* the things He said to do."

She looked heavenward, like a morning glory in bloom as the light of the Word filled her. Compassion made my own inadequate feelings melt away. I began to pray, and the floodgates opened for her, for the pilgrims, and for me. Although I didn't feel qualified, I knew that contrition is a great witness. I still find it amazing that the very sin that we feel disqualifies us for His work, qualifies us with the simple act of repentance.

II

I lived atop the column for the next 25 years. The pilgrims brought me food, water, and clothing. Some even gave valuables, but having no need for riches, I gave them away. I was there when the weather was cold and the wind made the desert sing mournful dirges. I was there when the heat seemed it would turn the stele and every rock into molten lava. Hundreds of travelers came weekly on the way to Jerusalem. The Lord supplied all my needs, and I felt as if I were doing something for His kingdom. I prayed and I preached every day: repentance, forgiveness, salvation, and healing.

As close as I was to the Lord at that time, I found the subject of healing bewildering. I remember on one occasion a man and woman brought a blind child and asked me to pray for her. I didn't feel anything tangible, not even the heavy presence of the Holy Spirit. I prayed a simple prayer then felt compelled to sprinkle the girl and her parents with some water from a basin that I kept on the column. The child's eyes opened. She and her parents gushed with delight. Another such incident happened with a man who had come all the way from Rome on a pallet. I prayed for him, and while we sang spiritual songs he was instantly raised from his litter.

The most remarkable healing I witnessed there came in the form of deliverance. A young man cursed, pulled his hair out and cut at himself with a sharp rock. Foam spewed from his mouth, and his eyes were wild and glassy. His mother said he was possessed by a demon. The youth was laid at the base of the pillar where pilgrims tied him to a makeshift seat. They took a heavy rope and threw it up to me. I lay the rope over the top of a beam and let it down below to three men who hauled the boy up. I pulled the youth on top of the porch. Before I could untie him or even begin to pray, he turned his head and his tongue darted at me like a serpent. The boy's eyes and skin became yellow, and he howled a dark and beastly bay as if the hounds of hell were inside of him. Perhaps they were.

Suddenly a voice coming from within the lad spoke to me. "I know you," it growled as the young boy's eyes began to bleed.

Fearful, I was completely caught off guard.

"You are Lazarus. You were taken from my master," it hissed.

For a brief moment hell flickered to life in my memory, and how Jesus' words had saved me.

"No!" I shouted, staring deep into the bloody eyes of the youth, and said, "You cannot have this one. In the name of the Lord Jesus Christ I command you to be gone from him." I took the boy by the head and forced him to drink water from the basin.

The young man emitted a scream, at first a high pitched shriek that grew louder and longer, finally becoming a low guttural moan. The boy writhed and jerked but was finally calm.

"It's gone, and it can never return. The Lord told me!" he exclaimed. "Finally it's just me."

His mother cried tears of joy as the pilgrims eased him down from the pillar.

On other occasions I prayed for the sick and they were not healed. Sometimes nothing happened even on those days when I felt a strong presence of the Lord. I don't know why some are healed and some are not, but I believe God's power and willingness to heal are always there. Somehow the problem is with us. Do we try too hard? Do we desire the healing more than the healer? I don't know. After all these years it is still a great mystery.

III

One day a flickering light shone far off in the desert. Like a wavering, blazing candle, it moved slowly, toward my tower, through the radiant desert heat. The entire horizon seemed to squirm to the flame's torrid, shimmering dance. But the flame dissolved into a broad glare that eventually revealed three men.

A man on a mule accompanied by two monks came to the foot of the pillar; the man on the donkey wore fine red clothing embroidered in gold. Upon his head he wore a red hat with a brim. One monk carried a long oak staff topped with a large, shimmering silver cross. The other carried a brown leather bag. He approached the pillar and pulled a scroll from the sack. He began to read:

"Simon of Stylites, hermit of the pillar, your presence has been requested by the Holy Father, Innocent, the Bishop of Rome. News of your piety has spread far. We would be pleased if you would grant us your company back to the city of Rome. After meeting with the Pope, you will be given return passage to Antioch so that you might resume your hermitage."

Although I hesitated to leave my post, I felt that I might be called to serve the church in some capacity. Though my reverie with the Lord atop this isolated pillar was fulfilling, I also longed for a change. As the years had passed, I had missed the events and challenges of the world. It had been almost a century since I had seen Rome, so I decided to honor the Pope's request as much out of curiosity as duty.

Of the trio, Father Marcus and Antonus kept to themselves somewhat, but Brother John and I became good friends. It was almost three weeks before we reached the third largest city in the Empire, Antioch. From there it was only a few days to Seleucia where we boarded our ship. The voyage to Rome went by quickly, and the warm friendly summer breezes of the Mediterranean set us down at the ancient port of Ostia.

Only twenty miles from Rome, Ostia had changed since the last time I'd been there. Once thriving, the city was in severe decay. Larger trade ships had difficulty making port because of the silt. While not deserted, it was obvious that the port of Ostia was slowly dying. Many of the shops and roads were in disrepair.

Brother John explained that the country was just beginning to recover from a Visigoth invasion two years before. The Visigoth chieftain Alaric, had descended on the capital and besieged it. In order to avoid bloodshed, the Roman senate offered the Visigoths a bribe, but the Romans and Emperor Honorius had not made good on the promised tribute. Now there was concern that the Visigoths would return to collect.

I was indeed amazed at how the western Empire had gone into decline since I had soldiered for Rome. According to John, corruption had grown like a cancer, and the rulers had become progressively weaker. Pleasing the mob was the government's policy. Roman rulers made laws that led to moral hazard for the people. Honest men and women who worked to build better lives for themselves and their families suffered while crooks and scoundrels prospered. The Roman civilization was failing.

It was the middle of August of the year 410 when we arrived in Rome. I was given a bath and new monk's habit with which to meet Pope Innocent. I sat on a wooden bench in the hot summer sun, eyeing the beautiful flower garden as I waited to meet the Bishop of Rome. The roses were in full bloom, their essence overflowing the garden like a bubbling brook. The music of the trickling fountain made it easy for me to meditate. I pulled a blossom close and touched the velvety smoothness of its scarlet petals. A thorn pricked my careless thumb, and a large

101

drop of blood dripped into the fountain. I wondered why the Pope would want to see me, but there were no answers from anyone, even Brother John.

The door to the chamber opened, and John peered outside. "Simon, the Bishop of Rome will see you now," he said quietly.

IV

My leather sandals slid on the stone as I entered the room where the Bishop sat. He looked much as one would expect the Pope to look. Father Innocent had brown eyes and dark hair. He was clean shaven and wore a white miter, an oval shaped hat, trimmed in gold with a large red cross in the front. His ecclesiastical garb was also white with gold trim. Near the neck a long red horizontal stripe extended from shoulder to shoulder, forming a cross with the vertical crimson stripe that ran from the collar to the hem.

"Simon, you look quite different from the way you were described to me," he said. "I was half expecting a wild man who ate locusts and honey."

"Bathing and a new garment can do wonders," I said.

"You look much younger than I expected."

"The life on the stele appears to agree with me, Your Grace. I can honestly say that I don't feel I've aged at all since I climbed the pinnacle and gave my life wholly to God."

"Simon, your piety is known throughout the Empire. Seldom does a week go by without hearing some story about the pillar hermit in the desert. Why have you retreated to such a place?"

"I have discovered that it is the only place where I've understood my purpose, a place where I can live apart from the world, a place where I can remove myself from earthly pleasure. I had no intention of anyone ever seeing me. I simply wanted a place where I could meditate and pray. One morning a host of pilgrims beset my column. Although I tried to convince them that I was not a holy man, my denial convinced them all the more that I was. If my simple life on the pillar leads some to repentance and prayer, then the body of Christ benefits," I said.

"Would that all of our decisions were so uncomplicated," the Pope said, pressing his palms together and resting his chin upon them. "Upon your column you trust the Lord for your well being. Here in the great city of the church, we live in fear." He pulled close and whispered, "There is a rumor that even now the army of Alaric is marching on us."

"Do you think the barbarians could be dissuaded from attacking the city again?" I asked.

"No, I'm sure Alaric would not be very pliable after the Emperor promised tribute from the Senate two years ago and failed to pay. We almost starved then, and I'm sure if the Visigoths return they won't be lured to leave by a promised payment."

"Perhaps the Lord might find a way for you to speak with Alaric. Perhaps you might be able to sway him or to at least minimize the effects of a siege."

"You may be right, Simon of Stylites, but I digress. You are probably wondering why we brought you here."

"Yes, Your Grace, I was wondering what the head of the church would want with me. Some call me the lunatic on the stylus."

"This time Alaric's army is more than just a rumor. The city of Rome cannot withstand such brutal power. We need a miracle, and I was hoping that miracle was you."

"I'm afraid I don't understand."

"My advisors and I have discussed and debated who you are for years," the Pope said, unable to control the excitement in his voice. "I will be direct. Are you the prophet Elijah returned?"

"No, I am not Elijah," I said.

"Then you must be Enoch or Elisha. The scriptures speak of their return. Surely you are one of them," he insisted.

"I am neither Elisha nor Enoch, Father."

"Then it must be as I first thought. You must be John the Baptist returned, living in the desert, eating locusts and honey.

I felt sad. The holy man was almost begging for my assent—the head of the church thinking I was John the Baptist.

"No, Your Grace," I said. "John was a great man. Those you mentioned were all great and godly men. I'm just a man. I can work no miracle to save Rome, but God is merciful."

He suddenly looked old and deflated.

"I will tell you who I am," I said, "if you make a solemn promise never to utter a word of what I say to you to anyone."

The Pope, the leader of Christendom, quietly nodded. His brown eyes looked into mine with silent expectation.

"I am Lazarus, raised from the dead by Christ almost 400 years ago."

The Pope squinted at me inquisitively. I don't think he believed me; in fact, I believe he thought I was crazy.

"Hmm," he said with a hint of disbelief. "I'm not sure what I expected, but I was hoping for an answer. I was hoping for a miracle." His features became heavy with age, and his eyes seemed to tear. "Very soon barbarian armies will fill the streets of Rome. To stop this destruction I have grasped at straws, hoping for a godsend. I sent for you, the holy man from the East, looking for a sign, some message of earthly deliverance."

"I understand, but the Lord seldom answers prayer the way we believe He must. I have served as a soldier, Holy Father. I will do whatever the church requires. How can I help you?" I asked.

I could tell he was deeply troubled. His brow was furrowed, his speech slow, deliberate. "No, no, my son," he replied. "You are only one. There is too much work here for one man. We are facing the end of an age, the end of Rome as we know it. Rome is about to pay for its vanity. Return to Syria, my long-lived friend. Though you are not one of the prophets returned, you have given me hope," he said. "I know that God is, and that He has His own ways of answering prayer. I sometimes forget that."

103

At that point we were interrupted with urgent papal business and I was dismissed. The Pope eyed me kindly as I left.

The next morning Brother John and I headed back to Ostia for my return to Syria. In our ox cart, we were only a few miles from the city, nearing Ostia, when some Roman riders came from the port road.

"You brothers need to turn around and go back to Rome," the stout cavalryman said. "Alaric's forces have already taken Ostia and are sure to surround Rome itself. They're not far behind us." The riders galloped off, up the road toward the city.

I told Brother John that we should continue on and not to worry.

"We are clearly Christian brothers," I said. "Alaric's forces are Christian barbarians. I'm sure no harm will befall us."

"I admire your faith, but these Visigoths are not as churchly as you might think. I've dealt with them in the past," he said.

Before I could say anything more, we heard clopping hooves nearby and saw a cloud of dust. Cavalry was coming up the road, and it wasn't Roman cavalry. I regretted that we hadn't immediately turned back for Rome. I would never again gamble with the lives of others as I might gamble with my own.

The Visigoths

...a sinner's wealth is stored up for the righteous. Proverbs 13:22

I

Helmeted, barbaric figures riding frothing warhorses charged down the road. In an instant they were upon us; the ground trembling, the dust choking the air. The loud guttural grunts of the Goths' heathen language sounded more like that of pigs than of men. John's eyes said we were dead men. A rider grabbed the reins of our ox and signed for us to climb down from the cart. The Goths bound us with heavy rope and loaded us onto the back of the cart. We were prisoners.

John and I were taken to a camp where we were whipped and forced into labor for the barbarians. While the Goths were not totally ruthless, they were firm in what they expected from their slaves—complete and total obedience. Anything less meant being run through with a sword or being clubbed to death. I saw one obstinate captive. He was told to move but refused; eyes defiant, he stood with his fists clenched. A large Goth walked up to him with a mallet and with a bash to the stomach doubled the foolish man over. Bent double from the monstrous stroke, the slave clutched his ribs. A second blow from the giant hammer crushed the man's head. He fell dead instantly, falling like a slaughtered calf. This brutal example helped most of us decide to do what we were told. Because John and I were monks, and because the Goths were Christian barbarians, the two of us were relegated to simple cooking duties.

We were only a short distance away from Rome on the day that history has recorded as the fall of the Eternal City. Midway through that day our captors broke into song, followed by a corporal yawp that resounded like that of howling dogs. The barbarian King Alaric's forces had broken through at the Salarian gate and were wreaking havoc in the city. Days later I found out that the gate had been opened through treachery. Rome was looted for the first time in 800 years. Thousands of Romans were brutally killed, buildings were burned, and the streets were littered with rubble. For the victims of Rome, the city's destruction seemed inadequate retribution for the Empire's many sins, for the innumerable thousands who had died at the hands of the Romans. But for many, Rome had been our dream of a nation where commerce, thrift, and good works prospered. Now that dream was coming to an end.

The days continued with only sketchy news from the city. Though its capital city had been sacked, as a nation Rome continued to function. The Visigoths were like an army of locusts that had consumed everything, then moved on. Brother John and I eventually found ourselves in the midst of a large group of slaves forced to load the pilfered treasure from the great fallen city. In my two millenniums of life I've never seen more gold in one place as what lay before me—eight centuries of wealth. For 800 years Rome had plundered countless kingdoms and tribes, bringing the stolen gold and riches to Rome.

We loaded the choicest treasure onto 50 carts for King Alaric. The rest was heaped onto hundreds of other wagons. After we finished this work, our overseers grunted an order, and we began to move south with Alaric's trove. We were part of a huge golden caravan led by the barbarian war chiefs. In the coming days these chiefs would offer treasures to their favored warriors in loud, drunken orgies of violence and boasting, more like brawls than victory feasts.

The lumbering treasure train snaked its way along the roads of Italia, the rest of the Visigoth army rag-taggedly keeping pace and ravaging the countryside like a pestilence. The stench of horse dung, sweat, and human excrement marked our trail. We crawled along for almost a month to the creaking rhythm of the heavy carts when suddenly the train and the entire army came to an abrupt halt. Shocking news moved like dark thunder clouds from the head of the train to the rear. Alaric, the first man to conquer Rome in 800 years, was dead!

We never learned the cause of Alaric's death, but there was much grieving within the camp as these Christian barbarians mourned their fallen leader. I wondered why the Visigoths were called Christians until Brother John informed me that missionaries who traveled outside the Empire often reported that entire tribes were evangelized in one single prayer of salvation. These Goths sang mournful dirges in the darkness—stirring music that wrung wailing and tears from both men and women. For three days the Goths were motionless, like a ship in calm water. At the end of the third night we were on the move again. John and I were penned among 200 slaves assigned to the 50 oxcarts of gold. Our group was guarded by about 100 well-armed soldiers. Our golden caravan left the main army and traveled separately all night and the next day. We stopped to make camp at the confluence of the Busento and Crathis Rivers near the town of Cosenza in Calabria, southern Italy.

The sun had just begun to set in the foothills, and violet patches of sky were easing their way into the western horizon. We were all weary. As Brother John and I sat to rest upon some rocks, I noticed a large stone with a vertical crevasse running down its center from years of water erosion. The boulder itself looked as if it had been slammed down on top of the rock beneath it, forming a horizontal fissure. Standing next to it was a robust evergreen through which the fading sunlight filtered. The fissures in the rock combined with the light of the setting sun and the evergreen to form the semblance of a cross. John and I felt comforted by this natural phenomenon and began to sing praise songs. The evening air was cool, and we could hear the river serenading the countryside with mournful melody. Despite the solitude and the cross revealed at sunset, I had an uneasy feeling about the place. John voiced my doubts.

"Brother Simon," John said, "Something here seems out of place. I do not believe we will make it out of here alive."

I offered a distressed smile, feeling guilty because I knew I would live no matter what happened.

"You've been a good brother and have led many to the Lord," he continued. "I know you will find great treasure awaiting you in heaven."

"Aside from being in the presence of God, the greatest treasure will be seeing old friends," I said with a reassuring pat on his back.

II

The next morning we awoke to grunts and kicks. Our barbarian captors made us take picks and shovels to the other side of the river where we began digging a large trench. The ground on the other side leveled off and was much less rocky than where we had encamped.

The river itself was deep and fast flowing. In most places it ran about twenty paces wide and sloped to a depth of about fifteen feet. The Goth engineer lined us up away from, but parallel to the river and then forced us to dig. Our shovels and picks heaved up piles of dirt and pried rocks out of what became a large trench. As the day wore on, it became evident that we were digging a ditch that was as wide and deep as the waterway, parallel to the river.

The Goths worked us in shifts, with fifty resting and one hundred and fifty digging at any one time. For two full days we dug and burrowed like miners, stopping only for about six hours of sleep during the night. It became obvious to all that we were going to dam up and divert the river. The work was tedious, but on the morning of the third day we opened the giant trench. The last group of slaves dug closer and closer to the river, struggling to get out as it became obvious the ground was becoming saturated. One slave drowned when the river suddenly gushed into the canal before he could climb out. The poor man was buried beneath a mound of mud and died before we could rescue him.

Next we were forced to cut down trees and dam up the small river so that it would flow only through our waterway. This part of the task was easy compared to the digging. We finally dropped the last log onto the dam, and the river was almost completely diverted from its natural path. The bed of the river was mostly a slick and muddy sludge comprised of earth, rocks, and silt.

Our captors intended to dig a large grave in the bottom of the riverbed, then hide it underneath the river; however, as the riverbed dried, we discovered a honeycomb of underwater limestone caves that led into the hills from the banks of the riverbed. John and I were amongst those forced to explore the subterranean chambers, and we found that one of the caverns was large enough for a tomb. The grotto went deep into the hills beneath the place where we had slept fitfully the night we arrived at this site.

Some of the slaves died of exhaustion, but our captors were in a hurry. We were allowed no respite. Instead we began the slippery task of unloading the treasure from the laden oxcarts and moving it into the giant cave. After some hours, piles of gemstones sparkled in the torchlight of the cavern. The sheen from the gold lit the grotto as we toiled in the eerie light. We had hauled in most of the treasure when a group of soldiers appeared bearing the body of Alaric. We kneeled as the Goths placed the corpse in the tomb. Then we were forced to lead the war chief's horse into the cavern.

The beast was immense, and the entrance to the cave was near the bottom of the river bed which was slick and gritty. The only way to move the animal was to hoist it down into the damp river bed and then walk it up over the slippery stones that led into the cavern. Eventually the steed was blindfolded while we put a wide canvas under it. Next we attached to two long beams to the canvas in order to guide and lift the horse. Two slaves were crushed as we lined up on each side of the contraption to hoist the frightened, kicking creature close to the cave entrance.

Struggling with the animal, we finally led the charger into the tomb. Some of the treasure still remained outside. Fatigued, muddy, and sweaty, some slaves continued to unload the last of the treasure. Again, John and I were excused from heavy labor and designated instead to adorn the tomb with the treasure. We piled chains and gemstones; we placed magnificent shields, helmets, and statues around the cavern to make a stunning display of wealth. When we finished, the entire floor of the main cavity was carpeted with gold coins.

There was more gold there than I believed existed. More than seven centuries of Rome's riches seized from that chief plunderer of all time. Rubies, diamonds, emeralds, sapphires, opals the size of grapefruit, bloodstones, and gold filled the cave. There were so many coins that they spilled onto the riverbed below.

John and I placed bejeweled crowns, embellished staffs, and priceless religious ornaments from all over the Mediterranean world around the fallen leader. He lay upon a golden litter that rested upon two ornate chests of precious stones and incredible baubles. Near it we placed sacred relics, both ancient and religious, golden statues of a dozen forgotten gods. There were jewels of every kind as well as vases, flowers, masks, armor, plates, and chalices—all of them gold. We piled and displayed the treasure around the dead chieftain and his steed. Even Midas would have been jealous.

"I hope they kill us," Brother John said somberly. "I'd hate to be buried alive in this place."

I dreaded the thought.

"They'll murder all the prisoners in the work party after they finish putting the river back on course. They'll even kill their own soldiers who know where the treasure is, so that no one will ever know where Alaric's burial place is."

The captain of the guards watched us while we worked. When he was satisfied with the tomb, he said, "Our King will need a horse to ride into the unknown." He assigned two guards to slay the animal. "Alaric will also need priests in the afterlife."

John looked at me helplessly while the stone-faced captain coldly drew his sword and plunged it into my friend's sternum.

Brother John slid from the gory blade and with a heavy groan dropped to the floor. Furious by John's sudden murder, I turned my rage upon the guard who easily buried his steely sword into my own chest. So great was the pain that I thought my heart had exploded. I fell with a thud and drifted out of consciousness to the faint, strange, grunting sounds of my captors.

Thursday, July 11 8:00 p.m.

"That's twice you were buried alive," Father Braden said grimacing. "That's always been one of my greatest fears." Involuntarily, he took a deep, gasping breath.

"For good reason," Lazlow said. "I've been buried alive several times, and knowing that I wouldn't die made the experience all the more dreadful. But as horrific as those experiences were, I know God has never forgotten me because he's been faithful to deliver me from those dark and terrifying places."

The Treasure of Alaric

Where, O death, is your victory? I Corinthians 15:55

I

In shadow I drifted in and out of thought and time. Dazed and afraid, I couldn't be sure if I had come to my senses, for I could see nothing. The darkness was so disconcerting that I wasn't sure if I were alive or dead, and in the dense blackness I thought I might be somewhere in between. In my confusion, fear's icy tentacle reached into my brain and wrapped itself around my mind. Shaken, I reeled, my senses whirling in disordered wonder. Where was I and what had happened?

The darkness was impenetrable and confounding. I've never felt more totally abandoned as I lay there. I could see nothing in the absolute void. Unsure, I realized that I could feel my body. My chest ached as I sat up, and as I did the gold coins stuck to my arm jingled to the cavern floor.

Then, like icy water, the hard memories of Alaric's burial and Brother John's death engulfed me. Trying to gain some sense of the physical, I felt along the ground with my left hand. My fingers clinked through the layer of coins on the cave floor before I touched something covered with fabric. It was John's body. He had been on my left before he was run through. I quickly turned and searched for any sign of life, but there was none in him. I pressed his cold hand to my cheek and sobbed at the loss of my friend.

I cursed the void and then I yelled at God and asked Him how many friends and loved ones would I lose in my lifetime? How many would I have to watch die? And as I wept I thought I heard a somber voice from the hollows of the cave whisper—*all.*

The darkness then reminded me again of how alone I was. I didn't know how long I had been in that pit, but the mouth of the cave was sealed, and I could hear the flowing river echoing within the cavern. Terror gripped my soul, and my heart froze as I realized I was buried alive.

Anxiety overcame me as dozens of scenarios raced through my head, each one worse than the next. I would be alive forever in this darkness, a stranger to light and life. I would be an insect, crawling beneath the rocks, a worm. I would be worse than dead, alive in a crypt with no way out and only the pain of hunger for companionship. Terror again filled my hollow gut and threatened to consume me. Already my mind said I would descend into madness! I would become an animal!

I became enraged, then despondent, asking God why He had sentenced me to this prison of blindness and forlorn seclusion. As I sat there contemplating existence in eternal darkness, I remembered how the Apostle Paul had prayed and praised God even when it seemed as if he'd been abandoned. I felt ashamed. I pulled myself to my knees, bowed my head, and repented before the Lord. I then began to praise Him in the midst of my trial, and I meditated for a time about the wonder of Jesus as well as the wonder of my own life.

Though the situation didn't miraculously change that instant, I felt the oppressive hand of darkness lift. I was strangely at peace as I waited on God. Though no audible voice broke the silence, the comforting presence of the Holy Spirit strengthened me. I heard a still, small voice from deep within—or was it an impression—whispering that God had not raised me out of my own tomb to have me buried in someone else's.

Even though I hadn't found a solution to my problem—a way out—my entire attitude went from one of defeat to one of victory. I quickly set about devoting my energy to being productive and finding a way out of the cave. I knew that God would be faithful to me.

II

My first step was to concentrate on what I remembered about the cavern. In my mind I tried to picture precisely the layout of Alaric's tomb. I focused on the details, trying to remember how Brother John and I had decorated the cave with Roman treasure. Holding fast to those images, I began to crawl around the cave, short distances at first, then further, counting, measuring, always returning to the same spot.

I don't know how long it took for me to become familiar with that pitchy place, three days perhaps? I could only measure by sleeps since there was no light. After that time, I knew by touch where virtually everything was: gold coins, gemstones, jewels, and other larger objects such as crowns, shields, armor, and even Alaric's dead steed. I wrapped the King and his horse in some tapestries that had been buried with the King. Brother John's body was near the mouth of the cave. With a heavy heart I enshrouded my friend with gold coins.

While covering the body, I made the first of two wondrous discoveries in the cave. As I scooped up gold coins from the floor of the cavern, I touched and recognized several unused pine pitch torches that had been left behind by my slave brethren. The second and most important find was a solid gold tinderbox that I literally stumbled over near the body of the Visigoth chieftain.

When I tripped over the small heavy box in the darkness, I didn't know what it was, but my fingers slid over the cold, smooth metal to find a lid and a clasp. Unlocking the latch, I found flint, a small steel piece, and what felt like dried moss.

Giddy with excitement, I attempted to light one of the torches. I took the flint and sparked it against the steel, setting a small patch of moss aflame near the pine torch. The moss flared up, momentarily blinding me. I had to turn my head away while my eyes streamed with tears from the bright ball of flame.

My eyes soon adjusted, and I could see. It was wonderful just to have light in the darkness. The torch light was bright yellow, and it hissed and exhaled thick, black smoke that flew upward to become part of the shadows. The floor and the walls of the underground chamber twinkled like a golden grotto; the exotic treasure trove shimmered in the torch's iridescent glow, dancing with light and life.

I had only a limited amount of light, so it was imperative that I move quickly to do as much exploring as possible. I lit a second torch and walked toward the back of the cave. The cavern grew smaller and branched off in three different directions.

The tunnel on the left sloped downwards, and I decided against taking it. The middle and right tunnels seemed to run parallel for a few yards before veering away. I chose the middle portal and began to creep along, the two torches lighting the tunnel as I moved slowly forward.

The way was craggy and sharp, and I had to hunch down, eventually crawling on my hands and knees, my eyes adjusting between the darkness ahead and the flames of the torches. The air was dank and thick, and I was sure it had never been breathed by man. The passageway grew ever smaller as I inched forward, shoving the flickering torches ahead of me along the tunnel floor. As I pushed one forward, it suddenly vanished into an abyss.

Foolishly, I lunged to try and rescue the light. The rocky floor began to give way, and I slid forward while the earth shifted beneath me. The sounds of the stones echoed as they bounced along the sides of a long, hollow shaft. Gravity tugged at me, and the earth and falling rock offered no traction as I tried to scramble away from that black unknown.

I finally lodged my knees against a large rock which stopped my momentum, and I was able to scoot backward. A bit shaken, I quickly crawled my way back to the mouth of the three tunnels.

The remaining torch was almost consumed, so I decided to try the passageway to the right. I walked slowly for about fifteen paces before the channel began to turn upward. It became somewhat steep and narrow. Like the other crawlway, the diameter of the shaft became more constricted as I moved further forward. I crawled underneath the rocky canopy, gouging my back as I struggled uphill.

The torch died, and the darkness encased me. Again, fear tried to pry open the door to my mind, its voice saying *buried alive forever*. But I shut it out, and I began to pray, thanking God for my deliverance. My eyes could see nothing. I edged forward, crawling and tapping with the dead torch, like a blind man rapping with a cane.

I moved ahead a few more yards, creeping along like a wounded animal, aching, groping along the floor of the passage. Suddenly I noticed a waft of fresh air. There was no breeze, but the air was cool and smelled welcoming. Excited, I kept moving forward, and the cave began to open again, and eventually I could stand up.

Rising on shaking legs, I rapped against the wall and floor of the cave with the dead torch. An echo told me I was in another large cavern. I could see nothing yet. Weak and overcome with trembling, I sat for a moment. My body ached from head to toe, my knees and hands raw from crawling. I had no way of knowing whether it was night or day, but it didn't matter. Encouraged, but overcome with fatigue, I drifted off to sleep.

III

Hours later I was dreaming of food when I was awakened by a sunbeam. A single shaft of light shone upon my face in the darkness. The light found its way into the cavern through a hole near the top of the cave. I became so ecstatic that I forgot my hunger, and I praised God for the light as I began to look around the cave—larger than I had thought, and up near the top was the sunlight that had found its way into the darkness. From what I could tell, the gap through which the light came was about the size of a large coin, though it was partially obscured by what appeared to be a stalactite hanging from the roof of the cavern. With the skill of a mountain goat, I climbed up the side of the cave toward the light, tiptoeing on rocks, finding crevices to hold onto, but there was no way to reach the sunny portal.

For most of that day I sat and contemplated my options. God had provided me with a way out. I knew there had to be a way to get to it. I considered tying a rope to a spear, throwing it through the hole, then climbing up. I had neither rope nor spear, and even if I had, the opening was very small and obstructed by the stalactite. The only solution that made sense promised to be a long and tiresome process. I would haul in the treasure piecemeal, heap up an immense pile, and climb on top of it to get to the opening.

Bringing in so much treasure took weeks and was agonizing at times. Gold is heavy, and I had to use a shield and a wooden box I found to haul it with. Hauling the treasure wasn't the only problem, however. My knees, hands, and elbows became raw from crawling back and forth, unable to stand upright. I was finally forced to tear some strips of cloth from a blanket that had been on Alaric's horse. The stench from the dead animal was horrible, but my elbows and knees welcomed the padding.

Another problem was the lack of food. My body cried out for nourishment. Even though I'd dealt with fasting before, this was different. I learned that the harder I worked, the more my body wanted something to eat. It was a grinding hunger that made me feel as if my stomach were trying to feed on itself. I did my best to ignore the pain, but it was always there.

Even with no food and the absence of light in the pitch black treasure cave, the escape mound grew, slowly at first, but steadily upward and outward. I relentlessly crawled, hauling gold from the lower cave to the upper cavern. I estimated that it would take weeks to bring enough gold up to reach the height of the cavern, which was more than three times my own height.

After days and days of crawling on my hands and knees I developed heavy calluses. Like a mouse building a nest, back and forth I brought in Alaric's hoard. The process was slow, but I had finally amassed a mountain almost large enough to reach to the top. I had also left a thick trail of gold coins back to the trove that reflected some of the morning sun throughout the tunnel. The entire cave was lit up with a golden glow.

When I attempted to climb my mountain, the footing shifted at times, and I was forced to pack down the gold and use the shield and a couple of gold trays I found to steady my ascent. I scaled the mass of treasure; at times my feet sank up to my thighs. The footing was firmer near the wall of the cave, and when I stood I found something in the roof of the cave that had been hidden by the darkness—a large tree root that snaked in and out of the cavern's ceiling. I could reach it.

Hanging from the root, I nudged my hands along until I was close enough to raise my fingers up through the hole into daylight. I sobbed with relief as I felt the warmth of the sun. I first had to dig around what I had earlier mistaken for a stalactite. It was a mass of tangled roots, part of which hung like a lion's mane. After shaking some of the dirt from it, one branch of the mass was large enough to offer me a natural foothold so that I was able to use it as an anchor for climbing out of that grave, that black hole of madness.

I squeezed my right shoulder and then my head up through the knotty hole and was able to grab hold of a low tree branch to pull myself out. I rolled over onto my back and lay on the ground, just staring up at the sky in awe. I cried at the beauty of its blueness, inhaling deeply the pine-scented air. In my mind I saw the tomb's fingers open and release me. I raised my hands and shouted "Hallelujah" at the top of my lungs. Then I rolled over, rose to my knees and praised God.

IV

When I finally began to look around, I was at the base of the same large evergreen tree that Brother John and I had observed the night we arrived at Alaric's burial site. Again I fell to my knees and thanked God for his mercy; I thanked Him for everything, even the wonderful air I breathed.

I knew I needed to hide the cave entrance and accidental access to the treasure. I took care to cover the hole with some large flat pieces of sandstone along with some branches and pine needles. Before leaving, I took note of the tree and its location in relation to the river, which was running fast as usual. Alaric's men had been careful to disguise the burial site so that only a keen eye could tell anything was amiss. In only my ragged monk's habit, I set out on foot, determined to find my way back to the pillar of Simon of Stylites and the peace I had found there.

My journey back to the desert took months. When I returned to the great stone pillar it was only to discover that someone else now occupied my former aerial home. A man with long, wild hair and a tattered robe preached and taught about Jesus, and people were edified by his words. Although I was a little angry at having been replaced, it was evident that I was no longer needed there. I wondered if God was finished with me.

For the next two years I lived as a vagabond, questioning my life and living in poverty. I wandered the streets observing man's inhumanity to man, watching the human race prove that the love of money is the root of all evil. I was disgusted with all of the wickedness I saw. Swindlers, flesh peddlers, and thieves seemed to lurk on every street corner, but thankfully for every knave and villain I met, there were a hundred people struggling to make an honest living. I found myself helping families often by working in their fields and performing tasks for them like mending fences. But many remained impoverished and needed help that only money would provide. I had no valuables, and I realized I could help more people if I had wealth. I knew where to get it.

V

My travels during that time eventually took me back to the city of Myra in Turkey. I knew that Nicholas of Myra had died long ago, but his followers carried on the bishop's work, giving to people in need. The city of Myra was much the same as when I was there before. All in all it was still a picturesque, sea-trading town. The followers of Nicholas were led by a stocky, gray-robed monk named Brother Eustace.

Eustace was one of those people you feel you've known all of your life. His disposition was so pleasant and his manner so warm and kind that you knew he was always about the Lord's business. He had bright eyes, a quick smile, and he genuinely loved people. We became instant friends and took the noon meal together at the kitchen of what was one of the first monasteries.

"Brother Lazarus, it is strange that you come to us at this time." His voice was deep and resonated in his rotund frame. "It is said that Bishop Nicholas often spoke of a friend by the name of Lazarus who gave a fortune to the bishop's cause of providing for the needy."

"With a name like Lazarus he must have been a good man," I said, laughing at my own joke.

"It is unfortunate that the donations have slowed to a trickle with these hard times. We now barely have enough to meet our own needs, much less the needs of others.

"I suppose it's purely coincidental," I said. "But I've come to help you solve that problem."

"How is that?" he asked, plucking a clean chicken bone from his mouth and dropping it onto his plate.

"I can provide you with enough funds so that it will be years before those doing the good bishop's work will run out of money. What I need from you is your time, passage for two to Rome on a boat, and enough money to purchase a large wagon, some tools, and two mules."

"What did you say?" the good brother looked stunned.

"I said I needed your..."

"No, before that," Eustace said.

"I said I could provide you with enough funds so that it would be years before those doing the good bishop's work would run out of money."

"I've been praying a long time, and now you come in and use the exact words I've been praying. Coincidence or confirmation?" Eustace asked. "One thing is certain. The Lord Our God has an incredible sense of humor." The jolly monk cut loose a belly laugh that reverberated throughout the room. "I've always wanted to go to Rome."

VI

Later that week we boarded a merchant ship headed for Rome. Once there we procured a large wagon, rope, canvases, crates, and the two mules. As soon as we moved outside of Rome proper, I blindfolded Brother Eustace who spent the next five days at my side. By the end of the fifth day, I had returned to the spot where Alaric's treasure was buried.

"This is very strange, Brother Lazarus. I hope you're not planning to do away with me," Eustace joked.

"If I were going to kill someone, I surely wouldn't go to this kind of trouble. Besides, we're here. Take off the blindfold. I'm sorry that you will, of course, have to put it back on when we return to Rome," I explained.

We found the tree that marked the spot where I had clamored up and out of Alaric's tomb. Since it was late in the day, the rays from the sun again made the shape of a crucifix on the boulders behind the tree, and I was reminded of my friend Brother John. Eustace and I moved some brush and peered down into the cavern. The treasure was untouched.

Brother Eustace's jaw dropped in amazement. For a while he could only speak in a series of "ooohs" and "aahhhs" while he gazed at the size of the golden hoard.

"How did you come to know of this? I've never seen, or even dreamed, of so much gold and jewels," he said.

"It's a long story, but I will assure you that I'm the only one who knows of its existence."

The next morning we set about our work of bringing up and loading as much of the treasure as the animals could haul. By the end of the second day the wagon was ready. We hid the entrance to the cavern again and fell into an exhausted sleep. The following morning we began a slow and laborious trip to Rome.

The followers of Nicholas would have enough money to continue their good work for years to come, and I would again be a rich man.

The Gathering Storm

Prepare your shields, both large and small, and march out for battle!
Jeremiah 46:3

I

I settled in Aquitania for another 30 years. During this time I refurbished my estate which had become dilapidated from years of neglect. Feeling restless once more, I left the care of vineyards in loyal and capable hands in order to continue my service to the Lord. Shortly afterwards, I joined a colony of monks near the town of Turonum, present day Tours, introducing myself as brother Simon.

Life there was quite simple and therapeutic. The daily routine of serving God, working and fellowshipping with believers who had a common goal, was deeply satisfying and peaceful. Such a life is accentuated even more in a pastoral setting where monks sow and reap and worship the Lord; however, the serenity of my monastic life was soon challenged when a dark cloud descended upon all of Western Europe.

In the middle of the fifth century, the Hun nation began to flex its muscle under the leadership of the man whose very name is still synonymous with barbaric evil—Attila. After bringing Europe to its knees years before, the Huns had settled in what is today Hungary, but the Hun warlord, still greedy for power, turned his eyes to the Eastern Empire. For years the East had paid tribute to the Huns, but the bloodthirsty Huns were gathering their forces, and rumors of Attila's plans to descend into the Balkans were rampant.

Western leaders were uneasy though glad to learn that Attila's strike would be aimed elsewhere; however, the Roman Emperor Valentinian and his sister Honoria despised each other. A family squabble drew Attila's attentions back to the West. The Emperor discovered his sister having an affair with a servant and had Honoria's lover put to death. Valentinian then promised his sibling to a Roman senator in marriage. Furious, Honoria had sent a message to Attila proposing marriage and offering the King of the Huns almost half of the Western Roman Empire as dowry. Attila realized that the West was weaker than the East and made plans to attack and claim his bride.

Valentinian was outraged at his sister's betrayal and sent emissaries to Attila stating that Honoria's offer was false; however, the wily Hun leader declared to the Roman delegates that the marriage proposal *was* true and that he would personally come to collect his consort. The western emissaries returned to Rome and reported the grim news to Valentinian.

Soon afterward Attila led his horde throughout Germany and parts of Gaul. More than a hundred thousand of his followers murdered, pillaged, plundered, and completely destroyed anything in their path. A column of vile heathens several miles wide, they crawled across the continent like a plague. Maiden, monk, woman, child, none were spared. After the Huns crossed the Rhine, one city after another fell as Strasbourg, Cologne, Metz, Cambrai, Rheims, Amiens, and Worms were all put to the torch. At Trier, the Huns left so many

117

human bodies piled along the Moselle River, that the water flowing down river carried the stench of death for months. All of Europe quaked with fear and would tremble at the mention of this unspeakable terror for centuries to come.

The Western Roman Empire, an empire in name only, was already frail. Barbaric Christian tribes ruled most of Gaul and Germany, and the tribes viewed Rome warily. The cautious eyes of the Alans and Visigoths grew wide when the great Roman general Aetius approached their leaders. Seeking an alliance, the tribes were forced to choose between fighting for the Romans or against them. If they fought against them, the tribes ran the risk of destroying the only force that would have any chance of stopping the Huns. If the tribes fought with the Romans, they might be annihilated in one battle.

Valentinian was weak, but his best general, Flavius Aetius, had once been a hostage of the Huns and knew their ways. Aetius sought allies to side with the Romans against Attila. The Huns' primary weapon for years had been the mobility given them by their horses. The Huns' ways were simple. Their speedy, mounted troops could steal, kill, and destroy quickly. They left a path of murder and destruction throughout Central Europe which included the razing of countless monasteries and convents. Even though Attila was successful, over the years the general had supplemented his army with foot soldiers like the European armies. The addition of these troops took away some of the horde's mobility.

II

While we monks had been going about the business of winning the lost for the Church, convincing clergy and lay people to take up arms and fight against the Huns was another matter. The primary problem was that many Christians believed that it was wrong to take up the sword—violating "thou shalt not murder" of the Ten Commandments as well as Jesus' example of turning the other cheek. Hundreds of lay people and monks took passive stances when it came to war, preferring to become refugees, slaves, or worse. Many died for their beliefs.

After leaving the Roman army I, too, had struggled with the issue of taking human life, but a chance meeting with Brother Augustinus (you know him as St. Augustine) changed my mind once and for all on the subject. While Augustine's principles for "just war" were convincing, what he said to me about the nature of humanity and Christianity still resounds deeply.

Augustinus was more than 50 years old when I met him in Gaul. He was visiting a church in southern France. Because I had served as a soldier, Augustinus sought my insights concerning war, violence, and injustice. During the course of our discussion he laid out his causes for "just war" which he later wrote about in his work *The City of God*. He described the circumstances and reasons why Christians should take up the sword. In spite of the beauty of that treatise, it is the words of Brother Augustinus that have served as my compass all of these years.

"No matter what anyone believes, common sense and practicality dictate the foundation that a person with any moral standards should have," Augustinus said. "It is wrong for good people to stand idly by and watch evil men harm the innocent when the good people can prevent it. For that reason, I believe it is a sin for a Christian not to act on the side of the right."

With those words in mind, I made a point to visit as many of the villages and monasteries throughout Gaul as possible. It was at one such town that I accidentally met General Flavius Aetius. Both he and I spoke fervently of the need to stand and fight Attila to anyone who would listen: monks, nuns, laymen, mercenaries, even refugees from cities that had been sacked by the Huns. One survivor told a tale of seeing his abbot's brains bashed out with a golden crucifix. Another had seen his mother and sisters raped and murdered, and his brothers impaled by the vicious barbarians.

It was early spring when I decided to raise a band of warrior monks whom I would teach to use a pike. We would at least try to help Aetius stem the tide of the Hun menace. The lessons went well considering I was training passive monks to fight with a spear. Many of my fellows had held only garden tools, but some such as Brother Ells and Brother James had military backgrounds. All were eager to fight for the Lord, and we concentrated on combat skills, drilling for hours each day.

Brother Horace, a former centurion, became my second in command, and Brother Thaddeus was an officer as well. With our years of experience and expertise, we were able to forge the men into a cohesive unit, a group of about 5000 fellow brothers who had joined together to fight the barbarians.

One afternoon Brother Horace presented the men to me as their commanding officer. They all stood at attention wearing brown robes and holding long pikes.

"As you are our commanding officer, the men and I would like to present you with a gift," Horace said in his gruff voice.

"Your gift is your service," I said to them.

"Our service is our gift to our Lord and to men. But this is our gift to you." He pointed behind me.

I turned to see Brother James with a beautiful roan mare. I don't know how they were able to procure such a horse, but I was touched beyond words. For a brief moment in my mind's eye, I was with Zenobia again; I was remembering Bark.

"Bark," I said aloud, the word rousing me from my daydream.

"Bark?" Brother James questioned. He looked at Brother Horace.

"Bark—her name will be Bark. Thank you all for such a wonderful gift," I said to the men as I admired my horse.

III

I sent a message to General Aetius that we were ready to join him in the battle against the Huns. His courier sent word that our allied forces were to gather near the city of Orlans. Aetius also asked me to seek an audience with the prefect of Orlans, a man named Sangibon, to entreat him to join our cause. I then left my band of men for Orlans proper, a city defended by the Alans, an ancient tribe of golden-haired, light-skinned people. Under the prefect's leadership, Orlans had prospered. Sangibon was a ruler whose political ties to the Empire were tepid, and whose communications with Aetius were also lukewarm.

It was late afternoon when I entered Sangibon's court with a brief introduction. He sat upon an austere chair in a throne room that was also unimpressive. Just as I had found true of so many other city leaders who thought highly of themselves, I had expected to find yet another small-minded leader who thought he ruled the world. I was surprised to find that Sangibon was earthy and friendly. Though he was pale and gaunt, his soft, gray eyes were as warm as his smile. His round, balding head made him look comical as it seemed to be placed between his shoulders without a neck. Standing by his side like a watchdog was his advisor, Vermis.

As I entered the room, Vermis watched me like a snake eyeing its prey before striking. He had reptilian eyes that closed from the sides when he blinked. His forehead and nose were pitched forward, and he wore his brown hair combed back, giving him the appearance of a weasel. One look from him told me that my arrival was unwelcome, and he kept his distance as if I were an enemy.

"Sangibon," I began. "I regret that I have ridden a hard day's journey to bring you ill news. The scourge of God is upon us, indeed at your very door. I come to implore you to gather your Alans and fight alongside the great Aetius in the coming battle."

"Your information is incorrect, Brother Simon. The Huns are nowhere near us. Besides, my most trusted advisor tells me that even if Attila does venture this far, there will be no battle," he said.

"Attila has always been our friend and ally," Vermis nodded to his master. "This priest would have us back under the heel of the Roman boot."

"Prefect Sangibon," I said, "Attila will come here, and soon. Yesterday his army was less than two days' march from here. The Huns have already sacked Beauvais and razed Reims. They murdered all, not just men, everyone. They leave nothing but a path of death and destruction."

"Great Sangibon," the wormlike Vermis said, "I'm sure that this so-called monk exaggerates beyond belief. Besides, even if the Huns do come our way, that is all the more reason that we should open the gates. Nothing can stop the Huns. No army has been able to defeat them. Besides, other cities have been spared."

"I'm sure that the victims of Chartres, Metz, and the other dozen cities that have been leveled would have been spared had they simply left the door unbarred," I snapped in reply.

"Chartres? Metz? Sacked? Why was I not told of this?" asked Sangibon.

"The Huns are an honorable people, Brother Simon," Vermis quickly interrupted. "Surely even you know that! They have no quarrel here. Attila has promised friendship. And you of all people Simon, a man of the Church, would be well advised to heed Jesus' example of peace and love."

"Jesus died and descended into hell, but you won't have to do that. Hell will come to you," I said. "Sangibon, how is it that you do not know that Attila's horde is so close?"

"I have had a lengthy illness and am only recently recovered," the prefect said. "My trusted advisor has been in charge of all my communications these past months. Vermis, do you know anything about the Huns being nearby?"

"Rumors, only rumors," the advisor said, his shifty eyes cutting back and forth.

"You must know that the Huns are almost upon us," I said. "Even the townspeople know it. You are Sangibon's counsel. Why haven't you advised him of this?"

Vermis recoiled like a snake. "Be careful what you say, holy man," he countered. "If the Huns were coming and if there were going to be a battle, why didn't the great Aetius come himself?"

"Flavius Aetius came here more than a month ago, but he was sent away."

"Is this true?" Sangibon asked Vermis.

"Sire, this man must think there is no order here in Orlans. Surely if the great General Aetius was in Orlans, you would have known of it. I will go to the captain of the watch to see what he knows of these matters." Vermis hastily left with a curt bow to the prefect and a black-hearted smile directed at me.

IV

"Sangibon," I said. "The outcome of this war may depend upon whose side you take in this upcoming battle. By all accounts you are a good and honest man. Men like you and I cannot stand by and watch this evil perpetrated by Attila's forces."

The leader looked down and sheepishly asked, "When and where will this battle take place?"

"The Romans and their allies are encamping on the Catalaunian plain even as we speak. I myself have 5000 warrior monks bivouacked not far from there. We expect a battle within days."

"That soon?" he exclaimed with a start.

"Yes, there is no time to lose. I have brought maps. I will show you Attila's approach as well as that of the Romans and Visigoths," I said.

"Theodoric is coming to fight alongside Flavius Aetius?"

"Apparently the Visigoth chieftain believes the Hun threat is great enough for Theodoric to side with Rome," I explained.

For the next few minutes we poured over the maps detailing the Hun line of attack on the city and the allied approach. Sangibon had about a thousand troops in the city proper. Another 25,000 Alans tribesmen had been gathering for some time, probably under the direction of Vermis.

"Your tribesmen have been gathering for days," I told him. "But they wonder which side they will fight for."

"The Huns are the enemy of all," Sangibon said. As he drew up orders we heard a commotion outside that grew louder by the second.

"Guard," he said. "See what that noise is and report back to me."

121

"It may be the Huns," I said. The prefect nodded and we hurriedly walked into the streets. People were fleeing. Soldiers were running away from the city gates.

"Soldier!" Sangibon barked. "Why aren't you on guard?"

"Counselor Vermis gave us your orders to abandon our posts and flee the city before the Huns arrive."

"Vermis," I spat. "I should have known."

"Get back to your posts!" Sangibon shouted. "Ring the alarm bell. Vermis is a traitor."

The soldier turned and began yelling to his comrades to return to their duty. We pushed through the throng toward the gate, ordering people to go to their homes.

The guards were hurrying to their stations when the clanging sound of sharpened steel rang through the air. Peasants came running toward us at full tilt.

"The Huns! The Huns! Run for your lives!" they screamed.

Moving quickly against the fleeing mass, we finally were within sight of the Orlans gate and saw enemy cavalrymen. The portcullis was up and several mounted Huns were already inside the walls of the city, viciously striking down those who stood in their way.

"Don't let them have the city!" Sangibon yelled, drawing his sword. "Close the gate! Close the gate!"

But as he barked orders, more Huns on ponies entered through the portal. Having no weapon, I picked up a shield left from a fleeing guard and moved toward the gate and the enemy. One bold Hun turned to attack me. I blocked his slashing sword with the top of my shield, then with all of my strength, I flipped the bottom of the buckler upward, breaking his arm. The blade fell from his grasp as I slammed the shield against his leg and knocked him from his mount.

Picking up the dropped sword, I then fought and parried my way toward the portcullis. Sangibon had rallied some of his men and was advancing on the gate as well. I pressed onward in the long shadows of the setting sun, slashing man and beast. One horse went down, toppling its rider. Another Hun fired an arrow at me, but my shield took the dart. I broke his bow with my blade and severed his leg with a hack.

The percussive melody of more cavalry rumbled from outside the city walls. The din of hand-to-hand combat ensued—grunts, gurgles, and the clatter of swords and shields. The Huns battling us inside the city turned and fled through the gate. We looked out to see the Hun riders retreating in disorder with Roman cavalry at their heels. Sangibon and I were surprised when we were greeted by Flavius Aetius and his men.

"General Aetius," I said. "Your arrival was most timely."

"It appears so, Brother Simon," the Roman Commander said. "Attila's vanguard was already in the suburbs. We drove them out. It looks as if you've been doing some fighting as well. Not many priests wield sword and shield."

"He brandished them with complete command," Sangibon said, trying to catch his breath. "I've never seen such prowess. What would he be like if he weren't a monk?"

"General Aetius," I said. "This is Sangibon, the prefect of Orlans. He will be fighting with us in the upcoming battle."

"That is good news indeed," the Roman leader said. Aetius then climbed down from his saddle and stood, extending his right arm to the Orlans prefect.

Sangibon reciprocated the action. "We must put an end to this evil," he said.

"We will," Aetius said. "How many men can you bring to bear?"

"If the numbers are as Brother Simon reports, almost 30,000, including his fighting monks," Sangibon responded.

"Excellent. Even with such an addition as that, we will still be outnumbered, but our chances of success have increased dramatically."

"One thing is certain," I said. "If the Lord is not with us, it won't matter how many men we have."

"I have to believe He is with us," Aetius said.

"Let us go inside," Sangibon nodded. "I would like to see your plan of attack."

V

As we began to move toward the palace I looked back toward the gates. I noticed an old hermit in a wagon pulled by a mule. The man's cloak covered his face while the wooden cart creaked and moaned, limping toward the gate. Sangibon saw it too.

"Stop that cart," the prefect yelled to one of the guards.

A soldier sprang to the wagon and grabbed the reins of the mule, slowing it to a halt. The driver looked back at us.

"Vermis!" Sangibon said with disgust. "I could tell by your crooked posture that it was you. Where are you going in this disguise?"

Sangibon pulled back the man's hood, revealing the traitor's face. I searched the cart and found a small strongbox beneath a blanket. By this time a small crowd of peasants and soldiers began to gather around us.

"It's Vermis," said one of the guards. "He told us to abandon our stations."

"They misunderstood my orders, sire!" Vermis interjected. "What I said was, if the Huns attack, we might as well abandon our posts, and before I could say anything else, the men started running away."

"He lies!" another soldier said.

"They all just started running away?" Sangibon asked sarcastically. "I'm glad that's cleared up. What's in the strongbox and where are you going?"

"I often go to visit my sickly mother. I was just taking her some money I saved for her."

"Open the box," the prefect said.

"I do not have the key," Vermis said reluctantly.

"No key!" the prefect said. He then turned to a large, rugged-looking soldier. "Sergeant, open this box!"

The gritty veteran took his sword and hacked the small chest in two, revealing a large cache of gold coins that spilled out onto the wagon bed.

"I wish I were his mother," someone in the crowd jeered.

"You must be well paid to have saved this much gold," I said, examining one of the coins.

"It is truly a wonderful son who would take such a trove to his sick mother," Sangibon said. "Vermis, you have spun your last lie. You have duped me for the last time." The prefect looked around at the crowd which grumbled viciously at Vermis. "Do with this traitor as you please. Share the gold," and he motioned for them to take him away.

"Tear him apart," someone screamed.

"Kill him!" another yelled.

The angry crowd dragged the squirming traitor away.

We went back to the palace and met with Flavius Aetius who quickly explained the battle plans.

"My legions will take the left flank and Theodoric's Visigoths the right. We will each have the high ground. Sangibon, your fighting Alans warriors will have the honor of taking the center," Aetius said.

"The honor? You mean we will take the brunt of the attack from the Huns," Sangibon said pointedly.

"That is true," Aetius said grim-faced, "but I have good reasons for placing you there. First of all, you don't have to win. You just can't lose. While your troops are holding the center, I believe we can win on the wings, envelope the Huns, and be rid of this menace once and for all. We will assemble at dawn three days hence."

After a brief exchange regarding our assembly point, Aetius left to make final preparations. I also excused myself to return to my monks and went to the livery to get my mount. I found a small crowd there, and when I entered the shed I saw Vermis lying on his back, tied to a rough-hewn chair. Seared flesh, pink and bloody, was all that was left of the traitor's eyes, which had been gouged out with a hot poker. Blood trickled from his wrists and neck where the rope burns cut into him as he'd struggled while tortured. The men wanted more.

"He sold us out for gold; now make him drink it," someone said.

Groaning from the pain, Vermis moaned and gasped. He'd been beaten and most of his hair had been pulled out. The blacksmith had poured molten lead in a steel ladle and was threatening to spoon it into Vermis' mouth while the others jeered.

"Open up and I'll give you a nice drink," the smith said to the pathetic prisoner. "You love gold so much...see if you like this!" He then began to drizzle the molten metal onto Vermis' lips and chin. The terrified wretch writhed with a muted scream. His eye sockets streamed in agony as the liquid metal burned into his skin.

The crowd responded with a sickening laugh of approval.

Revolted by such brutality, I quickly took the smith's hot poker from the fire and stabbed Vermis through the heart with the red-hot tool. He died instantly. The smell of the burning flesh and blood was nauseating.

"What did you do that for?" the husky voice of a drunken ruffian challenged me. "The traitor deserved his punishment. We weren't done with him yet. In fact, we might want to have some fun with you."

The lout stood like a bear and came at me. I easily ducked his lunge and slipped behind him, twisting his left arm. I took the poker and held the glowing end of it close enough to burn his whiskers.

"God honors the just, not the cruel," I said loud enough for all to hear. "Soon there will be a great battle. Take your rage out on the Huns who come to destroy everything that is dear to you." I shoved the drunkard away, threw down the poker, and went to find Bark. The evening was beginning to grow late, and I had to find my men.

When Worlds Collide

Praise be to the Lord my Rock, who trains my hands for war...Psalms 144:1

I

Early the morning of the battle, we arose and prayed. I then went to my tent and pulled from my baggage a bundle of blankets. Inside the blanket roll was a large sword. Weeks before I had searched through my own hoard to find the blade that had been buried with Alaric. The weapon was chest high in length and as wide as the span of my hand. The sword was excessively heavy, but years of working in the mines and more than a century of soldiering had given me the strength to wield the massive rapier.

The hilt was gold and looked new. Perhaps it had been reworked by Alaric's best craftsmen as a weapon for their chief to have in the afterlife. The haft of the sword was as long as my foot and formed a great cross. The vertical shaft extended onto the blade itself and had been excellently crafted in order that a giant hand could easily grip it. The handle had been rounded for comfort. The guard, a horizontal bar that formed the cross, protected the hand. It, too, was gold. At the end of the haft was a large golden roundel.

The rapier had become tarnished over the years, and now as I cleaned it, I marveled at its exquisite workmanship. In spite of its length and breadth, it was well balanced and had a keen edge. As I buffed and inspected the sword more closely, I discovered for the first time a small inscription in ancient Hebrew that simply read: *King David.*

King David? But the rapier was so large. Of course! This was the sword of Goliath. David had slain the enemy of Israel, taken the giant's weapon and beheaded him as the entire Philistine army watched. With their champion utterly defeated, the Philistines had fled the field. It must have been a glorious victory for Israel, and now I had the very blade in my hands. The stories of the boy king had thrilled me as a child, and now I held the actual weapon the shepherd warrior had taken from Goliath.

Tracing the timeline of history in my mind, I concluded that the Romans must have pilfered the sword from Jerusalem several centuries before. It had remained in Rome until Alaric's forces had sacked the city, and I had taken it from Alaric's tomb.

My warrior monks had encamped on the Catalaunian plain near a stream. Brother Thaddeus had pushed the men hard. Despite cutting thousands of stakes from a nearby wood, the unit had arrived before twilight, and the men were now well rested. Early the next morning I called in my officers and anointed each of them with oil. After a time of prayer and meditation, each leader returned to his unit to pray with his men.

Aetius wished to take the field at dawn. I felt it necessary that we enhance our section of the battlefield to aid our defense. I had our men take the wooden stakes they had cut and prepare a field of caltrops and spikes. I remembered how effectively Aurelian had used them against Zenobia's cavalry almost two centuries before.

126

Sangibon's forces joined us before sunrise. The rest of the Alans tribesmen came in waves throughout the early morning, all answering the call to do battle against Attila. The first rays of dawn found the allied leaders meeting in the center of the camp with Flavius Aetius and Theodoric. The massive combined army was unlike anything I'd ever seen, even in my days as a legionnaire. Our forces had lined up facing east, expecting the Huns to take advantage of the morning sun glaring in our eyes, but no attack came. The massed Hun army strangely remained stationary.

Like the Jewish priests of old, my band of warrior monks covered the field with their praise songs and hymns as we bided our time. The civilized world waited for the lion to come out of his lair. Was something wrong? Was Attila waiting for Aetius to attack him? It didn't make sense. The Huns were always the aggressors in battle.

Tension hung in the air like a haze and still we waited. Just when I was beginning to think there would be no battle, Attila emerged from his laager, a huge protective circle of wagons. From our vantage point we could see almost the entire battle line. Aetius and his Romans were far to our left; Sangibon, his Alans, and my fighting monks held the center. Over a mile to our right were the Visigoths under Theodoric and his son Thorismund. The size of the Roman allied army was tremendous, the sight of thousands of pennants, flags, and tribal standards waving quietly in the gentle breeze, magnificent.

As large and as glorious as our forces were, the Hun ranks swelled quickly, their numbers staggering. An army from the Eastern Germanic tribes known as the Gepids held Attila's right flank. These were Christian tribes held in bondage by the Huns. Attila's far left flank was in the hands of King Walamir's Ostrogoths. They were another tribe subjugated by the Huns. In the center Attila's strength, the Huns, gathered like the dark clouds of an oncoming storm. The entire world had come together for one final battle, an Armageddon. This was a war of two vastly different worlds—Christians versus barbarians.

II

There was no standard uniform for the Huns. Most wore either round fur hats or pointed leather helmets along with burnished leather armor and leather breeches. They cheered and began to chant "Attila! Attila!" as their king stood in his stirrups and moved forward, his compact body clad in black. A gold helmet sat atop his long, matted, black hair, his face hardened and scarred from countless battles. His Huns raised their bows and spears and shouted wild battle cries—enjoying the thrill of the coming fight. Their loose cavalry formations moved like a horde of rabid wolves, around and about the mighty leader. Attila paused for a moment. I saw him turn and bellow at his comrades. With his right hand the Hun king pointed to his far right, then to his left. The enemy's ranks swelled as thousands of horsemen gathered near their leader in anticipation of their impending attack. The allied army braced for the onslaught.

Our forces occupied a slight rise on the plain from which I could see most of the field. I had never seen more men gathered for a single conflict, even during all the time I had spent as a Roman soldier. The rolling plateau was a dreadful panorama as both armies stood frozen in the moment, each in awe of the other. This was to be the battle of the age, the battle that would decide the fate of Europe and the world for generations to come. The two forces were poised about a thousand paces from each other across the long front.

I saw Attila lift his sword and then utter a barbaric howl that resounded through the enemy ranks. The entire Hun nation roared its approval. Their rams' horns blew a mighty trill and the enemy's entire front began to move at a slow trot, like a gigantic tidal wave of man, horse and steel.

Wasting no time in response, Aetius' war drums began a quick-time beat, and his red-cloaked, silver legions marched up the hill on our left. To the right, Theodoric and Thorismund took their Gothic cavalry and made for the high ground on our right. These warriors carried large round shields and wielded long spears. In the center Sangibon was in charge. His men were dressed in assorted battledress, while my own wore helmets and thick monk's robes. We all held some type of shield. We awaited the hordes of Hun cavalry that broke into a gallop as they moved toward our position. The ominous black swarm came on.

Many of the Alans were like my own men, inexperienced in battle. Combat always reveals whether a man's courage is greater than his fear. This is especially true for men who are not professional soldiers. Those who stood with us that day were no exception.

The usual style of attack for the Huns was to charge and then fire their arrows just before they retreated. Not today. The Huns stood in their stirrups—a device that had yet to be adopted in the West—and released their missiles at full gallop as they continued their advance. I am sure Attila believed that our center would crumble, and that we would turn and run in terror from the tens of thousands of horsemen who were barreling across the plain.

The ground reverberated with the shock of wave after wave of cavalry as they bounded toward us in a wild attack; the rumble of Attila's hordes made even the earth afraid. Yet not one of our men ran. On came the enemy, blackening the sky with their arrows. Everyone with a shield raised it to block the barbed darts. Even so, hundreds were killed or maimed. Our only hope was to withstand the onslaught without running away. Courage is easy to speak of in peacetime, but when lives are on the line, valor is sometimes a scarce commodity. This was a day for the brave.

We defended a slight rise, with a large hill to our left and a smaller one well to our right. All in all, the front stretched for several miles, the two sides separated by the peaceful stream where we had camped. To prevent being overrun by the Huns, I was depending upon the rows and rows of ground spikes to offer us protection. But I knew that such a briary thicket would work against us if our men fled the field. We had to hold. The right and left flanks were already engaged. Aetius' troops had reached the hill first and were exchanging blows with the Gepids. Theodoric's Visigoth cavalry clashed with Walamir's Ostrogoths for the summit on the far right, and Thorismund's troops were battling even farther beyond.

Sangibon had taken my advice, interspersing his best Alans warriors in between some of his untried "green" units. I had done the same, even placing unproven troops close to the caltrops in an attempt to make the men feel more confident. Of the 5000 warrior monks I commanded, only a handful had any military training, but the men stood bravely in their ranks, their spears ready, their faces grim and determined.

III

Now the charge of the Huns was almost upon us. The ground shook beneath us as if Vesuvius had reawakened. With the attacking Huns less than a hundred paces from us, I made my first move. For years legends had surrounded Attila's sword, the *Sword of Mars*, a great iron weapon of old that Attila wielded to show that the gods favored him. I now pulled my own great sword and held it aloft for our line to see. Even Sangibon's men gawked at the enormous blade.

"I hold the sword of Goliath, the sword King David took from the Philistine," I bellowed.

"It's the sword of a giant," I heard a man say.

"No, it's the Sword of Mars," said another.

"Just as our God did for David, this day the Lord has delivered these Philistines into our hands!" I shouted.

With a spirited roar the Alans, the Franks, my monks, and others cried valiantly in defiance, poised for the enemy charge. The Alans held their swords and shields in readiness, the Franks their axes and bows. I ordered my men to pack in tightly at the last moment. Like a phalanx, our pikes made a wall like giant porcupine quills against the enemy horsemen. The titanic clash was deafening as Hun ponies and swords crashed into our pikes and shields.

The Huns plunged into and through parts of our line and the shield wall which the Alans had made. Our men wavered but held. The sheer mass of the cavalry pushed us back. It was all I could do to swing my great rapier, but the sword's edge was true and cut through anything it met.

I impaled the first Hun who attacked me, then decapitated another who got in the way of the monstrous sword. Around me the battle was a mass of confusion. The conflict had only just begun and already the dead were everywhere. The ground began to become muddy from the blood. A Hun rider took a spear and ran through one of my captains, Brother Ells. The fierce enemy cavalryman cut into the ranks of my men with his savage slashing. I turned and with a deft cleave, hacked off the leg of the murderous Hun rider who tumbled from his mount; he was quickly skewered by a monk's lance.

A horn sounded, and the Huns retreated about a hundred paces before whirling about and charging into us once again. Sangibon led his reserves into the action to thwart the attack. Attila's advance was stymied, but Sangibon fell to a Hun who had lunged with his sword, then suddenly cast a lasso over the Orlans prefect and pulled him to the ground. The leader was trampled to death by the Hun cavalry.

Seeing their leader down, several Orlans warriors managed to cut the rope and scooped up Sangibon. Retreating, they left a small gap in our line. The pursuing Huns ran their ponies into the hole in an effort to outflank us. However, charging to our left, the Huns suddenly found themselves in the spiked thicket, which gored their horses and tossed their riders to their deaths.

Thankfully the spiny caltrops enabled us to retreat and to cover the space in the line, but we were still being pushed further back. The precarious center looked as if it were going to fall apart at any moment. The fighting was ferocious. In such tight quarters my sword was too long and became useless, so I made my shield my weapon, knocking my adversaries to the ground. Everywhere were bodies and blood. Thousands upon thousands lay dying or wounded in the center alone. There were so many bodies that the horses had difficulty finding footing.

The battle raged late into the afternoon with neither side gaining an advantage. Such hand-to-hand combat is both personal and impersonal. Sometimes you have to look into the eyes of a man you don't know, an enemy you might even like if you knew him, but you have to kill him before he kills you.

The Hun warriors were short and broad shouldered, their faces marred by cuts and burns inflicted on them as children, part of some tribal rituals to make them fierce. Their looks alone were enough to inspire fear, and they fought with great fury. With each retreat these barbarians would regroup like a black wave withdrawing from the shore only to swell and break into an even more ferocious charge. Our line had fallen back with each successive attack but had yet to break. I remained on Bark, fending off the enemy and encouraging our men.

IV

With all the confusion, it was impossible to determine what was happening on the two wings. The Roman wing did not appear to have given up any ground, but the Visigoths were in disarray. There was no sign of King Theodoric or his guard. Meanwhile we were holding in the center, but we were being stretched thinner and thinner as we gave ground with every successive charge.

A ram's horn sounded, and the Huns again retreated to regroup. They withdrew and reformed, this time throwing every man available at us. They fired every arrow in their quivers before their final onslaught. The field was littered with the dead, and footing was treacherous. Many soldiers tripped over their fallen comrades or slipped in gore.

In spite of the confusion, the assault came on, and the thicket was so clogged with horses and bodies that nothing could get through. In the areas where there were no spikes the Huns made headway. Their methods of attack were unparalleled in bravado as they slashed like wild men with no regard for their own safety. Pushed to the brink, our center began to break, and the Huns began tearing through our ranks.

I engaged Hun after Hun, directing both my men and Sangibon's troops. My warrior monks were exhausted but continued to fight. Many of the Alans tribesmen continued to battle bravely, but a few men lost hope and began to flee from Attila's advancing barbarians.

I turned Bark's head and whipped her into a gallop in an attempt to stem the tide of those running away. The trickle of retreating warriors suddenly turned into a torrent. I reached for the great sword to rally the men, but as I did so an arrow fell from the sky and pierced my chest. The missile struck deep, and the blow was so powerful that it knocked me from Bark. As soon as the troops saw me go down, the entire center began to waver. Even my own troops began to look for a place to run.

Like wolves smelling the blood of their wounded prey, the Huns increased the intensity of their attack. They pressed in as Brother Horace came to my aid. He looked at me and shook his head then seemed surprised to hear me speak.

"Help me to my feet," I told him.

"That might kill you," he said.

"I'm not going to die," I told him.

"But Brother Simon," he said. "The battle is lost. Hurry that we may escape with our lives."

"Help me onto my horse!" I said.

"You need a surgeon," Horace implored.

"Do as I tell you!" I ordered.

It took every ounce of strength I had and some help from Brother Horace to get back on Bark. I was still dazed and the wound was tender, but the climax of the battle was upon us as the men looked to me. They stopped in their tracks when they saw me regain my steed, the arrow imbedded in my chest. In the midst of the tumult, I felt an incredible sense of peace surround me. I asked the Lord for strength and for the right words to say. I then grasped the hilt of the great sword, drew it with my right hand, and held it aloft for all to see.

"Behold the power of the Lord," I shouted, and with my left hand I gripped the end of the arrow lodged in my chest and ripped it from my body.

V

For an instant all of the fighting stopped. Every eye was fixed on me with the sword of Goliath in my right hand and the gory arrow in my left. Even the blood-red sun paused to observe the scene. Suddenly and miraculously the entire center turned and rallied with a terrific roar.

My own men began to chant *Agnus Dei* and moved forward in quick-step, marching to the beat of the hymn. Their pikes bristled with strong resolve and determination. The Alans regrouped and, like men possessed, charged the enemy.

Having thought the battle won, the Huns were stunned at this turn of events. The Roman center was not only holding but gaining ground. Simultaneously, Roman war drums announced that Aetius had routed the Gepids from the field; his men were closing on Attila's left while the victorious Visigoths, having defeated King Walamir's troops, were enveloping the right.

Even as their own flanks crumbled, the overconfident Huns expected their attack against the center to split the Roman army in two. Such a result would have won the battle and given the barbarians another triumph. But as I led my warriors, now ferocious and undaunted in their determined attack, fear swept through the ranks of the enemy. Unaccustomed to defeat, a wave of terror overwhelmed the Huns; they panicked and ran. Hundreds were knocked from their mounts as they smashed into one another trying to get away. Attila, fleeing at a breakneck pace, avoided capture. The shock of the retreat was so powerful that the leader could not rally his men.

The macabre scene they left behind was one of incomparable gore. I had never seen more dead and wounded on a single battlefield. Severed arms and legs—gutted men were strewn everywhere. The beautiful stream that had separated the battleground was choked with bodies; its waters trickled a deep shade of crimson. Blood was everywhere, spattered on every warrior, pooling on the ground, and dripping from pikes and swords. Now that the fighting was over, the acrid smell of blood and the foul stench of death crept over the field.

Most of the allied generals wanted to attack Attila in his laager even though our forces were exhausted. The fighting had lasted almost the entire afternoon without pause, and tending to our own countless wounded and dead promised to be a Herculean task.

Meanwhile back at the Hun camp, Attila had made a gigantic pile of wood and wagons to use as a funeral pyre, believing Aetius would strike and finish the Huns once and for all. The mighty Hun warlord had finally been defeated, but our own army was so depleted that the Roman General decided not to resume the attack even on the following day. Perhaps Aetius considered the balance of power, concerned that destroying the Huns would open the door for another enemy, possibly even Thorismund's Visigoths, to attack Rome.

The losses on both sides were tremendous—forty thousand dead among the three allied wings. More than a thousand were dead from my own unit alone and a thousand more seriously wounded. The Visigoth King Theodoric had been killed along with most of his personal guard. Aetius and the Roman Empire had survived. As horrific as our casualties were, Attila's were catastrophic. Almost half of the enemy force lay dead or dying, many killed trying to escape the battlefield. The outcome of the battle of the Catalaunian Plain ensured that western civilization would live on.

For several days after the battle, we buried the dead. Afterwards, we gathered for a great feast where we gave thanks to the Lord for the victory. Meanwhile, Attila retreated to central Europe where he licked his wounds. He reemerged with his horde two years later in an attack on Italy, but because the area had been devastated by famine, the Huns were forced to retire to their homeland. Shortly after that invasion, the man whose name was synonymous with terror died of a nosebleed on his wedding night. The Huns faded into obscurity.

The Green Knight

...a king who will reign wisely and do what is just and right in the land.
Jeremiah 23:5

I

With the Hun threat eliminated, Europe breathed a sigh of relief. I returned to the farm in Gaul where, once again, I enjoyed the simple pleasure of working; however, after many years of tending the vineyard, overseeing the harvest, and making wine, I began to realize that simple life was not the Lord's plan for me. The world swirled around me, and I was blessed with too many skills to be set apart from it for too long.

My interest was piqued by the stories I'd heard brought to us from Britain. They told of a kingdom called Avalon where there were virtuous knights, a noble king, and an honorable code by which all lived. As I crossed the choppy waters of the channel to seek this place, the winds were gentle and the sky was clear. What would I do if I found Avalon? I couldn't serve the way I served Rome—with blind obedience. Many times as a soldier of the Roman Empire I simply followed my orders without thought because I was expected to do so. If the enchanted kingdom of Avalon did exist, I wanted to enter it on my own terms. I needed to find a way to test its king and his subjects.

I hadn't been to Britannia since the time of Boudica's uprising. Now, almost a century since the Romans had departed from the island, the people remained civilized. The inhabitants were more Roman now than in the time of Boudica. I proceeded to Londinium, and I paused just outside the city. There were now huge, knotted oak trees where I had buried Joseph so long ago. Much time had passed since he had taken me under his wing. Joseph had been a true friend and a good man. I sat down, leaned against a tree trunk, and reminisced. I missed my old friend and mentor.

"I suppose you know my little secret now, Joseph," I mused, speaking to the breeze and pondering my immortality.

Everyone I asked about Avalon said it was in southwestern Britain. I wanted to see with my own eyes this place of godly men and Christian principles. Arriving in southern England I found that King Arthur's name was spoken with great respect. In those days words meant more than they do now. The politics were simple then. Leaders led. The people of Avalon felt safe, and there was fair trade in the region. Commerce and security are two parts of the equation that result in prosperity, something I'd not seen since the days of the Pax Romana and Marcus Aurelius. Dressed in a brown robe with a hood, I felt welcomed by the people of Avalon.

I moved among the monks and priests who served a chapel near the palace. They all had the highest regard for the King and his Queen. The local rulers were pious and just and always made sure the churches had provisions to feed the poor. Near the chapel was a school founded by St. Patrick where monks were taught to become scribes.

Even at the local inns, merchants from Francia, Hispania, and the Rhine celebrated their profits. They often remarked how safe their passage was through Avalon with Arthur as King. Law and order were the rule, unlike Gaul with bandits lurking behind every shrub. Chivalry was the code by which every knight of the Round Table was expected to abide: the strong should protect the weak and see justice done. The effects of this code trickled down even to the common people.

Thus far, Avalon had exceeded my expectations, but I was still skeptical. I suppose 150 years of serving Rome had made me a little wary. I had to determine if the King and his knights actually lived according to their code. So I set in motion plans for a contest, a test of combat and truth.

As a monk, little personal information was required of me by the folk that I met. I spoke to them and spread the Word of God while I gathered the materials I would need for my plan. I had brought with me a large horse that I had again named Bark. He was huge, standing 16 hands tall and weighing more than a thousand pounds. It was harvest time and summer was at an end. The chilly hand of winter could be felt subtly guiding the autumn breezes. I found an abandoned cottage in the wood to use as my workshop.

I first set about to find some woad, a cruciferous herb; its leaves create a blue dye. I began by drying the leaves, grinding them up, and letting them ferment in water. They stunk worse than pig's entrails, but they did create an indigo blue dye the color of Celtic war paint. I mixed the blue with some tint made from wild mignonette, another plant used for dyeing. The yellow color from the mignonette combined with the blue made a bright Sherwood green. I took some pieces of Roman armor I'd brought, a breastplate and shin greaves, and plunged them into the green liquid. The dyed leather between the metal ribs of the armor gave it an eerie chartreuse sheen.

Next I dyed Bark, brushing the stain onto him. His coat became bright green, the color of grass. Even his hooves were emerald. I then hewed some holly branches and braided a crown for myself and a war mask for Bark, careful to keep the thorns away from his eyes. My clothing and Bark's saddle blankets turned green as they sank into the smelly, steamy cauldron.

Lastly, I climbed into the warm vat myself. The hot, slimy bath made my hair stand on end, the heat pricking the nerves along my back and spine. The sensation reminded me of the great bath houses in Rome as I sank my head beneath the murky green water. The warm ooze offered me the solitude of another world with its bubbly caresses. Moments later I emerged from the cauldron and was enveloped by a cloud of white vapor. My pine-painted skin looked uncanny as it was the color of a summer forest. I saw my reflection in a nearby puddle of water. My hair and beard were tinted as well, even my eyelids— their red rims made me look like a jade gargoyle, bloody circles highlighting the whites of my eyes and my green skin. Finally, early one morning during the celebration of Christmastide, I set off for the court of King Arthur.

II

What a sight we made in the sunrise as Bark stopped for water at a small stream. His blanket was the color of the forest and covered with braided holly. We looked monstrous. I looked every bit the goblin king with a nightmarish green tint to my hair, beard, and skin. Adding to the sight was my holly crown, green armor and gauntlets. Against the pure white snow, Bark and I looked even more phantasmagorical, as if we'd risen from the murky slime of the bowels of Hades. The new-fallen snow silenced the earth, the trance broken only by the muffled, frosty snorts pulsing from Bark's nostrils. Confident and determined, warhorse and warrior rode boldly for Camelot.

It was still snowing Christmas day as we neared the castle, the white ground crisping beneath Bark's hooves as we rode. We passed only one soul along the way, a peasant, on foot, covered with a hooded cloak. The wintry earth muted our approach. Startled, the man's eyes met mine, and after a muffled scream he dashed off into the pure, vestal wood. When I arrived at the chase, the hunting lands near Camelot, I waited to approach the palace until I was sure the feasting was about to begin. It was midday when I climbed atop Bark and rode for the egress. The portcullis was open, and peasants moved freely in and out of the castle, for all were welcome on this day.

Seizing an opportunity, I spurred Bark and charged up some flat stone steps and through an open gate. The horse's bulk sent frightened people scurrying as Bark's hooves clopped down the stony, torch-lit corridor toward the palace's great hall.

The aroma of the feast drew me to the hall's long double doors, and as I pulled Bark's reins, the horse reared up on his hind legs and charged into the chamber. The first thing I saw was a huge, round table, hollow in the center. It was oak and beautiful, and sitting around it were the great knights and ladies of Camelot. At the bottom of the table, opposite the King was an opening so that attendants could move in and out easily to serve any member of the court. Piled on the table were huge mounds of roasted venison, beef, and mutton heaped upon platters. There were buckets of mead, and music filled the air as a drum beat the time for the slippery strains of the cytere, a square-shaped stringed instrument from which poured out a merry song. Aghast at my appearance, knights and ladies leapt to their feet when they saw me.

I urged Bark onward, farther in, near the huge pit where a large blaze spat out sparks. The King remained seated in the most prominent chair at the head of the table. He was calm, looking as if he had expected me. I carefully guided Bark through the open space in the table and again pulled on the reins. Obediently, my steed rose up on his hind legs, pawed the air, and snorted with nostrils flared. The bewildered members of the court looked at me, at their king, then back at me in confusion. Circling within the table, I began to tease the knights. "Who is this King?" I roared, thrusting my sword in the air. "Who is this King?" I offered again.

No one uttered a sound. Only the fire spoke with its voice of crackles and groans. Knights, ladies, servants, attendants, all stood as still as if captured in a tapestry.

"Is this how the King's warriors greet a fellow knight?" I asked disdainfully. "I thought this was a table of honor." I cantered to one side, hacked a great piece of mutton with my sword, stabbed it through and tore it with my teeth, gnashing like a barbarian.

The silence grew louder as I smacked my lips rudely and ate while Bark snorted menacingly.

Finally, Arthur stood. "I am King Arthur," he said, his voice as masculine as the smell of burning oak.

"Mighty King Arthur," I said, tauntingly, cantering back and forth on the great green steed. "I challenge anyone at this table." I threw the mutton leg to the floor, and not even the dogs dared approach. "I challenge any knight from this table to exchange blow for blow with me. Is there a man among you?"

No one spoke; the silence now deafening in the prolonged moment.

"And I was told these were the finest knights in the world," I scoffed.

"I," said the King. "I will exchange blows with you."

The room was like a vacuum.

Incredulously I asked, "Must the King accept this challenge? Is there no knight here who will stand in for his King? Haven't you all taken an oath to protect him?" I scowled at them and then laughed.

Some knights nervously glanced around the table, not wanting to be cowardly, but not desiring to challenge so powerful an apparition. Finally, a deep voice came bellowing across the table from behind me.

"I cannot let the King accept this charge," a knight said. "I am Gavain, and I accept your challenge." He stood, broad shouldered, his hair and beard a fiery red that showed his Gaelic heritage, his voice aggressive and firm. "But whose challenge is it that *I* accept? Do such as you even have a name?"

Like the Israelite camp when David rebutted Goliath, I sensed an attitude of courage and strength from the knights. Reining in Bark, I turned to face my challenger.

"So there is a man among you, someone with some courage and honor." I paused. "I am called the Green Knight. We shall trade blow for blow with sword. I will take your blow first. Then, when and if I am able, you will take mine. However, there are ladies present, and this is Christmas Day. We are in a hall for feasting, not fighting—I suggest we remove ourselves to the courtyard outside."

The court looked to Arthur with an air of tense expectancy. Arthur gave a kingly nod and his men began to move. I guided Bark to a nearby door leading outside. Holding the postern, the gawking servant eyed us as we walked from the dark stony confines of the castle into the virgin white courtyard, where the snow continued spitting from the leaden sky.

III

The King and his knights were followed by an entourage of squires and servants. The ladies remained inside but flocked to the castle portals to watch. I followed Gavain into the open air as I led Bark through the bright, snow-covered courtyard. There was a pond with a few crude, wooden benches nearby. The knights gathered in a large semi-circle, white mist escaping from them as they breathed the icy air. The squires crowded in to watch.

I dismounted, crunching through the white crusted snow until I stood in front of Gavain. His squire handed the knight a broad sword. A little uneasy, I wasn't prepared for what happened. I had assumed the redheaded warrior would run me through, especially since my armor was old and didn't cover me entirely. Although there would be pain, I knew I wouldn't die from a stab wound, so I wasn't afraid.

With a wave of Arthur's hand, the courtyard became so eerily quiet that one could almost hear the snowflakes as they drifted to earth.

Gavain broke the silence. "Now Green Knight, lean over slightly so that I might have a swing at your neck."

In all my mind's scenarios, it never occurred to me that I might lose my head. Over the course of 500 years of life I had been burned, beaten, stabbed, sliced, stoned, shot with arrows, buried alive and boiled in oil, but I had never been beheaded. A familiar feeling slithered through me and made me shudder: fear. I remember thinking that throughout our lives we have to relearn certain lessons—for me, fear was one of those lessons, the fear of the unknown. I had become immune to it over the years. Warily, I embraced what was to come. I bent down and stuck my neck out like a turtle from its shell. I thought I might die, but in a curious way a part of me would have welcomed it.

There was a terrible, heavy, momentary silence as the gallery fearfully anticipated what was about to happen, like a crowd gathering at the gallows to see an execution. Slowly and deliberately Gavain's heavy sword rose above me, and then the blade sliced the air with a whisper. I felt sharp, cold pain sever my neck; I saw the snowy ground rushing to greet my face.

Landing first on my forehead, I felt my head topple over before coming to rest next to Gavain's boot. I could see it all from ground level, my blinking eyes distanced from my body. As if on cue, the onlookers cringed in unison, but the silence was broken by a tremendous cheer from the knights. I, or rather, my head, lay there, open-eyed, mouth gasping like a fish out of water. A snowflake parachuted down and touched my tongue, another landed on my eyelid. Lying there helpless, I stared upward; I could see Gavain as he stood, cocky and victorious.

He leaned toward me, and I saw his spider-like hand reach down for my head. Picking it up by the hair, he raised both of his arms in a victorious gesture, a sword in one hand, my head in the other. Then he turned to his fellow knights.

"So much for him," Gavain said, twisting my head so that we were face to face. "I don't think you'll be interrupting anymore Christmas feasts will you, Sir Knight?"

The gallery laughed at the jest. I tried to take the image in, but it was surreal to the extreme, unaccompanied by life's routine of breath and control. Strangely though, only a few feet away, my body remained upright, as if frozen. The pain was numbing and the cold severe, but then the unimaginable happened. As the knights stood chuckling and staring at the gory scene, my headless torso took a few steps and snatched my skull from Gavain's hand. The women screamed from the portals, and the men stood in jaw-dropping amazement at this unexpected twist.

IV

My green, armored torso stood boldly, blood oozing down my emerald neck. Even the King was astonished as my two arms triumphantly lifted my bodiless head into the air. I looked for my decapitator, my gauntleted hands gently guiding my lacerated neck and head back together. Gavain's eyes were as large as saucers, his face the color of watered milk.

My arms held my head onto my neck. Gurgling, I spat out a mouthful of blood, and I somehow, amidst frothy crimson bubbles, blurted out the words, "I will return. You will honor your oath."

Gavain was motionless; I could see fear in his eyes. Then, as if I were carrying a melon, I removed my head from my neck and held it under one arm, climbed back atop Bark, pulled his reins and rode away.

I'm not sure how, but Bark and I found the way back to the hut after dark. I lay down on my straw bedding and placed my head where it would normally fit on my neck and fell into a long sleep. I don't know how long I lay there, but when I awoke the wound was completely healed. The following day I returned to Camelot.

The gates were not open, but I was given immediate entry. I rode back to the empty courtyard, slipped down from Bark and, like the angel of death, silently waited for Gavain. Arthur came first followed by Gavain, who wore no armor. Like a prisoner before his execution, he entered the courtyard.

"Some of my knights tried to convince me that we should attack you when you returned," the King said. "But we have ascribed ourselves to a code, and the challenge must be met or we betray our honor and our faith."

Gavain stepped forward. "Of my own free will, I am here."

He bent down before me, offering his head. I said nothing but unsheathed my blade with its metallic voice. There was a solemn silence amongst the knights who stood and watched. Gavain looked down, awaiting death. I could sense the King's heavy heart, which made my sabre even weightier. I gripped the hilt of the sword and slowly lifted it. With all my strength I brought the blade down and purposely pulled it short of the mark, barely nicking Gavain's neck. He winced and immediately touched the cut. He looked at me, a smudge of blood on his fingers. I smiled.

"You passed the test," I said.

There was a collective sigh of relief by the knights who had gathered round.

I looked Gavain in the eye and said, "You are a virtuous knight. Serve your master well." Then I turned to Arthur. "This is an honorable court, and you are a great King. I must take my leave."

"I see the truth in your test," the King said.

There was great celebration as I rode away from Camelot. The church bells pealed, their song ringing throughout Avalon and in my own heart. I had finally found something worthwhile. I had found a home.

I spent the next few weeks scrubbing the dye off of myself. It took a while, but it finally wore off. I cut my hair, washed and brushed the dye off Bark, scrubbed and polished my armor and waited. Each day I went through the fighting exercises that were part of my Roman training for so many years, and I prepared to become a Knight of the Round Table.

Lancelot

...there is a friend that sticks closer than a brother. Proverbs 18:24

I

Several months later I returned to Avalon, this time as a knight looking to serve a king. I told the King I was from Aquitania where I was known as Lazarus of the Lake. This eventually became Laz du lac, or Lancelot. On this third visit to Camelot I would adopt a settled life once again. I would become what we called in Latin, Arthur's *fidus Achates*, his most trusted friend. I would love and serve him faithfully for fifteen years only to discover the greatest love of my life and in doing so, betray my King.

The sweet scent of a spring day greeted me as I rode up to the gates of Camelot. As proud as any knight of the Round Table, I'm sure Bark and I made quite a sight in our glinting silver armor. The massive snorting warhorse pranced and cavorted beneath the open portcullis as we entered Camelot proper. The saddle creaked as I pulled the reins, petitioning the guards to see the King. This time I was invited into the great hall where I had challenged Gavain. The spring sunlight warmed the stone inside the castle as I entered.

I strode in, awaiting the arrival of the King. Arthur entered quietly and unannounced. He came into the room wearing a simple brown tunic in warrior fashion. His friendly eyes met mine as he stared, bewildered for a moment, finally saying, "I know you from somewhere, Sir Knight."

I nodded acceptance, but said nothing.

"My attendant says your name is Lancelot," he said, studying me. "You are from a great house in Gaul?"

"Yes, sire. My home is in Aquitania."

"Yet you come to Camelot?"

"I've been looking for a king who is worthy of my service. I have heard of little else but King Arthur, his knights, and the code they live by. I am here to offer my sword."

"I welcome you to Camelot, Sir Knight. However," he paused and grinned, "we do not allow men into our company who just say they are knights. You must prove yourself in combat." He searched for the words. "Let me be direct. Many men try to join our ranks. Few do."

"What happens to those who fail?" I asked.

"The nature of combat is such that mercy is shown whenever possible during the bouts, but many are killed," he said gravely.

"I can assure you. I won't be killed," I said, chuckling.

"The words are easy," he said pointedly. "It is good to know that you have great confidence. Within the month you will have an opportunity to demonstrate your skill at our tournament. But until that time, you will dine with us and receive as much hospitality as we can offer you."

An attendant took me to my quarters, a stone chamber with a mattress of straw, dried herbs, and dried rose petals. I was assigned a squire whose name was Ektor, a broad-shouldered young man with a kind spirit. As my attendant, he showed me the ways and passages of Camelot and told me more of the great King Arthur and his knights.

Just before dusk everyone gathered for supper in the great hall. The amber mead flowed, but there was little carousing or drunkenness. I was introduced to the knights of the court, who treated me with courtesy but with a bit of disregard as well. The largest of them was Sir Kay. He was more than six feet tall and weighed almost 300 pounds. He looked agile enough to be a good fighter, but he was gentle in his demeanor and as kind to me as anyone else at Camelot. Gavain, Bors, Percival, Bedivere, and Tristan were there as well as many others. The night was fairly uneventful until I was introduced to Arthur's Queen and her sister.

I had seen beautiful women before, but none like Guinevere. She could have been Helen of Troy, whose beauty led kingdoms to war over her. Her eyes were gold, her hair rich chestnut. Her skin was like moonlight, but it was her face that was an artist's dream. The Queen's warm, delicate smile could have been that of a muse. There was an attraction between us from the beginning. Guinevere's eyes penetrated beyond the cursory glance to which I was entitled. I was also introduced to Guinevere's older sister Hecate who had flaming red hair and eyes the color of the sky. In some ways she was more beautiful than Guinevere, but somehow the Queen far outshone her.

Not yet a courtier, I was not allowed to converse with the Queen or Hecate, but I did find myself the object of approving glances from both women during the course of the evening. After dinner the ladies retired and the men drank more mead and finally settled in to playing Tali, an ancient dice game. After a few hours of play, everyone retired to their bed chambers. This was the routine for several weeks until the month of May arrived.

II

The first day of May brought with it the Spring Festival at Camelot. Avalon was filled with locals and travelers who came for the celebrations. Each day of the week featured something new as there were arts and crafts such as wood carving and whistle making. There was music and dancing as well. Maidens wearing white robes, a symbol of their virtue, marched in together in step to the music and waited to be chosen for marriage. There were even storytelling and writing demonstrations put on by the scribes of the school recently started by a monk named Patrick. One scribe drew symbols—letters for the crowds—while another captivated audiences with tales of the great knights.

The first part of festival week was fun and whimsical. Actors performed funny skits, musicians played joyful tunes, and jesters danced and showed their wit. All this jollity led up to the festival's much anticipated feats of might. These took place midweek. Many knights participated in the strength events, the first of which was a race in which opponents pulled wooden ox carts around a track. Another contest was to see who could heave heavy stones the farthest distance. Sir Percival won the final event as he hoisted a gigantic pine log over his head.

The last events of the week were for strength, skill, and combat. These would be the culmination of the festival, performed in front of Camelot's court as well as the peasants. I trained for some time with only my squire there to observe me. I demonstrated to him the advantage of stirrups when on horseback. Able to stand in my saddle, I swung my sword and thrust it to show my attendant the importance of footing and balance, but Ektor was not impressed.

"The other knights will just make fun of you before they humiliate you in battle," he said drolly.

Even King Arthur had doubts about my prowess as a warrior. "These men you're going up against are the best knights in the land, maybe the best in the world. Perhaps God has sent you here for us to train you. "

"My lord, I have some experience in combat," I said to the King, who could not repress a smirk at my impudence.

The Tournament crowds assembled just after second matins, the time of morning prayer. There was a good mixture of peasants and nobility. The people were jolly about the holiday and though they dressed mostly in drab colors, they wore brightly hued sashes or scarves for the festival. The nobles dressed up and were merry and joyful as well. All loved this time of year. I arose early that morning and went to the stables to check on Bark before having breakfast. He was being tended by Ektor.

"How is Bark this morning?" I asked him.

"He's very strong. I've never seen a bigger horse," Ektor said, smiling as he brushed Bark's golden coat. "He's like a pet the way he loves to be groomed. He moves into the bristles like he enjoys it." The horse leaned into the squire's strokes while Ektor grinned and continued his work.

After breakfast I returned to my lodging to prepare for combat. As I began to put on my armor, Ektor came to assist me.

"This is fine armor," he said. "It must have been very costly. I hope you don't have to be buried in it. You realize that the best knights in the world are here, don't you?" He smiled at me as if he knew something that I didn't.

"I'm not worried about getting killed," I said, taking no insult from his comment. "Just don't bury me alive," I laughed. "Now, tighten the cuirass."

He moved behind me to tie the leather breastplate. It was snug and fit perfectly. "Now hand me my helmet and sword."

"This helmet is most unusual," Ektor said. "It looks as if it were fashioned in the likeness of your face." He examined the helmet's nose and eye features that formed the front of the mask. "You have your sword, do you not, sir?" Ektor asked.

"No, I do not," I stated, trying to turn about in the cumbersome armor. "It was right next to my cuirass." I could tell from the squire's expression that he was as surprised as I.

We hastily began to look around the room, finding nothing. Ektor then went to the stable, but the sword was nowhere to be found.

"You must have a sword or else you'll have to forfeit. You'll be forced to leave in disgrace," he moaned.

"Disgrace? Even though my sword has been stolen?"

"That in itself is reason enough," Ektor explained. "The code requires that a knight protect the King, and how can a man be a knight without a sword? And what does it say about the knight if he let his sword be stolen?"

"What does it say about his squire?" I barked back angrily, upset that I had been so lax. Even as a soldier of Rome we had never let our weapons out of our sight. Had I learned nothing?

I felt unbelievably stupid. I backtracked in my mind to when I'd last seen the weapon and decided it must have been taken while I was at breakfast and Ektor was tending to Bark. The squire then went to the chamber maid to see if she had seen anyone enter the room, but she said there were people everywhere, all over the castle preparing for the tournament.

Encumbered by my armor, I sat down on an old curule, a type of Roman stool, and debated what to do. Finally, I sent Ektor out again to look for my blade. He still had found no trace of the weapon; the trumpets sounded "first call" to tournament.

I was imagining what I could say in front of the entire court that would explain my catastrophe, my stupidity, when another young squire suddenly arrived bearing my sword. The French workmanship on the hilt and the quality of the metalwork were unmistakable; there was no doubt it was mine.

"Your sword, Sir Knight," he said.

"How did this come into your possession?" I asked.

"I am not at liberty to say, sir. I have been instructed to tell you that it was somehow retrieved by one of the ladies of the court. It was given to me by her maidservant."

Ektor looked as puzzled as I felt; then he smiled and shrugged his shoulders.

"To whom may I address my thanks?" I asked the young squire.

"I can say nothing more," the lad said.

"You have my gratitude," I said, dismissing him with a nod and a smile.

Ektor and I hurried down to the stable.

"Are you sure you want to use these?" Ektor asked, holding one of the saddle's leather stirrups in his hand, examining it.

"They help the rider maintain balance and power," I said.

"They look silly to me, something like a novice might use. The best knights here have no need for such things and would never use them," Ektor said, embarrassed for me.

"We'll see about that. Attila's Huns certainly used them with great effect."

The trumpets blared again, the final call for those who were to compete. I mounted Bark and off we galloped to the arena, a remnant of ancient Rome.

III

I reported to the challenger's table with the rest of the knights who scoffed at me, pointing at me and the stirrups. We lined up in the coliseum, an old stone structure from the days of Rome's dominance. The competition began with the parade of the knights. The three dozen warriors each wore a bright scarf which bore the colors of one of the ladies of the court. The parade was a spectacle of reds, blues, greens, and violets waving gaily in the breeze. I had no colors; they had to be earned by sworn knights of the realm. The arena was packed full of standing, jostling, excited spectators; box seating was provided for members of the court. All were dressed in their very best. There was another separate box for the King and Queen. Arthur, golden crown upon his head, sat in a crimson robe on an elevated chair. Next to him sat Guinevere in a beautiful gown the color of the forest. Upon the Queen's braided hair was a golden crown adorned with emeralds.

The first competitions were combinations of feats of strength and skill. Those of us who did not participate in these events remained on our mounts tended by our squires. We sat abreast, awaiting combat. Not all of the knights participated, but the ones who did demonstrated great power and dexterity. Sir Mark was hailed as the strongest of all the knights. He lifted large oak logs over his head and could heave them incredible distances.

"It's too bad he doesn't fight as well as he can throw wood," I overheard Sir Mordred chuckle to his squire.

Sir Mackin's turn was next. His skill was with the bow, and his talent was unparalleled by anyone at the tournament. Somewhat small for a knight, Sir Mackin could take an arrow, shoot it up into the air, then draw another arrow from his quiver, fire it, and split his first arrow in two. I was as impressed as the wildly applauding audience.

"Bows and arrows," Sir Mordred interrupted with disdain. "That's the only thing he's good at. Battles aren't won with flying sticks."

I questioned Mordred's brazen arrogance with a raised eyebrow and a loud, "Hmmph!"

Mordred snapped back at me. "How does someone of such low birth afford such fine armor? You're not even a knight! What are those foot holders on your saddle? Are you so unskilled that you need those to stay on top of your horse?"

The knights and squires within hearing distance of Mordred's verbal darts let out a muffled laugh at the jest.

"Who are you and why are you here?" Mordred asked gruffly.

"I am one who is here to fight," I said.

This brought an even larger chuckle from the other knights, who apparently didn't expect much from me.

Sir Mackin's archery skills were followed by several other knights and squires who showed talents in various areas. Sir Vale could hurl a sword and hit a target the size of a man's head at thirty paces; Blakely, Sir Kay's squire, could balance on a tight rope.

It was late morning by the time the clash of arms competition began. The knights were paired one against another in mounted combat. The first pairings were for those knights who were young and of moderate talent, some novices, some hopefuls. All were looking for a place to sit at the Round Table. I was placed with this group. My first opponent was Sir Bors.

Bors was known for his skill with a sword and was considered a good rider, the best of our group. He wore the turquoise scarf of Lady Jane. Bors' silver armor gleamed in the bright sunlight. He approached me on his horse somewhat gingerly, apparently not wanting to embarrass me by defeating me too quickly. Our swords clanged together as I parried every blow. I fought defensively, and Bors simply wore himself out before I finally knocked him from his mount with my sword. I offered a bow from atop Bark and graciously extended my sword to my fallen foe. It was customary for opponents to shake hands after their bouts, and this we did. He was a gracious loser, although he eyed me as if he'd been taken by surprise as he walked off the field.

The competition continued throughout the day, and my next two rounds went just as the first had. I fought defensively and won after my opponents were spent. As the tournament wore on some competitors chose to fight on foot. My final opponent was the reigning champion, Sir Bedivere. He was a great rider and good swordsman. It was clear that he had studied my earlier victories as his tactics were different. He made a great charge with his steed as if to attack but then went on the defensive.

Taking the initiative for the first time, I began to hack and search for weaknesses in Bedivere's defense. Several times I could have struck him from his mount, but I desired to win in gentlemanly fashion. Bedivere realized that he had met his match as he became increasingly more cautious. My attacks clearly demonstrated the tremendous advantage of stirrups as I stood in my saddle and poured blow after hammering blow upon the former champion who could do no more than hide beneath his shield. Finally I found a large dent in the center of Bedivere's buckler; I took my sword and lodged it in the dent and simply shoved the dazed knight from his saddle. He was so exhausted that his legs could no longer hold onto his horse.

While Bedivere lay on the ground, I climbed down from Bark and helped the great knight to his feet before bowing to both him and the crowd as they continued to applaud.

"I've never felt such powerful strikes from a mounted opponent," Bedivere said.

"I do not deny that I possess some skill with a blade, but the secret to gaining advantage on horseback is the stirrups. Come and see." I pointed to my saddle. "It is said that the Huns used them."

"The Huns were great warriors," Bedivere said, "But you, too, are exceptionally skilled. How is it that we've never heard of you before?"

"I trained in Aquitania," I said. "I am certainly not the greatest warrior, but I have fought much in my lifetime."

"I never thought anyone would best me," Bedivere said. "Let us go and collect your prize."

IV

As we turned to walk toward the King and Queen, a voice cried out from the knight's gallery.

"I challenge you!" It was the screeching voice of Sir Mordred. "As I am a knight of the realm and you are not, I can challenge you."

"Can he do that?" I asked Bedivere.

"According to the law, any knight is allowed to challenge any man who aspires to knighthood here in Avalon," he said. Bedivere then whispered hoarsely, "Beware! Sir Mordred is a dangerous opponent. He doesn't play by the same rules as the rest of us."

"I accept your challenge," I called back to Mordred and the rest of the knights. "When and where?"

"Here and now," Mordred said, already swaggering toward me. "You thought you could cheat your way into a win with those foot holders on your saddle."

"They're called stirrups," I corrected.

An angry Mordred ran at me with spiked flail and shield. Although he had strength, his defense was weak. Each time the man swung his weapon he opened himself to attack. I exploited this weakness by stopping short of stabbing him each time. Both he and the observers realized I was toying with him. The knight became so enraged that he swung wildly. One of Mordred's angry blows buried his flail in the ground so deeply that the knight struggled to pull it out. Having to use his feet and legs to help pry up the weapon, the scene made him look ridiculous, and some of the knights began to laugh behind gloved hands.

I assumed my opponent would retire, but in an act of poor sportsmanship, Mordred flung sand in my eyes and attacked again. I held my ground as I struggled to see, blocking the blows with my shield. He began to swing his flail at my buckler, trying to lodge the barbed end of his weapon into the shield in an effort to snatch away my defense, but I remembered an old tactic from my Roman days. My commander once said, "If your enemy wants your shield, give it to him." That's what I did.

The next swipe from Mordred's flail snagged the shield, but I launched the buckler and my body forward and pounced on the unsuspecting knight. He fell backward like the opponent who has held onto the rope too long in a tug of war.

Struggling to our feet, Mordred attacked again, but this time I drew my blade, and slapped the shabby knight on top of his helmet with the flat side of my sword. The blow literally knocked him silly, and he stumbled around like a drunkard while all of Camelot roared in laughter.

Arthur stood and stopped the competition and motioned for Mordred and me to come before him. We both dropped our weapons. I moved toward the King while Mordred's squire helped him along.

"Sir Mordred!" the King said frowning. "Throwing sand in the eyes of this gallant knight was not chivalrous. You insult all of Avalon with such behavior."

"But Majesty, this low-born stranger does not fight with honor. He parries and steps away from my blows, refusing to be hit. On the tilt he cheated by using foot holders attached to his saddle so that he could deliver a stronger thrust. Sand in the face is the reward for this peasant with his loathsome guiles and trickery."

"Clever words will not win for you this time Sir Mordred. I am your King, and I see that the stranger has the ways of a winning warrior. You disgraced the Tournament Grande by throwing sand in the eyes of your opponent, against our code of chivalry. I could have you exiled for such behavior," Arthur said sternly.

"Forgive me, sire. I could not control my anger. I beg your forgiveness," Mordred said.

"Though you have dishonored Camelot, I forgive you, but you have affronted our tournament Champion," the King said, placing his hand on my shoulder.

Mordred turned to me and bowed. "I beg your forgiveness," he said, looking at me with cold, unmasked hatred in his eyes.

"I am not offended, my King," I interjected, coming to Mordred's aid. "It is difficult to control one's temper when one's blood is up. We have all sinned and fallen short of the glory of God."

Mordred bowed grudgingly, and the King smiled. I had won the competition and shown my fighting prowess, but more significantly, I had made my first enemy at Camelot.

The combination of my armor, sword, and stirrups, as well as 150 years in the service of Rome had made me invincible. Arthur presented me to the audience. I bowed gracefully and enjoyed the crowd's wild applause. I was the champion, and I stood nodding to Hecate and the other ladies of the court.

The King turned and said, "By our Saviour's blood, Sir Knight, you have trounced all of my champions. I have never seen such skill in a warrior. You've taken my rams and made them lambs. You are champion of the Avalon Tournament Grand, and you are now a Knight of the Round Table. I was wrong when I spoke to you earlier. You haven't come to learn from us; you have come to teach us."

That night was one of great feasting and revelry. The knights and courtiers all sat at the round table. I was placed at the King's left hand where we ate our fill of delicious meats and sweets. Afterwards, as we waited for the evening's entertainment, most of the knights welcomed me. They were keenly interested in my fighting skills and excited to learn more of my riding techniques. Other knights, Mordred and his friends at court, skulked in the background, hovering and muttering in the dark places in the hall like spoiled children who'd been punished.

A short time later as the great hall was bathed in light from its gigantic fireplace, music filled the room, and courtly dancing would top off the evening. Tradition held that the first dance be with the Queen and the tournament champion.

The stringed instruments began a sweet tune, and the timbrels and drums followed. The firelight flickered on the stone floor. The Queen's emerald gown was stunning, and her auburn hair gleamed from the blaze. I chanced a glance into her eyes—hypnotic, as we stepped to the center of the floor. She placed her left palm gently on top of my right hand and the music commenced. The dance itself was rigidly formal, but Guinevere was light footed and had a wild, alluring air about her.

"You are allowed to speak," the Queen whispered to me.

"Please forgive me, my Queen," I said, the words stumbling from my lips. "I haven't been in the presence of such beauty for a very long time." Until then I had never spoken to Guinevere.

"In becoming Avalon's champion, you have become my paladin, my protector."

"How lovely you are in your gown," I complimented her. "It is the color of the summer leaves."

"The King had this garment made for me because he loves green. Arthur's pet name for me is Greensleeves."

I was spellbound by the Queen's supple, velvety voice. Her tone was as rhythmic and musical as a Celtic wind. We spoke briefly about the tournament. Self-assured and confident, she was captivating. I felt like Ulysses sailing toward the island of the sirens.

At the end of the first dance, it was customary that the champion choose a partner for the second dance. I chose Hecate, her hair the color of fire, her eyes ice. I could see the desire in her as she touched me seductively whenever an opportunity arose. The Queen's sister made every effort to gain my affections through caresses and girlish giggles. Although I responded with smiles, my heart was elsewhere, and Hecate's piercing blue eyes said that she knew it.

Thursday, July 11 10:30 p.m.

"Camelot? King Arthur? We were taught even as children that it was all a myth," the priest said.

"Not all of it," Lazlow answered.

"And you were—you are Lancelot? Unbelievable! All of those Arthurian romances, those stories, are they all true?" Braden asked.

"Many of them are indeed fiction. With the end of Rome, all the lands I knew were in chaos. Arthur's court was a most pleasant and civilized place. It was Camelot. But forgive me, I realize it's late. Perhaps I should come back."

"At least finish this part," Braden said.

"The tale is almost done, at least the first 500 years of my life," Lazlow said, unable to keep a terrible sadness from his voice.

Excalibur

He took hold of the Philistine's sword and drew it from the sheath.
I Samuel 17:51

I

The fellowship of the Round Table provided some of the closest camaraderie I've ever experienced. Arthur's wise leadership was exemplified in the selection of these men, many of them renowned and valiant heroes. Trust and esteem for one another, our common dedication to Christ, and Arthur's vision of a just kingdom formed our band—a band which has now become legend.

As a knight of the realm I became Arthur's favorite, and he honored me with the privilege of sitting at his right hand. I suppose the bond between us grew so strong because of our respect for one another. Arthur marveled at my invincibility in combat, and while I appreciated my own abilities, I felt they were miniscule compared to the qualities I saw in Arthur: profound insight, great faith, and an even temper. The King had a singleness of purpose that most men can only dream of. He understood that he was placed upon this earth to lead, and he embraced the task fully. Arthur was an individual whose Christian walk often left me wondering if it were he who had actually known Jesus instead of me.

I remember a day when we had been campaigning in the north. An invading Saxon army was moving south toward Avalon. These barbarians were fierce warriors, strong and brave. We were deployed in a defensive posture along a ridge. The enemy was on the rise opposite us. Both sides were positioned so that either adversary would have to move down a slope, then march uphill in order to attack. That morning a heavy mist cloaked the wooded hills as well as the small vale that separated us. The haze was so thick that the scouts could only guess at the enemy's numbers. Though it was apparent that both sides expected a major battle, the day became nothing more than a series of probes and skirmishes, each side searching for weaknesses.

I led an attack against the enemy's left wing, but the fighting was light as the Saxon army remained stationary behind its line of shielded warriors. That afternoon the sun peeked through the clouds on the field and saw our cavalry squadron clash with the Saxons. Although it was a small skirmish on the right flank, the confrontation was ferocious but as brief as a summer rain. No one managed to gain an advantage, and the long day ended in a draw.

The following dawn the fog had cleared, and the enemy leader, Loth, stood on the hill opposite us; his voice boomed across the battlefield. His words resounded throughout the glen in the crisp, clear sunrise. Loth's speech swept over the morning noise of our army. Creaking leather, rattling pans, neighing horses, and grumbling soldiers paused to hear Loth's challenge.

The Saxon paced in front of his army which was already in line along the hill. Loth was tall and exuded strength and courage. It was obvious why men would follow him.

"There is our enemy," the challenger bellowed like Goliath, pointing at us, his words bold and brazen. "They could not defeat us yesterday, and they will not do so today." His tone then became insulting. "But today is the day that I challenge this so-called king to fight me, man to man! If I win, I will rule his tiny kingdom. And if he wins..." A sudden wave of laughter swelled from the Saxon army and filled the vale. They found the very thought of Loth losing to Arthur amusing.

Loth then continued, "Well, if he defeats me, then my men will serve him." And with that, the Saxon general belly-laughed; his army followed in a roar of hysteria.

Loth's echoing words demanded a response. With my many years of experience as a Roman soldier, I had seen this kind of challenge before, but on this occasion Arthur did something that took me by surprise. While most of our knights were angry at the insults, the King simply smiled, then took a white flag and headed across the battlefield toward the invaders. The hooves of our horses thudded as we hurried down the slope to catch Arthur.

"My King," I said, pulling alongside him. "Do you intend to discuss terms with this barbarian?"

"No," Arthur replied. "I must fight him."

"But Sire, you're ignoring your knights, your greatest strength."

"Nonsense, Lancelot," Arthur cried out as we rode, and then he turned to me. "My strength comes from the Lord."

I was taken aback at the truth and depth of the King's words as he charged ahead. I immediately felt embarrassed at my own hubris. How quickly I could be lulled into trusting in my own flesh; how easy it is to become arrogant. I spurred my mount and passed Arthur and the others.

"Make way for the King," I cried above the din of galloping cavalry.

The enemy lines parted, and there stood their leader. Loth was a man of unusual stature, a giant among his own men. He wore a brown, burnished leather breastplate and bronze greaves over his shins but no helmet. Instead, the enemy captain sported long, fiery red hair and a matching beard. He smiled confidently as he saw us approach.

II

Arthur held up his hand, signaling his knights to halt. He looked directly at Loth and without hesitation said, "I accept your challenge. This is between us now." Arthur leapt from his saddle. "My knights will not draw their weapons," he said. "Can you say the same for your men?"

"My men fight only at my command," Loth said, his iron voice hammering out the words.

"Form a shield wall around us!" Arthur commanded.

Both we and the Saxons formed a circle of shields around the two leaders.

Arthur unsheathed his sword while Loth wielded a battle axe. The two warriors stepped toward one another with weapons and shields in hand. Arthur was cautious and calculating while Loth was aggressive and bold. The Saxon moved forward and slashed diagonally with his axe; Arthur quickly stepped back and thrust his sword which was blocked by Loth's shield. The enemy leader moved like a bull, always on the attack as the two opponents battled hand-to-hand. Loth constantly moved forward trying to force the fight.

The axe Loth wielded would have been a two-handed battle axe for most men, but because he had such strength and size, the giant carried it in one hand. Though his weapon was slower and less agile than Arthur's sword, the Saxon swung it with such force that the blow couldn't be parried. Wherever its cutting edge fell it would sever shield, helmet, armor, flesh, and bone; nothing could stay it from its fatal course. The axe was too heavy for Loth to stab and parry with as a sword. Instead the red-headed giant swung it constantly in wide and small arcs, sometimes fast, sometimes slow. He swung the axe frontally and occasionally twisted to the side, always with horizontal or vertical slashes, seeking openings in Arthur's defense. All this Loth did with his right hand while his left hand held a small shield that fended off counterattacks from the King's sword.

While Loth was a brawler, Arthur was not. The King counted on intelligence and quickness. As his opponent would hack away, Arthur would dart and spin. It was obvious that the King was letting his adversary spend himself. Just when it seemed as if the Saxon should be tiring from the constant rocking of his huge battle axe, Loth suddenly switched the axe and shield from right hand to left and vice versa. With the fresh strength of his left arm the Saxon swung furiously at Arthur who barely sidestepped the vicious blows. Much to his chagrin, Arthur discovered that the giant was ambidextrous, a very dangerous opponent.

Though Arthur was quick, he also became fatigued. The contest was almost lost when a wild swing of Loth's axe found Arthur's helmet. The king's headpiece tumbled through the air. The blow was too close as the axe grazed Arthur's cheek, leaving a bloody laceration just below his eye. Stunned for a moment, the King brought up his sword to fend off Loth's following hack, but another powerful swing of the Saxon's axe broke the point of Arthur's blade. Although the sword was still a dangerous slashing weapon, it was now blunted and stabbing would be almost impossible.

Loth smiled and began taunting Arthur. "You're lucky," he said. "But I'm afraid you're about to be dead." The Saxon lifted his axe and feigned a slash, but instead he let the axe handle slide through his hands and tightened them just below its head. Loth then used the top of the weapon's head as a battering ram. A fearful blow to the midsection knocked the King to the ground. Loth again raised his axe, but Arthur twisted and kicked Loth in the stomach, turning him away. As the King regained his footing, the Saxon slashed at him with all of his might, delivering blow after blow; each one would have split Arthur in two had the King not ducked or dodged away. Loth's final wayward swing was so powerful that the axe imbedded itself in the ground. Seizing the opportunity, Arthur brought his sword down on the axe handle, cleaving it in two. Now with only a wooden handle and a small shield, Loth could only defend himself.

Arthur lifted his sword as if to slash. Loth used his shield to block, but instead of following through with the blade, Arthur pulled the Saxon's shield with his left hand. Using this opening, the King punched the Saxon's face with the hilt of his sword. This sent the enemy chieftain sprawling to the ground. Arthur then stomped Loth's chest and put his foot on top of the fallen leader. The King raised his broken sword high in the air as he readied to deliver the coup de maitre.

"Kill him," the knights began to chant. "Kill the invader."

With a mighty heave, Arthur brought the sword down, veering away from the head of his enemy. He plunged the weapon into the ground, missing Loth's face by a whisker.

Arthur's face was flushed with blood, his teeth clenched. "I will not kill him," the King yelled for all to hear. "There will be no death today. Let the laws that rule us all and the code that serves Avalon decide his fate."

The Saxons, seeing their leader lying helpless, grew uneasy. I sensed they might fight, but more strife was averted when Loth began to speak.

"We Saxons are men of our word. I yield to the King, and I ask for the mercy of the laws of this land. My life and my men are yours to do with as you wish. Serve him as you served me," he commanded them.

It was then that I understood just how kingly Arthur was. Not only had he fought this gargantuan beard to beard, but he had bested him. Even after Arthur's bloodlust was up, he had restrained his rage, and he still had the presence of mind to show mercy. The King knew that since he and Loth had fought individual combat, our code and laws dictated that the victor could be as merciful as he wished. Arthur's gambit had worked. Not only had he won the day with no warriors killed from either side, he had swelled our ranks to almost twice what we were before. The Saxons were far better than mere recruits; they were tried and tested soldiers.

Arthur's wisdom won the Saxon army and gained Loth, who would become a valuable knight of the Round Table.

I could not remember when I had last seen such strength in a leader. As I looked upon Arthur's broken sword, I realized that he needed a sword that was worthy of him, the sword that had been Goliath's, the sword that had belonged to King David, the sword of Alaric. I would return to Gaul and bring back the great blade that I had wielded against Attila.

III

I made excuses to leave for Aquitania, and for the entire trip I tried to devise ways that I could present the sword to the King. I considered simply giving it to Arthur, but that might have raised questions. Throughout the years I've almost always been discreet in order to avoid having my secret discovered. Usually it was easy to retire to private life after 20 or 30 years, and then return to the public as my own son. Such contrivances were not always effortless, but they were effective. My possession of this ancient weapon would raise unwelcome questions about my past.

I believe it was the Lord who moved me to give the sword to Arthur. Though the blade was so large that it was difficult to use in combat, it was more than a weapon; it was a symbol of power. I had seen its effect against the Huns. As I retrieved the rapier from its hiding place, I withdrew the magnificent blade from among the great piles of gold and other riches I had pilfered from Alaric's treasure. I gazed upon all of that worldly wealth until my eyes spied the wooden chest in which I had stored the Grail.

I carefully opened the box and gently lifted the golden cup. I removed the wineskin I had tied securely over the rim of the vessel and peered inside. It had been almost five centuries since the crucifixion and yet the blood in the vessel was still fresh. It was the same as the day Mary had collected it as it dripped from Jesus' fingers. I would take it to Camelot with me. I would give this wondrous treasure to the church.

While in the kingdom of the Franks, I purchased bolts of silk, fineries, baubles, and wine. Such gifts delighted the court at Camelot and enabled me to hide the sword and the Lord's Cup upon my return. The Grail I presented to the good priest Merlin. A converted Druid, Merlin was a devout servant of Christ. I explained to him that the Lord had led me to a cave in Gaul where I had found an old oaken chest covered with dust. I made the priest vow that he would tell no one that it was I who brought the Grail to Camelot. Opening the box, Merlin carefully took out the golden goblet.

"What is this writing?" he asked. "I believe it says: *the cup of the Lord.*"

The priest gently removed the Grail from the wineskin. The wineskin too remained new and supple. Merlin was awestruck. He took the Grail and put it in front of the large cross that adorned the chapel.

Word of the Holy Grail traveled fast throughout the kingdom, and the chapel became a site for pilgrims to come and pray. One day the King had his dying sister brought to the chapel. She told Arthur that she had had a dream that if she touched the blood in the Grail, she would be healed. While on a litter, Morgan took her little finger and barely touched the surface of the blood in the flagon. Instantly, she sat up and began to praise the Lord.

Afterwards, the sick, the deaf, the blind, and the dumb came for prayer and a drop of Jesus' blood. Some at court insisted that the blood would run out and that it should only be reserved for important people, but Merlin refuted such arguments, saying that the Lord cared for all, rich and poor. One day after praying for and healing countless throngs of people, there was no blood left in the cup. It was dry.

Early the next morning, pilgrims had lined up outside of the chapel which had now become a shrine. Merlin, heartsick that the Grail was empty, opened the doors sadly, prepared to turn people away. He peered into the Grail again, and to his amazement, it was full.

"A miracle, a miracle!" he shouted. The blood in the Grail had renewed itself.

IV

Meanwhile, the sword remained hidden as I had found no good way to discreetly present the weapon to Arthur. With the return of the spring berries, the King asked me to go hunting with him. There were to be no squires, no other knights, just Arthur and me.

It may sound silly, but I had been praying about the sword and Arthur. For months I hadn't felt it was the right time to give it to him, but oddly enough I felt moved to bring it with us for the hunt. Though I had to hide it in a blanket roll beneath some spears, the King suspected nothing as we left. I didn't know what to expect.

We traveled northwest for several days before we arrived at a series of ponds and a lake that sat amidst a primeval forest. Arthur and I split up. He traveled south along the water's edge, while I went north. The area was serene, and as I circumvented the shoreline, I could see someone at the northernmost point of the large lake. As I drew near, it became obvious that what I saw was too large to be a person. It was a statue of a beautiful woman, and the warm breeze from the lake hummed a song as it caressed her.

Unlike other statues, this figure wasn't made of marble; it was carved from the trunk of an ancient oak, now long dead. The girth of the olden tree was almost twice the height of a man. The roots of its once-great trunk reached into the ground like massive fingers prying into the earth. At the base of the woman's feet were two inscriptions, one in some archaic text that I couldn't decipher; the other just below it was in old Latin script. It read: *The Lady of the Lake.*

The carved maiden was larger than life, almost twice the size of a normal woman. She was exquisitely graceful. The taupe-colored carving stood upright, leaning out toward and overlooking the lake; her goddess-like hair looked as if the wind were blowing it away from the water. Her willowy sculpted tresses were fashioned from hundreds of long, interwoven branches. Such craftsmanship had been done lifetimes before, when the tree was still alive. Now, many years later, the graceful carving's gown still billowed as if blown by angel's breath.

As beautiful as the hewn gentlewoman was, her most striking feature, her eyes, peered out across the lake. She looked so eerily alive that I almost expected her to turn and stare at me. The woman's arms, which must have been tree limbs at one time, had been so skillfully wrought that they looked real, her palms up as if presenting an offering to the Lord. She was more than a wooden sculpture, more than a work of art. There was a peaceful presence and awe about her akin to what one feels upon seeing the ocean for the first time.

As I sat atop Bark, immersed in the serenity of the beauty and grace of the Lady of the Lake, the Lord spoke to me in a still, small voice. Somehow I understood that the Lady should give Arthur the sword. So I stood up in my saddle, took the great blade, and laid it in her outstretched hands.

The next morning the King and I were to begin our hunt, but there was a strange stillness around us. No birds sang, and the rest of nature's background noise was muted.

I motioned for silence and whispered, "Be still, my King, for we are being watched."

We then spied a late prowling lynx which must have frightened the birds. We laughed at our warrior's caution and proceeded to join our horses for the day's hunt. We were dressed only in our leather hunting tunics and breeches. Arthur and I had brought bows and arrows as well as spears. As we tightened our saddles, the forest magically began to move.

A host of Druids suddenly surrounded us. Some were armed with spears, others with bows. These men were so well camouflaged in their dark green cloaks and tree branches that neither Arthur nor I had detected their presence. I turned to the King, but he was already a prisoner. There was no fight. Our hands and feet were bound with vines as the leaders met to decide our fate.

At first the pagans spoke in an old tongue, one I could recall only in my distant memory of 400 years before. The only word I could specifically remember was one that meant "sacrifice." I could only surmise that we were both to be killed. As the leaders spoke, an argument ensued. From what I could tell there were two leaders. One was tall and lanky as a pine, the other shorter and stout as a stump. The short man did not wish to kill us. The longer they talked, the louder and more heated the debate grew; the two finally began to speak in language we could understand.

"This is the King and his knight just as we were told by the Witch of the White Stag," one said. "We should take them to the Lady of the Lake and sacrifice them."

"Kill the King? Should we not ransom him?" the other said.

"He cannot be King! How can a Christian be a Druid king? The Witch demands their sacrifice."

While the debate continued, Arthur and I sat with our ankles and wrists tied together. All of the Druid followers stood and jostled in the clearing, grunting their approval or dissention as their leaders quarreled. The young Druid guarding us forgot his prisoners and rushed forward to join the others in the argument which grew louder and more hostile. Like our kidnappers, the guard carried a silver sickle, a weapon that could be used to harvest mistletoe as well as for sacrifice. The instrument fell from the man's belt.

V

I edged forward slightly and retrieved the glimmering tool from the ground. By now the argument had become violent, and as the two leaders came to blows, I managed to cut my own bonds quietly with the curved instrument and then severed those of my King.

A moment later we were slipping away to our mounts, but the ease of our escape was short lived. Someone shouted, "They're escaping!"

We flew like the wind, running toward the horses at the end of the clearing. Arthur reached his mount first. Mine was just beyond when I heard the familiar sound of arrows whistling through the air. The King reached his saddle as a Druid appeared, ready to unleash an arrow at Arthur. I lunged in front of the King, the bolt lodging itself in my shoulder.

Crude shaft jutting from my back, I staggered toward Arthur, who pulled me onto his horse.

"Hold on," he said.

I gripped the saddle and was dragged along the ground until Arthur, by pure strength, pulled me up over the rear of the horse.

"We'll never be able to escape them with two of us on one horse," I moaned.

"God will provide a way," Arthur said.

I held on to the King with my right arm. My left arm was limp.
We rode along a path that took us north and came out just behind the Lady of the Lake.

"What's this?" Arthur said, staring at the wooden maiden who faced the blue water. She stood like an angel on the shore, overlooking the lake, and in her hands, an offering; she held King David's sword. The sunlight shone upon her and the blade gleamed in her hands as we drew near.

"I've heard tales of the Lady of the Lake," Arthur said. "But I've never seen her until now. She holds the sword of a great warrior. By my faith, Lancelot, you are my best knight. The sword must surely be for you."

"Arthur," I muttered. The pain in my back was still sharp as a knife. "She holds the sword of a King." I slid to the ground.

Suddenly the Druids were upon us again. They had followed us along the shore.

"There they are!" one shouted as they began to run toward us.

Arthur quickly guided his mount beneath the outstretched arms of the Lady of the Lake, reached up with both hands and wrested the sword from the statue. Perhaps it was the wind, perhaps it was that I was dazed, but it looked as if the carved Lady actually leaned down to bestow the sword upon the King.

"Look," the tall Druid leader shouted. "The Lady presents the King with a great sword."

"It can only be a sword of great power. He is King," the stout one yelled.

As if on cue, Arthur took the great weapon and held it aloft, straight in the air. The sun gleamed off of the shiny blade as every one of the pagans dropped to his knees.

"But what about the Witch?" I heard the tall commander ask.

"What about her?" the stout pagan leader responded. "This is a sign from the Lady of the Lake."

The Druids immediately became respectful and humbly asked the King's forgiveness. These strange priests of the woodland took me and put a soothing salve on my wound. What should have been a fatal wound healed so quickly that they believed it was another sign from the Lady. This is how Arthur united both the Saxons and the Druids to bring peace throughout the land.

VI

The following day we were on our way back to Camelot. As we stopped to rest along the way, Arthur took out the sword again, obviously in awe of the great blade.

"This must have been made for a giant," the King said as he held the heavy sword.

The truth of the matter was so humorous that I had to laugh.

"Why are you laughing?" the King asked.

"No reason. I find great joy in the way God chooses to work," I chuckled.

"The sword is beautiful. I've never seen anything like it," the King said as he examined the shining blade. "Look at the width, and the hilt is exquisite. The craftsmanship is so intricate and so beautifully wrought that it must have belonged to a king."

"I believe our Lord had it fashioned for you from the days of old."

"God has blessed me," Arthur whispered. "I am undeserving of such great favor."

"God is able to do more than we can ask or think," I said. "The fact that you understand and are awed by God's grace is why you have such favor. It is why He chose you to be King."

Arthur paused for a moment and gave thanks to God. We then prayed for the kingdom.

Once back in Camelot there were grim tidings: the Holy Grail had been stolen, and Merlin was nowhere to be found. We scoured the castle, the chase, and the villages near Camelot but found nothing. We knew only that the Grail was missing. We did not know what had happened to Merlin. Signs of a struggle suggested that the Priest had been abducted.

Even though the Grail was missing, excitement over the great sword spread throughout the realm. The King had his finest sword makers examine the weapon. We all knew that the hilt was beautifully wrought gold and brass, but the blade was the finest steel any of the smiths had seen. No one but I knew the meaning of the small Hebrew inscription that said the sword had belonged to King David.

Arthur declared that the blade was from God, so it was placed behind the throne of the King in a granite boulder carved into the shape of a clinched fist. The fist's polished stonework was beautiful, and at the base of the hand was the name that had been chosen for the sword. Chiseled into the rock was the word *Caliburnus*, a derivative of a word from the Welch tongue *calad* or hard, and the Latin *burnus* for "steel." Eventually the sword became known as Excalibur.

Since Excalibur was difficult to wield in combat, it became the Royal Sword and was used in processions and ceremonies. The weapon stood upright in the great boulder behind the royal seat, the blade's shaft pointing straight down, its haft forming a cross directly behind the highest point of the throne. Only Arthur was permitted to remove Excalibur from its stony sheath. Throughout the land the sword was called The Sword of the Stone.

Although Excalibur was a powerful symbol, all of Camelot was devastated at the loss of the Cup of the Lord as well as the loss of Merlin. Arthur held a council of the knights and charged each of us with the task of finding the Grail. The entire Round Table became obsessed with finding the Holy Grail, none more than myself. Stories of sightings of the Grail or of Merlin often prompted knights to ride off, seeking answers. We searched for years, but we never found the cup, and we never discovered what had happened to Merlin.

Guinevere

Stolen water is sweet; food eaten in secret is delicious. Proverbs 9:17

I

Over the years I became like a brother to Arthur. We fought together, supped together and fellowshipped together. There were great battles, wonderful feasts, and incredible adventures. The kingdom was at its zenith, a time of prosperity and safety. There was an abundance of food and comfort.

I introduced two games to the court. The Roman dice game *tesserae* became popular, but it was *lantrunculi*, a game much like chess, that fascinated the court. Because of the nature of the game and the exquisite wood-carved pieces, courtiers considered playing it to be genteel and elegant. Arthur and I enjoyed many battles on the chessboard and became friendly rivals. The other knights were fond of it as well. It was a happy kingdom, a joyous time. Arthur was a great king and a wise ruler. Camelot prospered, but success does not always bring out the best in us. Petty jealousies arose among the knights of the order, especially against me.

It was a well known fact that I was a pet of the court, especially of the Queen. I never gave my love for the Queen an opportunity to be seen as anything but courtly love, and I managed to conceal my feelings from the rest of the Table. I could not, unfortunately, hide my love from Guinevere, nor could I disguise those feelings from her beautiful sister. More than once I saw Hecate's scarlet-browed blue eyes take note of the stolen glances between the Queen and myself. When I was with Arthur, I placed Guinevere in an unseen corner of my mind. When I was with Guinevere, I forgot about Arthur.

One warm summer's day the tapestry of life in Avalon began to unravel. I was riding in the wood north of the castle late one July afternoon. I often rode in the primeval chase surrounding Camelot. It was a beautiful and tranquil wooded place where one could meditate and pray. The heat was intense that day. The earth's warmth shimmered near the shore of the chase's tranquil lake which glistened in the afternoon sun. My solitude was interrupted by giggling voices coming from a nearby cove. I went to investigate and as I neared the water, the female voices grew louder. Quietly, I moved to the edge of the wood, peered through the greenery, and sat unseen behind a shrub.

Before me were the Queen, Hecate, and two attendants preparing to bathe. The moment turned inwards. I froze, hypnotized. Guinevere's beauty had never been in question in my mind, but I had always fought the urge to think beyond her knee-length sunlit tresses. Her angelic, aquiline face and golden eyes were stunning amidst the ancient, pristine setting. Before that moment, I had always been able to temper my thoughts. She was my Queen, and Arthur was not only my King but my best friend.

Now Guinevere was standing in front of me, disrobing. I do not know if she intended to be seductive, but her manner was so sensuous that she might have known she was being watched. The attendants helped her and Hecate undress. They were voluptuous in every possible way. My eyes led me onward to

158

my sin. My kindled desire overpowered my guilt as I became a willing voyeur. Finally, Hecate and Guinevere stood before me perfectly revealed. Their beauty blinded me from my purpose, prayer and meditation.

Completely still, I could hear my own heartbeat, my blood pumping as I sat gazing at Guinevere and Hecate in all their loveliness. Both women were flawless, but I couldn't take my eyes away from the Queen. She was enchanting. The lake reflected her image against the blue sky, and she looked up as she untied her hair, letting it fall slowly, gracefully. She stood next to the edge of the lake, serene, beautiful.

"The water's so warm." A voice startled me from my trance. It was one of the attendants.

She looked directly at the shrub that concealed me and then again fell back into the water.

"It is quite wonderful," the silken voice of the Queen responded as she slid into the water.

Waist deep, she turned to face me as she arched her back and dipped her hair into the water. She then fell back in the lake and stood up again, the clear liquid caressing the curves of her body. She looked directly at the shrub that concealed me and then again fell back into the water.

I was breathless as I watched for some time; it was intoxicating. Long after the Queen and her attendants had gone back to the castle, I was still there, drunk on passion. I had initially gone there to pray, but sin is never very far away. That summer the women went to the lake to bathe frequently, and the scene repeated itself each time. I became obsessed with the Queen, but at the same time I loathed myself for violating the oath I had sworn to Arthur. He was my friend, my King. But I couldn't stop thinking of Guinevere.

II

Against my will, my mind began to make plans to betray my friend and to betray my God. I tried to fight it, but I lost the battle. I gave in to lust. In anguish I fought the urge to go into the chase, but I succumbed. Temptation overtook me like a rider on a swift horse. For the rest of the summer, any time the Queen went to bathe I fought desire but inevitably found myself there, yielding to temptation, like David watching Bathsheba. It was late that month when the forces of wantonness and desire aligned the circumstances for our capitulation.

Arthur, the knights, and most of the garrison had gone north to deal with some raiders. Because he feared for the safety of Camelot and the Queen, I was left in charge of a small garrison—our orders to keep both the Queen and Camelot safe. How ironic that I would be the one to destroy them both.

The Queen had once again gone to bathe at the lake. I had taken up my usual perch behind the shrubs close by. It was beautiful that afternoon, warm and peaceful, the light sparkling on the water. The Queen and Hecate had just arrived, Guinevere disrobing to her underclothing, when the maiden Jean began to shout.

"Look!" she said, pointing to the eastern shore of the lake. "It's the stag. It's the stag of legend!" she exclaimed.

There, standing next to the shoreline was a massive white hart, its huge antlers proudly adorning the mystical beast as king of the wood. The animal stood there, its deep blue eyes staring at the four women.

"We must give chase," said Lady Hecate. "It's waiting for us."

"But we cannot leave the Queen," the maiden Brynn said.

"You can hardly give chase dressed like that," Hecate said, pointing to the Queen who was undressing. "This is a divine moment that awaits us."

"You all must go. Now hurry!" said Guinevere. "I'll be all right."

Lifting their ankle-length dresses, the women daintily ran toward the animal. The beautiful creature didn't stir, but as Hecate and the two attendants neared, the deer turned and trotted a few steps up the hill near a clearing, slowing to turn around and look at the women who followed after.

"It is beckoning us," Jean said.

"Hurry! Hurry!" said Hecate. "We are being summoned by the gods."

The process continued with the beast drawing the attendants away from the lake, stopping and turning until they were all lost from sight. I sat in complete stillness, observing the Queen as she removed the final article of her clothing. Once done, she turned toward the shrub behind which I sat and began to walk toward it, stopping to pick daisies as she came up the slope.

Guinevere was so pure and beautiful, placing the flowers in her auburn colored hair. She looked angelic as she continued picking the white and yellow blossoms, drawing nearer, ever nearer to my hiding place. I held my breath to quiet my rapidly beating pulse. I was silent as the fire of love burned through my veins, the object of my desire within my grasp. A few feet away, she turned toward the slope which the white stag had crowned so recently. I'll never forget what Guinevere said no matter how long I live. She was so nonchalant that I was completely caught off guard.

"Lancelot," she said, a willing Bathsheba. "Are we ever to become lovers or am I only to be your Queen?"

Her words hung in the air, like honey slowly dripping from the bough of a tree. Then she reached through the shrub with her hands. I looked at her golden eyes which locked onto mine. I was mesmerized as a part of me wanted to turn away, but the fear and the guilt burned away with the heat of love. I stood up, drawn into her eyes, and I took her in my arms.

III

The scene was magical: the warm orange sun, the yellow daisies in her dark chestnut hair, the caressing sound of the water lapping against the shore, the warm summer air, the deep golden gaze from the most beautiful woman I'd ever met. Time stood absolutely still. And then, with a fire I hadn't felt in centuries, our lips met. There was a violent power in our kiss that I can't describe, and in that searing moment, every trace of loyalty for God, King, and friend vanished. All semblance of honor left me. In all these years, I've never known such passion. Afterward we gazed into each other's eyes.

"This is not the first time I have spied on you," I confessed.

"I know," she said. "I could tell you were there that first day almost two months ago."

"You've known since then?" I asked.

"Don't you know that I've been in love with you since you first arrived at Camelot?" she said. "Do you remember when your sword was stolen, the morning before your trial in combat? Squire Robert, Maid Jean's paramour, recognized your blade among the others in the armory. When he told Maid Jean, she informed me, and I had the weapon sent to you as quickly as possible. I was so afraid you'd be forced to leave Camelot. I thought I would go mad without you."

She kissed me full on the lips, then again, hard and passionately. I met her embrace equally.

"I have loved you from the first time I saw you. I've been torn between my love for you, my duty-bound honor to my God, and my loyalty to Arthur," I whispered.

"Oh Lancelot, I too have wept and prayed to remain true. But my love for you overwhelms my prayers."

As we lay there in each other's arms, we declared our love. I sat up, pulling her to me, and I noticed something on the ground, protruding from the leafy underbrush. I bent down and picked up what was a piece of a stag's antler. It was curved, and it resembled a heart that had been cut in two. The antler was pure white and had three points, one at the top, one at the bottom and one that jutted outwardly from the horn's curve, like a thorn. That point was blood red.

"It's so pure," I said, examining the horn.

"It's beautiful," Guinevere said, clasping it in her hands. "I shall treasure it."

We heard a rustling in the wood and saw the white stag standing directly behind us. The beast was only an arm's length away, shining majestically in the sunlight, its cold blue eyes glinted like frost.

"Hecate and the others won't be far behind," I said. "I have to leave."

We jumped to our feet, and I hurriedly began to dress. I was desperately in love. But I thought of Arthur and felt the guilt return, heavier than ever before, for I had now crossed a threshold. Nothing would ever be the same.

"Hecate will be so excited," Guinevere said giddily.

I froze. "The Lady Hecate?" I asked.

"Yes, when I tell her about us."

"You intend to tell Lady Hecate about us?" I asked dubiously, my blood now cold.

"Oh yes. We keep nothing from each other."

"*You* may share everything with *her*, but I doubt…"

"She is my sister," the Queen interrupted. "Besides, she arranged this."

"What do you mean?"

"Hecate has known for years that I've loved you; she suspected that you loved me as well. My sister came to me in June and told me that it was your custom to go into the chase each afternoon during the summer. We both agreed that it would be normal for the Queen to bathe frequently here and that you might be emboldened to declare your love under the right circumstances. She was right," she said, staring at me.

I was dumbfounded.

"But don't worry," Guinevere said. "Hecate is my sister and confidant."

I kissed her again as we parted. And although I'm not sure if the Eden-like setting really changed, it suddenly looked drastically different, spoiled and ravaged. My guilt and my shame grew heavier with each step, and I had a leaden, uneasy feeling about Lady Hecate's role in this affair.

IV

Hecate was a lady by definition: she was the sister of the Queen. It was rumored she dabbled in the black arts. Courtiers said Hecate's practice of witchcraft caused her engagement to Arthur's brother, Prince Urbanus, to dissolve, and no man would marry her despite her beauty. Common people claimed to have seen her dancing with a two-legged deer in the moonlight, one of the pagan rites of the Druids. The commoners feared the woman. Whenever a calf died or a tool broke, they whispered that Hecate had cursed them with a spell. She was almost as beautiful as Guinevere, more alluring in some ways. While Guinevere was auburn-haired and fair-skinned, Hecate was a flaming redhead with skin as pale as an opal. Her features were sharp: pointed chin, high cheekbones, and a short nose. She was pixyish in a way, but much harder, stern, as if her beauty had been chiseled from a glacier.

Hecate had made advances in my direction more than once. Not long after I first arrived at Camelot, she had arranged to be alone with me on several occasions. The first time she asked me if I found her fairness pleasing. I told her that her beauty was nonpareil but that such a countenance would inhibit me from my knightly obligation to Arthur and the Round Table.

A year later she asked me if I had ever considered taking a wife, and if I thought she were attractive. Again I assured her of her beauty; however, I made a mistake in telling her that my heart belonged to another. The look she gave me was demonic. Her penetrating blue eyes set like flint, aflame with rage and hatred. I feared I had created another enemy at Camelot. I was sure of it when I saw her with Sir Mordred.

Now that I had committed adultery, I suspected that Hecate would use my sin against me and Guinevere. But like the fool whose burned hand goes warily back to the fire, I found it impossible to keep my distance from the Queen. My attraction to her was an addiction. After being with Arthur for so long, Guinevere was as giddy as a maiden at first love. We both knew the King was campaigning in the north for a limited time, and we desired to be together whenever possible.

The next two months were wonderful and horrible. I was in love, and when Guinevere and I were together: duty, vows, common sense, routine, everything fell by the wayside in the wake of our infidelity. When apart, I knew my obligations were to God, Arthur, and Camelot. I knew I was breaking my vows of knighthood. More importantly, I knew I was sinning against God. I knew I was wrong and there would be a price to pay. I wanted to stop. I was sick with grief for my dishonor, and I pretended to ignore the low, dark clouds looming on the horizon. I was willingly seduced by my lust.

Each night that I was with Guinevere made my need for her greater. Every time I left her I asked God for forgiveness and for the strength to resist temptation, promising myself that I would leave Camelot. I knew the proverb: *whoever touches another man's wife shall not be innocent*, yet I ignored it for my own desires. I was torn between loving a God I knew personally, a God whose Son had brought me back from hell, and loving His creation, a beautiful woman, another man's wife. I remembered Jesus' words: *The spirit is willing, but the flesh is weak.* I knew the affair would end badly, that the cost would be too great to bear, but I was weak.

While Guinevere and I were able to constrain ourselves at court, rumors of our illicit love swirled like March winds, and knowing glances from Hecate, her new lover Sir Mordred, and other ladies at court suggested that our love was no longer a secret.

In Flagrante

...be sure your sin will find you out. Numbers 32:23

I

I had packed most of my belongings and had the squire prepare my mount. I entered the heart of Camelot for what I believed would be the last time. In my leather vest and riding breeches, I had gone into the great hall to have one final look and to make sure all was as it should be. The red cinders were settling, and their orange glow cast a sunset sheen on the round table. I tossed two oak logs into the pit and sat staring into the hungry flames. My guilt was so heavy that I had to leave Avalon before I did any more damage. How could I have sinned against God and hurt my King, my friend? How could I ruin everything? I was a thief, taking what was given to another man by God. Even if I could have stayed, even if I could have had Guinevere for my very own, how could I live knowing what would happen? Guinevere would grow old and die before my eyes, and I would again become a helpless spectator. I'd been in love many times; sometimes I'd resisted. But I'd never felt this way before. Was it because she was forbidden?

I sat and revisited my loves, my pain. Why did it have to be me? Why couldn't I have died all those years ago? I lost myself in morose contemplation, staring at the dancing flames and listening to the garrulous fire hiss and crackle. My reminiscing was interrupted when I heard the door to the great hall creak open. I peered into the muted shadows, but they revealed nothing. Like a candle, Guinevere's voice lit up the darkness.

"Lancelot, 'tis I," said the Queen, her words like a song.

My heart leapt and fell in the same instant. She stood next to me, wearing a long, white silken gown; the satiny touch of Guinevere's fingers ran through my hair.

"Are you leaving?" her voice quavered. "I was told your squire was readying your horse."

"Does Hecate have eyes in every room in the castle?"

"So it must be true," she said, teary eyed.

I swallowed hard and said, "I cannot stay."

Guinevere gently pressed my head to her bosom, holding me, caressing me. I stared into the fire, avoiding her eyes. Then I felt her teardrops raining on my cheek. Weeping, she sat down next to me, taking my hands in her own, her liquid eyes streaming, her lips parting with trepidation as she trembled.

"Take me with you," she whispered.

"You cannot leave. You're the Queen."

"You are my love, and if I cannot be near you, I cannot live."

We held each other, seeking the healing comfort that all lovers seek from one another.

"I will not ask you to live your life in exile," I said.

"We can go away, far away from here."

"You would leave your kingdom to be with me?"

"I cannot live without you; I will follow you."

Brushing a tear from her cheek, I slid my hand behind her neck and pulled her close. I should have turned and left, but instead I kissed the Queen passionately and thought about taking her to the far away capital of the eastern Roman Empire, Constantinople.

With a sinking feeling at my core, my voice was low and dry. "How soon can you be ready?" I asked.

"I need only one night. I must put my affairs in some kind of order and write a letter to Arthur. He will return in three days. We can ride to Londinium where we can find a ship to cross the channel. But we must do it before he returns. I cannot bear the thought of seeing him hurt, and I would not then have the strength to leave him."

I knew we were venturing even further into sin, and a voice from within warned me of dire consequences. I ignored it.

"You shall be mine, and I shall be yours," I said, knowing that she would perish with age while I lived on. I held her tightly as she began to cry, but her sobs became whisperings of love.

"Come to my chambers. We shall have our last night of love here at Camelot," she said, sliding her hands slowly and seductively around my shoulders. Her lips sparked the flames of love as she covered my face and neck with kisses.

The firelight teasingly accented the curves and suppleness of Guinevere's figure as she left the room for her apartment. I was persuaded to wait another night; I was drunk from the liquor of love. I turned and slipped up the castle steps, sneaking into the Queen's chambers, giving her time to excuse her attendants as I had often done before.

We kissed passionately in the dim light of her room and held each other in a quiet embrace for hours before finally falling asleep.

II

I had a disturbing dream that boiled in my mind. In the dream, someone was trying to get into the castle. I could not wake up. The gate was opening and two shadowy figures stood peering from a gray light. Groggily I tried to awaken myself. When I finally did, flickering torchlight at my feet revealed Arthur and Sir Mordred standing at the foot of the bed, an empty expression on Arthur's bearded face, a smirk on Mordred's. The King held a piece of parchment in his hand which he let fall to the ground before he turned quietly and staggered from the room like a man run through with a sword. Torch in hand, Mordred turned and followed.

In the yellow light of the chamber, I looked over at Guinevere who now was also awake.

"How could this be?" she asked.

I picked up the paper, reading it aloud in the fading light:

165

My Beloved Guinevere,
  I am retiring from the field early so that I might gain two evenings with you. How I have missed you. The campaign went well, but I thought only of you.
    Arthur

"Did you know about this letter?" I asked, holding it in my fist.

"I never saw it before," she said.

"Hecate!"

"She would not do anything to harm me."

"Are you sure? Then she must seek to harm me and the King. What other explanation is there? I must go and speak to Arthur."

"And what will you tell him that he does not already know? That you forced me to break my vows as Queen? He knows better."

"I have made you an adulterer; it was of my own doing," I said.

"I committed adultery in my heart the first time I saw you," she said, tears streaming.

"You must get dressed. We must leave."

"You must go alone," she said. "I cannot leave, not like this. I told you I would not have the strength to leave if he returned. In Arthur's presence I am his subject and bound by my covenant."

"But the scandal..."

"Yes," she interrupted, the distance between us suddenly as deep and wide as a chasm. "The cost will be great."

My heart fell. Only moments before, Guinevere and I were ready to embark on our new life together. Now she was suddenly distant, the Queen. I had convinced myself that our expressions of love were tender and beautiful, but now the veil was torn away and I saw our actions for what they were, illicit and ruinous. In the back of my mind I had known our affair would be disastrous, but I had been selfish and weak.

I was stunned. My mind swam in a sea of guilt and shame. "What have I done?" I murmured in a state of shock. I left the room and staggered down the stone steps that led to the great hall.

The King was sitting in his place at the head of the Round Table, his back to me, staring at the fire's embers, dawn creeping into the castle. I stood silently, not knowing what to say. I had come to Avalon to serve a King. Instead I had betrayed him.

"So you are the friend who sticks closer than a brother?" Arthur said with a sarcastic laugh. "I thought you were my friend, the champion of honor and loyalty. And I left you here to protect the Queen and the kingdom." Arthur looked to the floor with a laugh that was low and sardonic. "You were my brother in faith. I thought your heart was so pure that in my mind I imagined you actually knew our Savior. Now this! The faith I thought we shared made me blind to the evil in you. You have stolen her from me, Lancelot. My Guinevere. My Greensleeves."

I loathed myself and my duplicity. Tears streamed down my face, full of regret and shame. Sin blinds us to the depths of harm and injury it causes until it is too late.

"Forgive me," I uttered meekly, my heart sick as I turned and faced my own wickedness. How had it come to this? My own lust had let sin take root when I had first spied upon Guinevere bathing. Now I seethed with self hatred, fully aware of the injury I had caused. I went to the stable, saddled my horse, and left Camelot in disgrace.

Sanctuary

...if he have committed sins, they shall be forgiven him. James 5:15

I

For the next year I lived as a hermit in the abandoned cottage that I'd inhabited years before when I first arrived in Avalon as the Green Knight. I kept to myself, living as a recluse. The heaviness of my sin was crushing. It weighed on me daily like a nauseating darkness. How could I have done what I did? How could I have turned my back on my faith, my duty, my honor? How could I have betrayed my God, my King, my Queen, and my friend? How could I? I, who had known the Savior personally. I mourned sorrowfully. I fasted and prayed, asking God to forgive me.

Yet even at the doorway of repentance, I held on to a seed of anger and hate. The thought of Hecate made my jaw clench and my mind burn with loathing. I had convinced myself that it had been her meddling that had brought all this about, instead of my own lust and duplicity. My bitterness grew because I needed someone to blame. I felt like such a hypocrite, knowing that a part of me would want to do it all again if it meant I could have Guinevere. Such is the power of love even when wrong.

Early on one cold sunny day, I walked to the village livery to purchase some leather. The air was crisp and dry, and the patchy bed of snow that lay on the ground was frozen. The blacksmith was stoking the fire when I overheard him talking to Fergus the ostler.

"There's been little law for almost six months now," the blacksmith said.

"Aye, not since half the knights have sworn allegiance to Mordred."

"Sir Mordred and his lot will carry out the sentence some time in the late afternoon," the smithy continued. "I'll be closing in a while. People from all the villages will turn out to see the Queen's execution."

"The Queen? Executed?" I asked.

"Aye man, have you not heard she was found guilty of treason?"

"By whom?" I asked.

"By the law and Sir Mordred's court."

I was thunderstruck at the news. I turned and left immediately, retracing my steps as quickly as I could. The return trip to my cottage seemed twice as long as I replayed over and over my role in Guinevere's guilt. I felt as if a great hammer had knocked the breath from my body. I was on foot, but I hurried as quickly as I could. I had to ride to Camelot. I stopped only to saddle Bark and take my sword, riding only in my monk's cloak.

I rode my mount at break-neck speed, pushing the poor animal so hard I thought his heart might burst. The journey seemed endless, but I arrived at the castle by mid-afternoon. Peasants were pouring in through the gate, all coming to see the Queen. I entered unrecognizable to everyone as I hadn't cut my hair or shaved since the day I left Camelot.

I entered the castle freely as there were no guards; the place was deserted save for a chambermaid who eyed me warily when she saw me. I entered the great hall only to see Arthur, sitting in the same position as when I had left him a year before, his back to the door, his figure silhouetted by the afternoon sun.

"My King," I said as I knelt.

He turned and looked at me coldly. "Lancelot? I was hoping you'd come." His voice was impotent. Arthur looked pale; his eyes were expressionless.

"How can you ever forgive me?" I asked.

"There's no time for that, no time. You'll be too late to save her."

I was stunned at how aged and powerless Arthur looked; the life had been drained out of him.

"How could you sentence the Queen to death?" I stammered.

"It was you who sentenced her to death." The fire of anger kindled briefly in his eyes; then Arthur looked down, the brief fire again drowned in his despair. The King managed to speak in slow and measured words. "Mordred. Sir Mordred's scheming used the law against her, against me, against you and our whole nation. The law says any crime against the King is treason. You have also been sentenced. Sir Mordred's court has made him and his followers the richest men in the land. There is no justice. You must go and rescue her if you can. Take her to the Convent of St. Agnes; there she will find sanctuary. The knights loyal to me will not stop you, but Mordred and his men will kill you both without hesitation. Save her!" Arthur implored.

II

I turned and ran from the castle to my mount, and spurring his sides violently, raced to the keep. From a distance I spied the Queen being led forth in leather bonds like a common criminal. The crowd was divided over the execution. Many were crying for mercy, others antagonistic and angry. I slowed and guided my steed through the roil of humanity; the closer I came to Guinevere, the thicker the masses of people. Then, in blind haste I spurred Bark through the masses without regard for the innocents who might be hurt. People screamed, bullied out of the way by my steed. The throngs parted like the Red Sea before me. Those who failed to move were trampled as I pushed forward to the Queen.

I could see Sir Mordred and his knights who were all on foot. They were obviously disconcerted by the commotion, caught up in the panic of the masses. Mordred was visibly shocked when I suddenly appeared before him on horseback. He looked incredulous as I drew my sword and brought it down sidewise on his helmet, knocking him unconscious. Sir Lucius, who led the Queen, tried vainly to pull me from my saddle, but I kicked him down under the hooves of my horse. Mordred's other lackeys stood by and did nothing. As I neared Guinevere, Bark skittered nervously.

I had hoped to pull the Queen up, when unexpectedly I saw her lifted above the crowd. Beneath her I saw Sir Ektor and Sir Percival bear her aloft and place her belly-down across the neck of my mount. I harshly tugged the reins, and the horse reared, the onlookers once again opening a passage before us. I headed for the gate, faintly hearing someone yelling for the archers to shoot me.

I heard an arrow whiz by as I rode, trying to shield the Queen. A sharp twinge made me quiver as a shaft found my right side. The pain meant nothing as my heart raced and we galloped away from Camelot. When I was sure we weren't followed, we stopped. I eased the Queen to the ground then cut the leather straps from her wrists. She pulled the arrow from my side.

"Why did you come for me? I was ready to die for my sin," she said, as I pulled her up on the saddle directly behind me.

"The Nazarene already did that," I said, as we were once again on the move.

"Where are we going?" she asked.

"You will find sanctuary at the Convent of St. Agnes. It is the only place where you will be safe. We must move quickly."

"Oh Lancelot, this last year has been...I'm so ashamed. Arthur was so devastated. He is no longer himself. I never dreamed that it would come to this."

"Dreams are for the immortals. We can live only moment by moment, and try to right any wrongs we have committed, my Queen."

Arms draped around me, Guinevere held on as we rode through the wood, away from the main road, finally arriving at the convent under the cover of darkness. I knocked repeatedly until someone opened the door, an older woman with gray hair. She bore a torch and beckoned us enter.

"You are the Queen," she said to Guinevere. "We freely and openly offer you sanctuary."

"You have my gratitude," said the Queen. "I place myself in your care with the hope that I may one day become a sister. Now, if I might have a moment with this knight."

The abbess stepped back and bowed, leaving us in the torchlight of the foyer.

"How did you come to be convicted of treason?" I asked.

"Sir Mordred insisted. As the offended party, the King forgave the offense, but Mordred argued that it was more than a crime against the person. He contended that the crime was against the crown and state. I was tried and found guilty. You were to be hunted down and killed. Where will *you* go?"

"I don't know."

"I wonder what would have happened had we left that night," she said.

"We were never meant to be together. I had no right. I took what was not mine."

"I loved you, Lancelot."

"I will never love another as I have loved you, my Queen."

As badly as I desired to take her in my arms, I refrained, fighting the temptation to take her with me.

As she offered her hand, I took it and knelt, holding it next to my cheek.

"Please forgive me," I whispered.

"There is no ill between us. Our guilt is shared. Forgiveness isn't needed."

I looked at her, my lost love, tears trailing down her pale cheeks. I gently kissed her hand and walked out the door of the convent.

Vengeance

For the wages of sin is death. Romans 6:23

I

I found a small, austere monastery in Scotland where I could lead a simple life once again. The weight of my sin was so great I could barely function. Each day I asked for forgiveness, knowing that God would absolve me but realizing that remission for me was to be a long road. My shameful actions followed me every waking hour and haunted me in my dreams for years. I was weighed down by my folly.

I had given up all the trappings of knighthood, repented, and lived as one of the brethren of St. Phillip. My daily life at the monastery was unassuming. I took on the most difficult tasks as a form of self punishment. I couldn't believe that God could still have a use for me. Working in the fields, laying stone, cooking, and cleaning the barn filled my days with routine, something I needed in order to live with myself.

One day after vespers, a mute peasant came to the monastery. I don't know where he came from or how he found me, but he stood in front of me dirty and bruised. His attire couldn't be called clothing for he was in rags, but as he stood there, hunched over in the hallway, he reached into his pocket. He handed me an object that was wrapped in a cloth. I carefully unfolded the tattered fabric and was astonished at what I saw. It was the broken stag's horn that I had given to Guinevere years before. The white, heart-shaped antler was exactly as I had last seen it; even the tip was still blood red. I stood for a moment, bewildered, hoping to find some explanation.

"Is this from the Queen?" I asked the ragged man.

The poor wretch stared back blankly, then turned and walked away. I was mystified. Was it sent by Guinevere? Was she in trouble? I had to find out.

II

It was almost ten years since I had taken Guinevere to the cloister of St. Agnes. This time I approached the doors of the convent as a brother of St. Philip. It was late afternoon when I arrived on an old plodder that I had borrowed for the long journey. The horse clomped along in the warm weather. The lazy summer sun hung in the sky and watched me as I dismounted and rapped on the large oaken doors that opened into the convent.

Little had changed since the day I had left the Queen there. One of the sisters ushered me in. Her manner was meek and humble, her body covered head to toe with the drab, colorless cloak of her order, her face hidden deep within its hood. I was taken before the head of the convent, an older woman whose teeth were brown with age and disease. Plain, pale, and with eyes deep-set, she scrutinized me as I approached. She hadn't changed either.

"What is your business here, brother?" she asked.

"I desire to speak to the Queen."

She paused, momentarily puzzled.

171

"You mean Sister Guinevere," she surmised. "We have no titles here. Sister Guinevere is very ill, too ill to entertain guests."

"You say she is ill? Please, I must see her."

With a resigned look, the woman let out a deep sigh. "Perhaps you must," she said somberly and turned to speak to a second cloaked figure behind her. "Sister, take this brother to see Sister Guinevere."

The hooded woman nodded and passively motioned for me to follow her. She led me into the cloister through the main hall where the tapestries with their beautiful stories were displayed. The hall was cool, and the light shone on the rich, golden brocade needle work of the sisters of St. Agnes, intricate in every detail, great stories told painstakingly in lavish thread. I followed my guide up the cold stone stairs, noting the ill-fitting robe that hung upon her. I thought it odd that this one walked upright—almost gliding—her head and shoulders proudly thrown back, unlike the other sisters who humbly scuffled about, hunched over with time and duty.

The stone steps were worn in the middle from long use; our footsteps whispered in the empty hall. She pushed open a large door which groaned audibly. The room had a sickly, yellowish tint, and the afternoon sun filtered in through the chamber's windows. A torch lazily burned in the corner of the room near one of the beds, and next to the cot a candle joined the flame in its slow fiery dance. A woman in the brown cloak of a nun lay on the bed.

"She has a candle by her side always," said the sister in a soft, raspy voice. Turning, she spoke to the prostrate figure. "Sister Guinevere, you have a visitor," and then motioned for me to come near before she turned and quietly left us alone.

The room was completely still. Even the flickering candle seemed to wait, and for the first time I noticed the unmistakable odor of sickness, of vomit, sweat, and fever. I was greeted by a faint smile from my beloved Guinevere. Straining, she tried to bring her eyes to focus upon me. My heart sank when I saw her face in the saffron light.

Her once-beautiful skin was now reptilian, a scaly, sickly shade of yellow. Her breathing was shallow and weak, but most pitiful of all was that the light had gone out of her eyes. Those beautiful golden windows to her soul were now sunken and as dull a brown as the uniform she wore. Black circles and heavy bags accented them, made even more pitiful by the wrinkles that emanated from them like fleshy spider webs. The sad years had taken a terrible toll.

III

Guinevere was almost unrecognizable. She squinted, trying to focus. She looked far older than her years. She must have known I was staring.

"Forgive me; I've been so ill," she whispered hoarsely, peering at my bearded face. "Who are you?"

"A friend," I answered.

Like a drooping rose that is suddenly exposed to the sun, Guinevere's face regained a flush of its former beauty as she recognized my voice.

"Lancelot? Lancelot, can that be you?" She began to weep giddily as she smiled and struggled to sit up, reaching out to me.

I carefully sat down on the edge of the bed and gently met her embrace.

We held each other as she wept uncontrollably. Finally she pulled away, holding my hands in hers, gazing into my eyes and staring at my face.

"You've not changed, Lancelot. You haven't changed at all, not at all, not even a wrinkle?" Her voice held a question.

"And you're just as beautiful as ever," I lied.

"Look at me. These years—this sickness—horrible," she said. "I am as withered as a dead flower, but you haven't even a gray hair. How is that possible?"

"I do not know, my Queen. I too have suffered a deep sickness if only in my heart. Oh, my precious one. There is so much to tell, so much I long to..."

The door opened, interrupting us. Again the cloaked sister entered, this time bearing a dull pewter tray with two vessels and a small pitcher. She walked with her head lowered as she placed the tray next to the table.

"She must have her potion," the sister said. "It's medicinal. Brother, would you help with the sister's medicine?"

"May I?" I asked. She handed me the cup with the potion. I gently held it to Guinevere's lips so that she might drink.

"That's enough," the Queen said, forcing the drink away. "Thank you, my sister."

"This bitters tonic is for you," the hooded woman said. "It's—thirst quenching." The sister handed me another vessel and quietly retreated toward the door.

I took a draft of the vinegary green refreshment. It smelled odd, but its bite was strong and refreshing. I turned to Guinevere and asked, "When did you become so ill?"

"It's the penalty for my sin," she said. Her withered eyes looked into mine. "A few years after you brought me here it found me. I--"

Guinevere stopped mid-sentence, her words cut off by a spasm; her body began to jerk unnaturally. Her breath came too quickly. Again she shuddered, this time violently, convulsing and twisting in my arms.

"Guinevere!" Helpless, I tried to hold her writhing body.

"Help—me," she stammered, her body quaking spasmodically.

"Sister! Sister!" I cried out, tears filling my eyes. I lay Guinevere back down on her cot as the contortions began to subside.

The heavy door once again opened as the sister came in quickly.

"What's wrong with her?" I asked, searching for an answer. I turned back to my love as I cupped her hands with my own, trying to rub life into her.

Behind me, the sister looked over my shoulder, leaning in to do so.

"I'm afraid she's dying," she said in her throaty voice, the words piercing my heart. I clenched my eyes and pressed Guinevere's hands against my forehead as I began to pray. The thought, the pain of losing her made me sick to my stomach. Then, like a flash, a twinge of icy lightning spread up my spine and through my heart. I reeled as I experienced the pain of a sharp dagger buried in

173

my back. Dizzy from the wound, I heard a voice, cold, callous, and all-too-familiar.

"And you'll die with her, Lancelot."

My agony was so great I could barely turn my head, but I saw her, Hecate, her face now revealed, her hood fallen away. Time had finally wrinkled her skin. She leaned into me, pressing the dagger deeper, deeper, twisting it again as my insides wrenched from the steely invasion. I felt my heart stop pumping, the warm blood pouring down my back beneath the hilt of the knife, a strange stillness coming over me, cold, distant. Perhaps I could die after all.

"I've been waiting a long time," Hecate said. "It is I who summoned you here, not my sister. For years my spies have searched the realm for your hiding place that I might savor this moment. Now that you're a holy man, Lancelot, I have a little confession," she gloated. "The blade imbedded in your spine has been envenomed. The bitters tonic you drank, toxic. The potion you gave my sister, also poison. How ironic it is that the Queen would be murdered by her adulterous lover." Hecate then let out a long, fiendish howl of laughter. She snatched me by the hair of my head and twisted my neck, forcing me to gaze upon the smirk of victory, her venomous grin twisted with hatred.

IV

It was almost too much to grasp. The misery was unbearable, my back arched, my hands involuntarily raised in agony. I tried to move, but the pain was cold and numbing, the poison making me feel woozy.

"Revenge is always best when served to enemies who trust you." Hecate interrupted her own laugh, leaving her knife imbedded in my back. She ran to the door and barred it; then she returned. "We wouldn't want any unexpected visitors," she said. Like a lover, Hecate leaned in close behind me, pulling my head to her, her fingernails deep in my scalp, her breath hot on my neck, her lips teasing me. "Sir Lancelot," she whispered in my ear, twisting the knife again then moving around me to Guinevere, "and my poor sister," she crooned in mock pity.

Paralyzed, I watched the scene unfold, although the pain somehow began to slip away. Guinevere lay in front of me, gaunt and shivering like a frail leaf, her body in shock, the poison gradually invading her like a spider's venom sedating its prey. Hecate now moved close to her sister.

"Lovely Guinevere," she said, only inches away. "Lovely Guinevere," she repeated, petting her sister's hair as one would a lap dog. "You may be asking yourself why, and you too, Lancelot." She turned to me, and then began speaking as though she were telling children a story.

"There were two sisters. The younger daughter became the favorite, her father's pet and her mother's love. She was ever the darling of the court. It was always Guinevere, with nothing left over for me. You took my parents. You took the kingdom that should have been mine," her voice grew more menacing. "You even took my lover." She looked at me in a sickening, seductive way. "It was always Guinevere, Guinevere!" Hecate became enraged, full of hatred. "Guinevere, my little one! Guinevere, the baby! Guinevere, the King wants to marry you!" Then, in an instant, she was pitiful. "No one loved Hecate," she pouted.

My pain began to ease, my mind regaining its senses. Still, I was unable to move.

"How I loathe you," Hecate hissed at Guinevere. "I followed you here, sister. Remember how ill you became—after I arrived. I've been keeping you sick all these years. I knew he would come back when I sent a message, so I waited. I passed the time by making you a burden on this pathetic sisterhood." Hecate began to laugh. "It's really funny, you know, too funny. All this time you thought I was your closest friend," she giggled scornfully. Turning to me, "It was I who arranged for you to spy on my sister bathing. It was I who arranged for the snowy stag to appear. It was I who arranged for your meeting in the Queen's chambers. And it was I who intercepted the King's letter announcing his early arrival from the campaign. I have brought you all down!"

I looked at Guinevere. Her body was completely still except for her heartbroken eyes—her tears. I knew in a matter of moments she would be dead.

"And one thing more, sister," she paused, looking at Guinevere with an impish, sinister smile. She turned to me and reaching behind me she used the knife in my back as a handle to pull us closer together. "Did Lancelot ever tell you that we were lovers?" she said, seductively, kissing me full on the lips.

A heartbreaking wail escaped from the Queen who then dropped my hand as if I were Judas. Our eyes met, and I watched Guinevere's grow cold as she murmured something with her last breath. Eyes wide open, still stained from her tears, Guinevere entered eternity with Hecate's lie, a last great burden on her broken heart.

V

Flames of fury blazed inside me at Hecate's wickedness, but the poison checked my anger. I burned inwardly unable to unleash my seething wrath.

I felt the dagger pulled from my back, and I cried out in relief.

"Don't worry, Lancelot," Hecate said. "You too will soon be dead."

I turned to see her wield the dagger once more, only this time I caught her arm with my left hand. I had recovered somewhat, my rage strengthening me. Again she tried to force the blade, but I checked the blow.

"I'm just trying to end it more quickly for you," her voice almost compassionate. "You'll still die from the poison. Just think of it: Arthur's most formidable champion, the great Lancelot, yielding his life to a woman." She laughed.

"You're not a woman," I snarled, gripping the still soft and delicate hand that clutched the dagger. "You're not even an animal." I looked at the body of Guinevere, ravaged by her sister's years of torture, lying lifeless on the bed. "You're nothing more than a pathetic witch." I spat the last word. "A hag!"

Hecate growled. Her wrist was firm as I began to exert pressure on it. She tightened her grip and, with all her weight, tried to drive the blade home. She failed as I grew stronger, and in an instant the tables were turned. I stood and began to force her wrist inward toward her abdomen. "You!" I said, looking into her frightened eyes. "You will pay for all you have done."

I continued to twist her wrist, the knife inching its way toward Hecate who vainly tried to push it away. Her blue eyes suddenly widened as it dawned on her that I was growing stronger. Instantly she began yelling and flailing her fist at me.

"Help!" she screamed. "He's going to kill me!"

I coldly continued to turn the blade on her, and she whimpered in pain as her wrist snapped beneath my grip, the knife inches from her stomach. There was pounding at the door, but the witch had barred it herself.

Hecate's blue eyes spewed hellfire as she kicked and screamed, finally grabbing for the knife I held with her left hand but finding its poisonous edge instead. She shrieked like an animal when she saw her bloody palm and scratched like a wildcat, but I was undaunted.

Still standing over her and holding her broken arm, I took the knife and flung it across the room. With my fist I snatched her up by her fiery hair, so that we were eye-to-eye. She hung in the air, clawing at me, her face contorted in pain as she spat in my face.

I slammed Hecate to the ground and dragged her like a beast across the cold stone floor. Shoving her head next to the bed's wooden frame, I lodged my knee against her chest, grabbing the back of her skull with my left hand. I forced her face into the poisonous cup that she had brought to her sister. She tightened her lips, but I pinched her nostrils with my fingers so that she would have to drink.

"It's time for your potion, Hecate!" I said sarcastically. "It's medicinal!"

She squirmed like a snake. Gasping, she inhaled the poison through her lips, coughing and choking. Unwillingly, she drank more deeply than her sister. I stood up, tossing the empty cup into a corner of the cell. Hecate began to twist into a frenzy of violent convulsions. "How?" She struggled to speak. "How—can—you—still—live?"

I said nothing, but coldly watched in silence as the minutes passed and as she gasped one last time before the fury finally faded from her eyes. Her body writhed, contorted, and then stiffened. She died a horrible but just death.

I walked over to where Guinevere lay and lifted her in my arms. I wept because of the tragedy I'd brought upon her, the years of suffering. I wept because I loved her. I still love her. I will always love her. Though I was still smoldering over Hecate's vengeful role in her sister's life, I knew in my heart that my own lust was responsible for Guinevere's death. My own desire had led me to forsake my God, to betray my best friend, and to bring ruin to Avalon. I had even taken the life of Hecate. I was again a murderer. I had broken every vow I pledged as a knight. I wept for that too.

We buried Guinevere and Hecate the following morning. The abbess, finally recognizing me, accepted my story without question. The nuns wrapped the two bodies in shrouds and prayed over their pitiful souls in a mournful ceremony. I felt a deep emptiness inside as I left the convent of the Sisters of St. Agnes far behind me.

My culpability followed me as I rode, and my guilt battered me with the same thoughts again and again. I knew the Savior personally. I knew His voice. As a knight I had taken a vow before God and King to stand for honor and truth. I had committed adultery. I had murdered. How could God ever forgive me? How could Arthur forgive me? How could I forgive myself? For miles and miles, months and months these questions gnawed away at me like vultures on carrion. I could neither eat nor sleep, as every night the consequences of my transgressions revisited me. Wherever I slept, my bed swam in tears. Still I rode on, confessing all my sins to the Lord. Finally, one morning, the quiet, small voice of the Comforter surprised me and spoke to me from within.

"You must begin by forgiving Hecate," He whispered.

Hecate. Her very name stirred my blood with rage, but I knew forgiving her would be the key to my own forgiveness. It would be like painstakingly removing a deeply imbedded thorn. It would take time, but I had plenty of time.

Thursday, July 11 11:00 p.m.

Father Braden held his hand to his head, rubbing his brow. "This is too much. It's just too much," he said.

"Yes, you're right. I didn't mean to stay so long."

"Oh no, it's not that. It's just that this is so incredible, and you haven't even made it through the sixth century."

"True. But living for more than 2000 years doesn't exactly make for a short story." Lazlow smiled, stood up, and reached for his jacket. "I need to let you get some rest."

"Will you come back in the morning and continue?" Braden asked.

"Nine o'clock?"

"I'll have some coffee brewing," the priest said.

Both silent with exhausted emotions, Braden walked Lazlow back to the front door of the church. "Good night," he told Lazlow as he closed the door.

Returning to his study, the priest dropped to his knees and spoke aloud. "Lord Jesus. Who is this man?"

177

Epilogue

The sound of the harp filled the inn as the brown-robed friar asked for more ale. He sat on the wooden bench, elbows on the table, head in his hands. The server, a young man with red hair, brought a pitcher of ale and filled the holy man's cup.

"Thank you," said the monk.

"Was the soup to your liking?" the young man asked.

"Yes, quite good," the friar said. He looked to be 30, yet somehow much older. His cloak, black hair, and beard were still damp from rainfall. "How far to the coast?"

"One day by horse, two if you're on foot," the server said.

The young boy plucking the strings of the harp started another tune; the monk sat up, transfixed by his angelic voice as he began to sing:

> Alas, my love, you do me wrong
> To injure me so discourteously.
> For I have loved you well and long,
> Delighting myself in your company.
>
> You broke your vows, and you tore my heart,
> My queen, my lady, my lover.
> Now our world is torn apart
> For you gave your love to another.
>
> Greensleeves, you were all my joy.
> Greensleeves you were all my love.
> Greensleeves was my heart of gold,
> And who but my lady Greensleeves.
>
> I pardoned her for to ease my heart,
> And I ask the Lord that she might see
> I blame not e'n the errant knight,
> So deep is my love and my constancy.
>
> I loved and lost, but now I pray
> That ere I die I shall yet see
> Her shining eyes in the light of day
> And Greensleeves declare her love to me.
>
> Greensleeves, you were all my joy.
> Greensleeves, you were all my love.
> Greensleeves was my heart of gold.
> No one but my lady Greensleeves.

178

"Does that song have a name?" the holy man asked the boy.

"Yes it does," he responded. "It's called Arthur's Lament."

"It's beautiful." The monk nodded and handed the young man a coin. He pulled the hood of his cloak over his head and quietly slipped out the door of the inn and into the gentle autumn rain.

Preview
My Name is Lazarus
Book II

Prologue

September 25, 1066

Harald Hardrada's sword gleamed as he pointed the weapon toward the sky and shouted to his men, "Stand with me!" A full head taller than most Norsemen, the Viking leader's gold and silver locks waved in the late summer breeze as he tried to muster his fleeing men. The torrent of those who had escaped the surprise attack and made it across the bridge slowed to a trickle as Hardrada's invaders rallied to the great warrior.

On the west side of the river Derwent, King Harold and his Anglo Saxon army had appeared from out of nowhere. They had force-marched 140 miles from London to Stamford Bridge and suddenly fell upon the unsuspecting Vikings. The Anglo Saxon warriors were weary from the four-day march, but they found new strength when they attacked the invaders. The Saxons' brown, burnished leather armor and chain mail offered them more protection than what the Norse raiders wore, most of them clad only in leather tunics. Those Norsemen who were trapped on the west side of the waterway had been butchered by the advancing Saxons.

"Take the bridge," King Harold shouted to his housecarls, his personal troops, and thanes. The bridge was the only way across the tributary at this time of year, when the water was high. Four Saxon thanes charged the span, certain they had won the day as the stragglers from the invading army scurried across the wooden planks to safety.

From out of the pandemonium of the fleeing Viking army, a deep, guttural, mighty howl, like that of a bear, resonated over the battle din. A giant Norse warrior, a berserker, standing more than seven feet tall, double-bladed battleaxe in each hand, charged the bridge. With powerful strides he moved his massive frame to the center of the span. He wore chain mail from head to knee, a large, round shield draped across his back. A silver headpiece hammered into the shape of a bear's head protected the great warrior's skull. A nose guard protruded from the brow of the helmet, the berserker's ice blue eyes barely visible. He wore a breastplate, and mail leggings protected his legs down to his ankles.

Nothing had prepared the Saxons for this demonic predator who stood roaring with his battle axes raised in the air, defying King Harold's troops, but the Saxons believed that four of their thanes were more than a match for the giant marauder. The Saxon warriors advanced cautiously over the centuries-old wooden and stone structure that had been built by the Romans. Though it was 75 feet in length, the bridge's 10 foot width would allow King Harold's men to attack in unison.

The four men lunged together, two aiming high, two low, but the Viking stepped back, then quickly counterattacked. The Norse axeman worked his blades in such a manner that an opponent who dodged away from one axe would find the other axe slicing into his flesh from the opposite direction. Within seconds, two thanes lay dying on the planks of the bridge, one trying to hold in precious blood that spurted from his throat, the other rolling in pain, grasping for his own bloody entrails that squirmed in his fingers.

None of King Harold's housecarls or thanes had ever encountered an enemy with such savage power. This single Norseman was more deadly than two highly skilled axemen working together. No one could pass as he brutally swept away one Saxon attacker after another. Archers shot arrows at the Viking, but the brute was impervious to pain. One of the bolts lodged in his forearm, but the enraged berserker tore the arrow from his flesh with his teeth and spat the bloody bolt onto the bridge. His face red and contorted with anger, the Norseman again raised his axes in the air and yowled. With no opponent facing him, the madman hacked insanely at the bodies sprawled before him.

Fearful of the beastly warrior who had now butchered more than 30 men, King Harold's entire army stood frozen at the sight of the ghastly carnage. The man seemed invincible. Four axe-wielding housecarls futilely attacked the Viking. As they picked their way through the gore and the corpses that lay strewn on the bridge, the giant marauder bounded forward and with one monstrous swing cut two men in half. Both men toppled backward, blood gushing through their armor and their fingers as they clutched at their gashes. The third Saxon chopped at the Norseman, but the Viking dodged the blade and, with his left hand, the berserker buried his axe in his attacker's face. The fourth housecarl ducked away from one wild chop and tried to kick the berserker in the groin, but in that instant, the Viking's other axe found its mark. Half the thane's leg, hacked off above the knee, flopped onto the blood-drenched planks of the span.

On the east side of the Derwent behind the bridge, the Norsemen were reorganizing. They had lost many comrades, but Hardrada was determined to defeat King Harold and seize the throne of England. Each moment the berserker delayed the Saxons from crossing the bridge bought precious time and cohesion for the invaders. Hardrada knew the remainder of his army was marching from the coast to reinforce him.

The bridge was now so choked with bodies and so slippery from blood and gore that it was impossible for more than one man to get through to the snarling, bear-like creature blocking the way. Yet, one Saxon captain pointed at the water, shouting to a housecarl who nodded, grabbed a long pike, and ran down to the bank of the river. The officer then turned his attention to the bridge and strode forth boldly to meet the mighty defender. The captain carefully picked his way through the slaughter of his fallen comrades, fearlessly stepping forward to meet the blood-crazed gaze of his opponent.

The berserker swung the axe in his right hand first, followed quickly by the one in his left, causing the captain to dodge and duck. Carried by the momentum of the attack, the Viking twisted, and as he did, the Saxon struck quickly; his sword tore through an opening in the Norseman's chain mail leggings. Stabbed through the thigh, the berserker's blood gushed through his mail and onto the planks as King Harold's army cheered their Saxon captain.

The wounded marauder roared and with another powerful swipe of the axe in his left hand forced the Saxon to spin and dance away from its mighty blow as he had done before. Still unscathed, the Saxon feigned an attack and again drew the full force of the Norseman's swing. Timing his move perfectly, the captain dodged the Viking's vicious swipe. Seizing another opportunity to counterattack, the Saxon stabbed at the giant's head with his sword. The blow would have been fatal, but an arrow suddenly pierced the cheek of the Viking who jerked his head away from the Saxon's blade. Having avoided death, the giant Norseman quickly spun around and with a savage slash, cut deep into his opponent's breastplate. The Saxon staggered and dropped his weapon before the berserker kicked him off the bridge and into the bloody water below.

The battle of Stamford Bridge continued as the Viking forces of Harald Hardrada regrouped on the east side of the river. The corpse of the Saxon captain drifted slowly downstream a few hundred yards from the battlefield. High overhead the sun bathed the land below in its golden rays and looked on as the captain's body rolled with the current in the shallows and lodged against some rocks in the tall reeds. No one saw the dead man began to twitch. No one saw the chest wound mend itself amongst the swaying grass. No one heard the violent coughing as the captain's lungs purged the water that had seeped inside them. No one saw the man's eyes slowly open. No one saw the once-lifeless man rise up, reborn in the wet grasses of the river Derwent. No one except Lazarus.

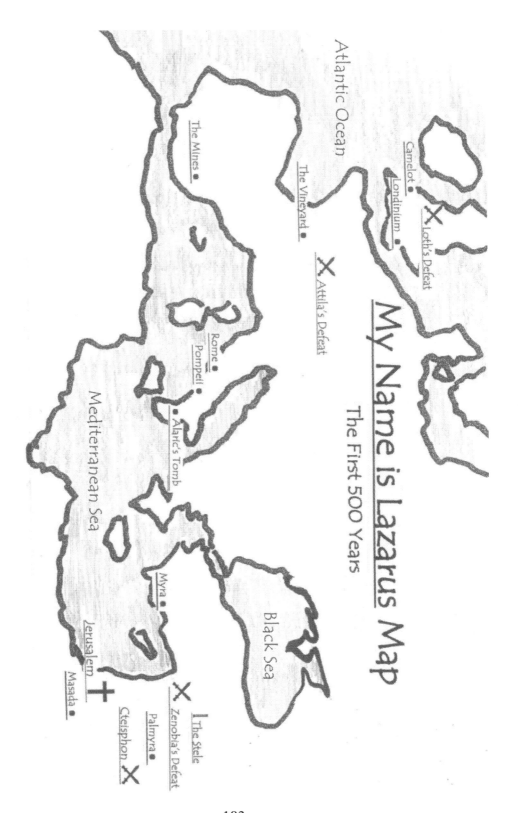

My Name is Lazarus Map

The First 500 Years

Atlantic Ocean

Camelot •

Londinium •

X Lotsi's Defeat

The Mines •

The Vineyard •

X Attila's Defeat

Rome •
Pompeii •

• Alaric's Tomb

Mediterranean Sea

Black Sea

Myra •

Jerusalem •

Masada •

X Zenobia's Defeat
I The Stele

Palmyra •
Ctesiphon X

34746551R00110

Made in the USA
Lexington, KY
17 August 2014